The

Chairmen

A Kurtz and Barent Mystery

by

Robert I. Katz

The Chairmen

A Kurtz and Barent Mystery

To

Jeff Palmer, Alan Santos and Peter Glass

Also by Robert I. Katz

Edward Maret: A Novel of the Future

The Cannibal's Feast

The Kurtz and Barent Mystery Series:

Surgical Risk
The Anatomy Lesson
Seizure
The Chairmen
Brighton Beach

The Chronicles of the Second Interstellar Empire of Mankind:

The Game Players of Meridien
The City of Ashes
The Empire of Dust
The Empire of Ruin
The Well of Time (forthcoming)

The

Chairmen

A Kurtz and Barent Mystery

Prologue

The letters were simple, crude and child-like, written in black crayon:

> **You don't know who I am but I know you. I've been watching you. I know where you live. I know where you work. I've waited a long time for this. I've had patience but my patience is at an end. Wounds heal slowly, by degrees. I'll be coming for you. Soon.**

He took one last look, folded the sheet of paper neatly in half, slid it into a brown envelope, sealed the envelope, and sipped his coffee. He had been mulling this over for months, not seriously, not at first, just toying with the idea, not really intending to go through with it, and now, suddenly, here it was, his decision made, the thought of turning back suddenly, finally unthinkable.

He smiled as he imagined the look on her face as she opened it. She would glance at it, frown, then most likely drop it into the wastebasket and do her best to forget it, but the next one would not be dismissed so lightly. She would look at the next one and ponder and begin to worry. Oh, *yes* she would.

He enjoyed thinking about. He savored it. Anticipation, he thought, was like a fine wine. *Enjoy it while it lasts.*

Bitch.

Carefully, he picked up the letter.

Tomorrow, he thought. *Tomorrow, it begins.*

Chapter 1

"Why me?" Kurtz asked.

Sean Brody smiled. It was a jolly smile, an easy, happy and confident smile, a smile befitting the Chairman of the Department of Surgery at one of New York's premier teaching hospitals. "Why not you?"

"I'm busy?"

"We're all busy. Nevertheless, we have responsibilities to the institution, and somebody has to do it."

"I'm a voluntary member of the faculty," Kurtz said, "I take care of patients. I don't do research. What makes me equipped to evaluate the credentials of an academic superstar?"

Brody made a rude noise. "Actually, it's policy to have at least one private practitioner on all the chairman searches. It keeps the air from getting too thin at the top of the ivory tower."

"Oh," Kurtz said. "I didn't know that."

"And the Dean likes you."

"He does? That can't be right."

"No accounting for taste." Brody smiled again and handed him a folder. "Look this over. The Committee will have its first meeting at 3:00 PM next Tuesday. Be there."

"Shit," Kurtz said mournfully.

Brody shrugged.

Kurtz sat at his desk, leaned back in his chair and glanced down at the file folder in his lap. A neatly placed sticker on the cover said, "Department of Cardiac Surgery, Staunton College of Medicine." Copies of the folder had been distributed to the Search Committee. Others would be mailed out to prospective applicants for the position.

There were eighteen academic chairmen at Staunton, which included the Chairs of Physiology, Biochemistry and the other basic science departments, as well as the clinical departments, and another twelve, all of them clinical, at Easton, the school's second largest teaching hospital. Since the average chairman served approximately five years before retiring or stepping down (or being fired…let's not forget being fired), there were at least four or five searches going on at any one time. In the past year alone, the chairmen of radiation oncology, physiology, anesthesiology, rehabilitation medicine and neurosurgery had all been replaced. This was Kurtz' first search and despite his half-hearted protest, he was just glad that he had not been drafted into any more of them.

The folder contained little that Kurtz did not already know. The Department of Cardiac Surgery consisted of six surgeons: three assistant professors, two associate professors and one full professor in addition to Peter Reinhardt, Professor and Chairman. It was a small department, but in most schools, cardiac was a division of surgery, not a separate department. There were also four fellows, three physician's assistants, two secretaries, two research assistants and an administrator, plus at least three residents from the Department of Surgery rotating through cardiac at any one time. The folder contained a summary of the departmental finances, which were excellent; a listing of research grants, ongoing projects and published papers, annotated by author and by year; an Excel spreadsheet with the surgical caseload; a listing of recent initiatives, which included a transplant program, an off-pump bypass program, an endovascular valve replacement program and a clinical protocol designed to reduce overall mortality, overall cost and length of hospital stay. Kurtz rolled his eyes at this last one. *Pick two out of three*, he thought. *Maybe*.

The department's caseload and research output had both stayed relatively constant for over ten years, until five years ago, when Dennis Cole, the only full professor other than Peter Reinhardt, had been recruited from Duke to be fellowship director. The obvious heir apparent, Dennis Cole had more than doubled the research funding, though he had done little to increase the caseload.

Chairmen…

Kurtz sat back in his seat and grimaced at the ceiling. Academic departments are not democracies. They're not meant to be democracies. Academic departments are dictatorships, and in the general opinion of the faculty, most of whom liked to cherish the illusion that they were independent champions for their patients' welfare rather than employees, chairmen are, at *best*, a necessary evil. The arrival of a new chairman, particularly a high-profile chairman, is always a time of both opportunity and justified concern, for both the department and the institution.

It is a sad but inevitable fact of academic medicine that most chairmen fail, for the simple and obvious reason that the talents and skills necessary to acquire the job most often have nothing to do with the talents and skills needed to actually do the job. Physicians who are good, really good, at patient care tend to do what they're good at. They take care of patients. They become physicians that their colleagues admire and their patients love and their students and residents, if they choose to pursue a career in academia, respect. And that's where they stay, content (sort of, most of them), with their chosen lot.

But you take a surgeon who can't tie knots, an internist who has no skill at diagnosis, a psychiatrist who sees nothing but his own neuroses when he looks at a patient, and the medical establishment is faced with a dilemma. What are you supposed to do with the guy? He's an MD, after all. He's a little clumsy or he tends to miss the forest for the trees or maybe he's simply nuts, but he's not stupid and he's not lazy, even if he's got no talent for the job that he's been training for. You can't just abandon him, not after four years of college and four years of medical school and at least three more years working his ass off in a residency program. The poor schmuck has debts to pay and maybe a family to support. So, you send him off to the lab, where he happily develops a career in research, killing rats and doing nobody any harm for the next twenty-five years.

Unless, of course, he is stupid and lazy, in which case you fire his stupid, lazy ass.

So how do you get to be a chairman? Well, first of all, you have to be famous, not famous like a movie star or a sports hero or even a politician, but famous among physicians. You can work on national committees, lobby congress and your state legislature on the issues that matter most to physicians, like managed care and governmental interference with physician autonomy. You can be a great clinician, so great that your expertise becomes universally acknowledged. But politics and clinical expertise will carry you only so far. Chairmen are in charge of academic departments and the academic mission most conspicuously includes advancing the science. No matter what else might account for your fame, if you want to be a chairman, you have to do research. For some, the research is a highlight to otherwise well-rounded careers, but for many, the research is all they know how to do. After twenty-five years, the guy who wasn't good enough to be a doctor has a hundred papers to his credit. He's well-known. He's got a national reputation. He's an expert on neuronal-glial interactions in the leach, or the effect of pepcid on bowel motility, or he's developed a new chemotherapy regimen that produces zero point two per-cent better results than the old chemotherapy regimen. He's famous.

Suddenly, a chairman decides to retire, and the Dean appoints a Search Committee. And who's on the Search Committee? First and foremost, a representative sample of the faculty of the medical school, many of whom are basic scientists: anatomists, physiologists, biochemists, pharmacologists—people who've never taken care of a patient in their lives, people whose sole criteria for evaluating excellence…is research. And so it goes. The guy who wasn't good enough to be a doctor is now the boss, telling all the real doctors how to do their jobs.

That, at least, is the worst-case scenario. Often, of course, you get lucky. You pick a guy who's got some common sense and maybe even knows his way around a patient. Maybe he went into research because he really liked research. Maybe he is competent. Maybe he's not out of his mind.

So it was with Peter Reinhardt.

Peter Reinhardt's grandfather had been a great supporter of German nationalism. He had won the Iron Cross during World War I and changed the family name from Stein to the more Germanic Reinhardt, none of which had impressed the Nazis. Peter Reinhardt was still Jewish. He spent a year in Dachau and was nearing death from starvation when the Allies finally liberated the camp. His father, mother and two older sisters did not survive. He was taken in by an uncle, became a physician and moved to America, doing a surgical residency at Bellevue, then moved on to Cornell for his cardiac fellowship and was recruited by Shumway to do transplant work at Stanford. He published his hundred papers. He became famous. He married a nice woman who thought he was God's gift to humanity and he in turn was fond of her and their three children. When the chair at Staunton became vacant he applied and was accepted.

Reinhardt's department did not love him but they did respect him. He was pompous and wishy-washy and vacillating but his heart—mostly—was in the right place. He was good with figures and he kept meticulous records and he never ran in the red. He cared about his people, he didn't hold a grudge and he stayed out of trouble. And if his department was well-known for nothing in particular, it nevertheless took good care of its patients and also produced no scandals. It was enough. Peter Reinhardt was successful.

And in his seventy-sixth year of life and his nineteenth year as Chairman of Cardiovascular Surgery at the Staunton College of Medicine, Peter Reinhardt chose at last to retire.

Two weeks had passed. Three notes had been sent. He was enjoying this. He sipped a brandy after dinner and thought about the future. Should he wait a little longer? Should he let the anticipation build? He had come to realize that the dance between predator and prey is a delicate one, anticipation on both their parts making the process all the sweeter. He smiled at the thought. Sweeter for him, at least.

He toyed with the idea of waiting but then shook his head. No, it was too soon to back off. Time enough later on to play with the timing, to let the fear die down, just a little, before stimulating it once again. Intermittent reinforcement, he had read, is always best. Never let it become routine, never let the subjects get their bearings. Never let them think that they know what to expect and when to expect it.

Smiling, he picked up a crayon (red, this time…) and began to write.

Chapter 2

It was 11 o'clock in the morning and Kurtz had his hands in an abdomen full of pus. "Give me a drain," Kurtz said.

The patient was a construction worker named Larry Reed, who had come into the ER complaining of abdominal pain. The pain had been building for almost a week. The patient had fever, rebound tenderness and was guarding the lower right quadrant—an obvious appendix.

A burst appendix, as it turned out. A burst appendix that had walled off into an abscess, which was the only thing that had kept Larry Reed alive. An abscess, while bad, is not as bad as acute, disseminated peritonitis. Unfortunately, an abscess, just as often as not, goes on to become acute, disseminated peritonitis.

Levine handed him a drain, frowned down at the abscess, gave a tiny shake of his head and wrinkled his nose. He didn't say anything but his posture radiated disapproval.

Levine believed in aggressive treatment. Levine was still young.

Kurtz believed in treating an abscess gingerly and with great respect. It was an old and still unresolved controversy: irrigate or drain? You irrigated the abdomen with about twenty liters of antibiotic saline, and maybe you could wash out all the pus and kill off all the germs that were left. Or maybe by trying, you just spread the stuff around and made the transition from abscess to peritonitis inevitable. Kurtz did not irrigate. Kurtz preferred to put drains into the center of the abscess, administer antibiotics and close.

Usually it worked. Sometimes, no matter what you did, the patient died.

"Sandra," Kurtz said, "would you please stand a little more to the side?" Sandra Jafari was one of five medical students currently on service. She was holding a retractor with her left hand, her body turned at an angle so that Kurtz could reach into the incision. Unfortunately for Sandra, in this position she could barely see the operation.

"So, Sandy," Levine said, "who invented rubber gloves?"

Sandra, a thin girl with a pale face and short brown hair, frowned uncertainly behind her mask. "Halstead?" She had a barely discernible accent. Something Eastern European, Kurtz thought.

"Very good," Kurtz said. "Most of the students don't know that."

"And why did he invent them?" Levine asked.

Sandra frowned. "To prevent infections?"

"Nope. Supposedly, he invented them because his girlfriend, who was an OR nurse, had a skin allergy."

"That's probably just a story," Kurtz said. "I don't think it's true."

"It's a good story," Levine said. "It should be true."

Kurtz rolled his eyes and Levine grinned behind his mask. "So, Sandy," Levine said, "what is the most common cause of appendicitis?"

"I don't know," Sandra said. She sounded worried.

"Neither does anyone else." Kurtz frowned at Levine, who shrugged. "Every once in awhile, you find a bit of food or something stuck inside. The appendix can't drain. It gets inflamed. Most of the time, you never do find a reason."

The anesthesiologist, Vinnie Steinberg, suddenly popped his head up over the drapes, looked at the abdomen and nodded. His head disappeared as he sat back down on his stool. Steinberg, thought Kurtz, looked glum.

"What's happening, Vinnie?" Kurtz asked.

Steinberg grunted from the other side of the drapes. "You hear Reinhardt is retiring?"

"Yeah, actually. What about it?"

"I'm worried," Steinberg said.

Kurtz didn't have to ask what he meant. A chairman retired, a new chairman came in, and suddenly the very next day, everything is different. In order to attract the right candidate, the Dean would have to give him at least some of what he wanted, and the first thing that every new chairman wanted was control: control of the hiring and firing, control of the curriculum, a significant say in the operation of the school, maybe his own institute funded by institution funds. Most of all, control of the money.

Say in his urge to exert control, the new chairman wants to bring in his own team of anesthesiologists, or even worse, wants to split the anesthesiologists who do cardiac off from the Department of Anesthesiology and make them a part of the Department of Cardiothoracic Surgery. That way, he not only gets control, he also gets to keep the money that the cardiac anesthesiologists bring in. Unlikely that the Dean would agree to that, but it could happen. For the anesthesia staff, it was worth worrying about. But more likely, the new Chairman of Cardiac Surgery would try to come in with a splash, do something to increase the prestige of his new department. The simplest way to do that was to do more cases. More cases meant more work for anesthesia, which, in the abstract, was a good thing. But the OR schedule was full. There were only three ways to do more cases. The first was to take time away from somebody else. This was possible but politically risky. The second was to build new OR's, also possible but time consuming and expensive. The most likely solution was to turn into a "twenty-four-hour" hospital. You let the guy work at night and on the weekends or even around the clock. You want to do a case? *Sure*, you can do a case. Oh, it's three in the morning? We have to pay overtime to the nurses and the pump techs and the lab boys? No problem. Nothing's too good for our new chairman, at least until the honeymoon is over and you start to piss off the wrong people. Anesthesiologists, like most normal human beings, do not like to work at three in the morning. A new surgical chairman was always cause for the anesthesia staff to worry.

"I'm on the Search Committee," Kurtz said.

"Yeah? I didn't know that. So, what do you think?"

"The first meeting is this afternoon. Moller is the Chairman."

"Moller is okay," Steinberg said.

Paul Moller was the Chairman of Surgery at Easton. Another chairman who was not a lunatic, Kurtz thought, except that Moller barely qualified as a chairman. Easton, though the residents all spent some time there, was not University Hospital. Moller had the title of Chairman, but it was a title at least one step down on the scale of academic prestige. For places like Easton, places that made their money by doing cases, not by receiving tuition or an enormous amount of grant money, the chairman had to be a clinician. Moller was a good surgeon. He had a few papers on his CV, but they were case reports and clinical studies. Moller was not a research clown.

Interesting that the Dean had picked Moller to Chair the Committee, now that he thought about it. Definitely sending a message.

Steinberg said, "Serkin is also on the Committee."

Kurtz frowned. "I didn't know that." Stewart Serkin was the Chairman of Anesthesiology at both Staunton and Easton, the almost new Chairman of Anesthesiology, speaking of things to worry about. The verdict was still out on Serkin. He had arrived only four months ago from Wisconsin, where he had been Vice-Chair for Research. An inauspicious title. "Not surprising, though," Kurtz said.

"No." Steinberg's voice was flat. Kurtz had heard rumors that the anesthesia staff did not exactly love their new Chairman.

"How's the patient?" Kurtz asked.

"Fine," Steinberg said.

Kurtz grunted. Larry Reed, aside from his abscess, was a healthy specimen. He didn't have atherosclerosis or diabetes or even high blood pressure. He had a functioning immune system. He wasn't septic. With a little luck, his abscess would drain, his infection would vanish and he would walk out on his own two feet, another miracle of modern medicine.

Kurtz hoped so.

Twenty minutes later, the patient tucked into a corner of the Recovery Room, Kurtz grabbed his white lab coat from the rack hanging on the wall by the OR and put it on over his scrubs. He glanced at his watch. Just enough time to grab a quick lunch before the first meeting of the Search Committee...

Staunton College of Medicine sat overlooking the Hudson River, a couple of miles down from Columbia-Presbyterian, which Staunton considered its principal competition. Columbia, one of America's oldest and most prestigious medical schools, was barely aware that Staunton existed, but Staunton liked to imagine that the two schools were fighting it out for dominance in the New York market. Of course, NYU and Cornell might have also had something to say on the subject, but they, too, were not exactly focused on the threat that Staunton represented to their own prestige.

Staunton was New York City's youngest medical school but maintained a solid academic reputation, with respectable (though by no means remarkable) levels of NIH and industrial funding. The school's primary teaching hospital was Staunton University Medical Center, 600 beds, fully owned by the school. In addition to CUMH, Staunton maintained affiliation agreements with a number of area hospitals, most prominently Easton, a 350-bed place only a few blocks to the west of Times Square.

Christina Pirelli had been the Chairman of the Department of Obstetrics and Gynecology at Staunton for a little over eighteen months. She had followed the usual academic path for an ambitious physician, a fellowship in maternal-fetal medicine with a follow-up stint in the lab. She then accepted a position at St. Louis and stayed for seven years, rising to Associate Professor, before being recruited to be Chief of Maternal-Fetal at Wake Forest. Five more years and she was ready. The Chair at Staunton opened and after a brief search, here she was.

Along the way, she had accumulated two ex-husbands and a daughter, now a freshman at Swarthmore.

Christina liked the job. Most of it was routine but solving problems and making things work better gave her a lot of satisfaction. Some of the staff were prima donnas but none of them were insane and all of them were at least competent. It was a good department and a good situation and she liked coming to work in the morning. Or she had liked coming to work...she frowned down at the brown mailing envelope sitting on her desk. Tentatively, she reached out a finger, gave it a little spin, then picked it up and opened it, already suspecting what she would find.

> **I'm enjoying this. I'm enjoying the look on your face as you read this. I'm imagining the questions running through your brain. You do know what this is about; oh, yes you do, though you may not know that you know, and when I come for you, you won't be surprised. Bitch.**

Actually, Christina had no idea what this was about, and she had no desire at all to find out. Christina began to crumble the letter, as she had crumbled the two previous letters, preparatory to dropping them in the wastebasket, then she slowly sighed, shook her head and picked up the phone. Three was three too many...too many to ignore, at least. She dialed Security. "Asshole," she muttered.

The Committee, aside from Paul Moller, who Kurtz knew pretty well, was comprised of Todd Dunn, the Chairman of Urology at Staunton, Stewart Serkin, John Nye, the Chief of Cardiology at the school, a biochemist named George Linn, Ralph Castillo, a pharmacologist, and Christina Pirelli.

Kurtz walked in five minutes late but still found himself the only one in the room. Moller walked in a few minutes later, shook his head, sighed, and sat down at the head of the table. The biochemist and the pharmacologist arrived soon after, opened their briefcases and proceeded to read student papers. George and Ralph had evidently done this before. The rest of the committee trickled in soon after. A good-looking brunette in a gray business suit sat down next to Kurtz, gave him a smile and said, "Hi, I'm Christina Pirelli."

"Richard Kurtz."

"I've heard of you. You're a surgeon, right?"

Kurtz nodded.

"This is my third search in the past year," Christina said. "It's getting to be a real pain."

"My first," Kurtz said.

"Lucky you." Christina shook her head, opened up a briefcase, pulled out a sheaf of papers and began to read.

The last one to arrive was Serkin, a short man with a thick head of graying hair, a brush moustache and a long, narrow face. Serkin walked into the room, smiled pleasantly and said, "Let's get going. I have things to do." Moller glanced at the clock, sighed again, and said, "Sure. First, why don't we all introduce ourselves? Richard?"

They went around the room, calling out their names and departmental affiliations, then Moller smiled and rubbed his hands together as if something had actually been accomplished. "Okay," he said, and glanced once again at the clock. "The Dean is supposed to be here to give the committee its charge. We'll wait another two minutes, and then if he doesn't show up, we'll begin."

At that moment, a tall man with a long nose, curly black hair and sad, hang-dog eyes walked into the room: James Kushner, the Dean. The Dean sat down next to Moller and smiled around the table. "Nice to see all of you," he said. A few inspirational statements, a couple of clichés, a rumination on the academic mission, a pronouncement on the responsibilities of institutions such as their own to bravely lead into the future, and a brief sentence of thanks followed. The only statement of any significance involved the finances, and how cardiac affected the public perception of the institution. "Cardiac surgery is high profile," the Dean said. "The public pays attention to cardiac surgery. Cardiac surgery makes money, and that money supports a lot of other departments that don't make money.

"Peter Reinhardt has been a good chairman. He's built a successful department. Replacing him won't be easy. What we need, obviously, is somebody who can provide leadership, somebody who the department, as well as the institution, is going to respect. The person you select for this position must be a clinician. He must also be a good clinical manager. Scholarly work is necessary, of course. The chairman must be a scholar. An academic department cannot survive if its leader is not an academic. The right person will not be easy to find. I want you to conduct a national search. Staunton deserves a national search." The Dean smiled. "Any questions?"

Nobody raised their hand. "All right, then," the Dean said. "Let me know if you need anything, and keep me informed of how it's going."

"Thank you," Moller said.

The Dean nodded, smiled again and walked out.

"Okay," Moller said. "The institution has hired the search firm of Bender and Boyd to do the leg work. They've already put advertisements in *JACC, Chest, Thoracic Surgery, The New England Journal* and *Academic Medicine* and they've written to all the surgical chairmen in the country asking them to submit the names of viable candidates. CV's from interested applicants have already started coming in. The search firm gives them an initial screen and then sends us the ones that make the cut." Moller smiled around the table and passed a series of file folders to each member of the Committee. "These are the first. I'm sure we'll get a lot more. Look them over. We'll meet weekly in order to decide which ones to interview. I hope to have a short list of the top three within three months.

"Any questions?" he said.

Dunn and Serkin exchanged looks. Serkin stared down at the pile of folders and wrinkled his nose. Both men shrugged. Serkin, Dunn,

Christina Pirelli and John Nash rose to their feet and trooped out. Castillo and George Linn followed. Moller looked at Kurtz and raised an eyebrow. "Well? What do you think?"

"I'm sure they're a really swell group when you get to know them," Kurtz said.

Moller puffed out his cheeks. "It's going to be a long few months," he said.

"Cheer up," Kurtz said. "Maybe none of them will show up for the next meeting."

Moller snorted. "Fat chance," he said.

Chapter 3

He sipped his coffee and closed his eyes, letting the rich, dark flavor roll around his tongue. He smiled. He didn't used to pay so much attention to his morning coffee, but he found that having a new purpose, a new cause, tended to focus him on so much more. Everything, he found, seemed suddenly filled with significance. *Life* had so much more meaning. He used to drink just about anything. Now, it was *Gevalia*. He sipped his coffee and pondered. Was it time to expand his activities? Yes, he thought. It was. It was time to take his campaign beyond the initial target, to let the institution itself know that it was under siege.

He selected a new crayon, one never before used for any lesser purpose (green, this time, yes, green would do nicely) and began to write.

For Kurtz, the next few days were uneventful: a few routine cases, patients in the afternoon, work out in the evenings, try to ignore Lenore's mother, who was calling about fifteen times a day. Lenore had had plenty of practice. Kurtz had not yet mastered the technique. Since the wedding was only six months away, Kurtz figured he had better learn fast.

Esther Brinkman wanted a big wedding. Anything else, it seemed, would scandalize the neighborhood. Kurtz tried to stay out of it. So far as he was concerned, his own role was to show up, look good, parrot his lines and smile. If Lenore wanted it, Kurtz wanted Lenore to have it. But a big wedding was not what Lenore wanted. Lenore wanted a small wedding, the immediate family, a few close friends.

"Did you know that getting married is considered to be one of the most stressful times in your entire life?" Lenore said.

"I believe I did read that somewhere, along with having a baby, starting a new job and buying a house. Could you pass the chicken?"

They were eating in a little restaurant just off Pell Street, in Chinatown. A long line of hopeful diners snaked out the front door and gathered on the sidewalk. "I don't want my wedding to be stressful," Lenore said. "I want it to be fun."

"I like fun," Kurtz said. "Fun is good."

"Mother is being difficult."

"Nothing new there."

Lenore grinned and spooned a generous helping of shrimp with chili sauce onto her plate. "The secret to dealing with my mother," she said, "is to keep things as simple as possible. Don't let yourself be distracted by what Aunt Mimi said about traditional weddings in 1947 or by the sacrifices that Great-Grandpa Isaac made back in the *stetl*, just so his daughters could be properly married."

"Did these sacrifices include a dowry? I wouldn't mind a dowry."

Lenore raised an eyebrow. "You don't need a dowry. You get to sleep with me."

"I already get to sleep with you. Isn't a dowry supposed to certify a change in the relationship?"

Lenore smiled sweetly. "I'll think of something special for the wedding night."

Kurtz smiled back. She probably would, too.

"You have to be firm," Lenore said. "Just say no."

Easier said than done but Kurtz was beginning to catch on. When saying no didn't shut her up, you smiled and ignored her. For this, it was handy to have a prop, maybe a newspaper to bury your face in. A newspaper, Kurtz had noted, was his future father-in-law's favorite method. Stanley Brinkman went nowhere without his copy of the *New York Times*.

Despite the occasional bout of lunacy, Esther Brinkman wasn't a bad sort, Kurtz reflected, and he had reluctantly grown almost fond of his future mother-in-law. She had grown up in an era when young women were expected to have babies, take care of the house and not pursue a career. That had worked fine so long as Lenore and her sister were children, but once they grew up and moved out, Esther Brinkman had nothing to focus her rather formidable intelligence on. Thank god, she had recently joined her cousin Sylvia's real estate firm. It gave her less time to drive her daughters insane.

Kurtz had met Sylvia and her husband, Milton Hersch, at a family dinner over the holidays. Sylvia was a hard driving, focused and successful career woman who nevertheless looked upon the world with benign good will. She seemed to regard family and employees as extensions of each other. She would bring chicken soup to workers who had minor colds and dispense advice freely regarding children, husbands and relationships. The employees, like her children, had learned to ignore her advice but tended to indulge her. The chicken soup was excellent, her matzoh balls as light and fluffy as clouds.

Esther, Kurtz was amused to see, regarded her older cousin as a role model, which made sense, since they were a lot alike. They even looked alike, being small, gray haired and round.

"Your mother still mad about the rabbi?" Kurtz asked.

The rabbi was reform. An orthodox rabbi would not marry a Jew and a non-Jew. "Probably." Lenore shrugged. "She's not saying. I told her that unless she dropped the subject, we'd go to a justice-of-the-peace."

Another secret, Kurtz had learned, was never to make empty threats. If you say it, you mean it. Lenore meant it.

Kurtz sighed. As Moller had said, it was going to be a long few months. At least Larry Reed was doing well.

A hospital never really slept, even in the middle of the night. The halls were brightly lit. Buzzers were buzzing. Beepers beeped. Nurses and doctors and even the occasional patient who couldn't stand the lumpy bed or his roommate's snoring, walked up and down the halls.

Nobody paid you any attention, though, not if you looked like you belonged and knew where you were going. You had to sign in downstairs, if you were a visitor, and visiting hours were long over, but of course, there were exceptions. If your loved one was having emergency surgery or your wife was in labor, you could hang around until the crisis was over. The staff was supposed to show an ID card but the guard barely glanced at it, and even then, you could slip past the guards if you knew how. The entrance to the staff parking lot had no security. The hallway leading to the back stairs, in the front lobby, started before the guard post. Walk in the front door, turn left, and you could go anywhere you liked.

No cameras either, not inside the building. Cameras represented a gross violation of patient confidentiality. No cameras, no sign in, no record.

So easy, he thought. So vulnerable. A hospital was its own little world, with its customs and rules and ways of doing things. So easy to wander through and blend in and then, when they were least expecting it, to *pounce.*

He almost laughed as he walked along, nodded to one nurse, smiled at another, tipped his hat to a third. *Soon,* he thought. Soon…he could hardly wait.

"You know," Mahendra Patel said, "the operating rooms could really use a little more direction."

Stewart Serkin stared at him. "What do you mean?"

"The surgeons overbook their rooms. There's no penalty for the surgeons for coming in late. The pre-op checklists are supposed to make the whole process safer but they're slowing everything down. The nurses won't let us bring patients into the OR's until they've finished with the checklists, and also counted their instruments. Housekeeping is slow and they need more help. We sometimes wait for fifteen minutes or more once a patient leaves until they get in and start cleaning things up for the next case. Our turnover times average nearly fifty minutes. That's way too long."

Serkin suppressed a sigh. None of this was particularly important, because the OR's had been operating in exactly this way for years. Patel was annoying. The Department covered three different hospitals, Staunton, Easton and St. Agnes, a small place downtown that did primarily plastic surgery and orthopedics. Serkin's goal was to take these three disparate parts and meld them into a coherent whole.

Patel's viewpoint was too narrow, Serkin thought. Patel lacked vision.

"And your solution?"

"We need an OR Manager, somebody with some authority to get things done."

Serkin considered this idea for a brief instant and gave a decisive shake of his head. "No way. I'm not going to add another layer to the departmental bureaucracy. And besides, good OR's run themselves."

Patel stared at him. He cleared his throat.

"Yes?" Serkin said.

Patel looked away. "Nothing."

"Bring your concerns to the Executive Committee. The Executive Committee is the decision making body of this department. We can discuss it on Wednesday."

Patel drew a deep breath. "Okay," he said.

"Anything else?" Serkin said.

"No."

Serkin smiled coldly. "Then thanks for stopping by."

Kurtz, way back when, had been the point guard on his high school basketball team and, in his senior year, backup quarterback on the football team. A height and weight of six feet, two inches tall and 220 pounds had been distinct advantages for both positions. In addition to his physical gifts, Kurtz was blessed with speed, quick reflexes, a facility for sizing up a situation and a conviction that appeasement only encouraged bad behavior. His time in the army, where he had clerked for CID, had done nothing to change his convictions. "What do you mean, I can't do my case?"

"Jerry Doyle has a hot gallbladder in the ER," Patel said. "He says the case can't wait. Yours is the first open room."

"A hot gallbladder?" Kurtz stared at the phone in disbelief.

"That's what he says."

Kurtz had a breast biopsy scheduled for 11:00 AM. It was now 10:15. "I've never heard of a hot gallbladder that couldn't wait for an hour."

"He's a surgeon," Patel said. Patel, the clinical director of anesthesiology at Easton, knew his surgeons. So did Kurtz. Doyle was most certainly a surgeon, the sort of surgeon that gave other surgeons a really bad name. "He's got the right to declare a case an emergency," Patel went on. "If he does that, we have to bump the first available room."

"But he's full of shit."

"Probably. But I'm an anesthesiologist. I'm not going to tell a surgeon that his surgical judgment is full of shit. He's supposed to be better at surgical judgment than I am."

"Well, he's not better at it than I am," Kurtz said. "What's the name of this hot gallbladder?"

"Susan Baum." Even through the phone, Kurtz could practically see Patel smiling. "Good luck," Patel said.

"Thanks."

Five minutes later, Kurtz was in the ER. The secretary at the admitting desk was a bleached blonde with big hair. She smiled at Kurtz. "You have a patient here named Susan Baum, Mary?"

Mary's smile grew wider. "Room Five," she said.

"Thanks." Susan Baum's chart was sitting in a small bin outside Room Five. Kurtz smiled. Ordinarily, it would have been a violation of the Health Insurance Portability and Accountability Act (HIPAA) for any health care provider who was not directly involved in a patient's care to look through her chart. This patient, however, had been declared to be an emergency, which meant she was, by definition, in serious distress. Serious distress meant that the resources of the institution had to mobilize around the distressed patient. Serious distress was an allowable exception. So...forty-three-years old, complaining of intermittent right upper quadrant pain. No other medical problems. Vital signs stable. Big deal, Kurtz thought. Big fucking deal. Just then, a small, balding man wearing a bowtie walked down the hallway. He stopped when he saw Kurtz.

"Hey, Jerry," Kurtz said with a smile.

"What are you doing here?" Doyle said.

"I thought I'd come down here and give you a little hand. I heard you were having some trouble with a hot gallbladder."

Doyle blinked at him. "Trouble?"

"Yeah. I heard it was an urgent case. Patient in distress, blood pressure dropping, probably septic, couldn't wait for me to do my breast biopsy. That sort of trouble."

"Oh," Doyle said.

"I guess I was wrong though, wasn't I?" Kurtz held the chart out. Doyle took it between a thumb and one forefinger, as if it smelled bad.

"It is urgent," Doyle said. "She's in pain."

"Intermittent pain. Sounds to me like she already passed the stone."

Doyle drew a deep breath. "Okay," he said. "Maybe."

"You can do her after I do my breast biopsy. Right?"

"Right," Doyle said reluctantly.

"Thanks," Kurtz said. "I knew you'd understand."

Dolye sniffed. He looked like he was about to say something, evidently thought better of the impulse, then shrugged. "Sure," he said. "You bet."

> How many people have you trampled on to get to the top? How many careers has your ambition ruined? You're going to pay for the people you've harmed along the way. I'm going to make certain of that.

Offhand, the Dean couldn't think of anybody he had either trampled on or ruined, though he was aware that not everybody would see it in quite the same way. He was a Dean, after all, and before becoming Dean, he had been the Chairman of Pathology at Seattle, positions that some, no doubt, would envy.

"Hmm," he muttered. He had received a couple of notes like this about two years before, both from a student who thought that he was being funny. The student had been suspended, sent for counseling and then reinstated. The Dean had followed his progress with some curiosity. He was now a first-year pediatrics resident in Syracuse, said to be doing well and not likely to be trying for a repeat performance of his youthful idiocy.

Carefully, the Dean opened the center drawer in his desk and placed the note inside. In a month or so, if there was no repetition, he would throw it out.

Chapter 4

Stewart Serkin was staring into space, thinking deep thoughts, when his secretary walked in, put a thick envelope down on the desk and walked out. Serkin smiled in satisfaction at the secretary's retreating back. He had instructed the staff that they were not to talk to him when he was in his office unless they had something important to say. The mail could be delivered without extraneous comment.

Stewart Serkin was pleased with himself. His plans for the department were coming along nicely. Form follows function, process determines product. Serkin believed strongly in both form and process, and bureaucracy, in his opinion, was an impediment to both. Since arriving at Staunton, Serkin had deliberately set about destroying the departmental bureaucracy. Patel, for instance, had to go. This had been obvious for months. Mahendra Patel had been the clinical chief at Easton for more than ten years. He was seen by both the department and the administration as someone with authority, as a separate decision making entity. Inefficient, at best, and quite possibly dangerous. Serkin wanted one department, not three. He wanted one chairman, himself, not three mini-chairmen.

It was not that Patel made bad decisions. He didn't. The problem was that he made decisions. Patel was accustomed to command, and that was a threat to the smooth and efficient running of the department.

Vinnie Steinberg, though he didn't know it yet, was the perfect replacement. A man with no administrative experience was not going to pretend to be a seasoned administrator. The hospital and medical school administration would have no confidence in him. He would look, talk and even act like the face of the department but the power would inevitably flow where it belonged, to the Chairman. Satisfied with this conclusion, Serkin opened up the packet and began to read.

Almost seventy applications were ultimately received, most of which were quickly weeded out, the majority being from recently promoted Associate Professors with a moderate number of papers, little managerial experience and no academic reputation. At least twenty were from more senior Associate Professors with a reasonable amount of administrative experience under their belts, either as chiefs of service or division heads. To his surprise, Kurtz found himself agreeing with the chairmen more often than not, at least when it came to the junior guys. What made them chairman material, anyway, except ego? Not much. Of course, you could only tell so much from the CV. An ability to see all sides of an issue and reach either consensus or a reasonable conclusion was not a trait likely to be apparent on a résumé.

The remaining fifteen or so were from applicants that the chairmen on the committee, along with the pharmacologist, the biochemist and the Chief of Cardiology, regarded as the serious candidates: full professors with fifty or more papers to their credit and a solid history of funding. Perhaps ten of these had administrative experience. At least six of the ten, to Kurtz' certain knowledge, had reputations as overbearing, egotistical shitheads.

"How about..." Moller peered down at a CV, "John Allen Kaplan? Anybody know him? Richard?"

Kurtz shook his head. "He has a good CV," he said. "I don't know him."

"Anybody?"

"I concur," Nash said. "Sixty-seven papers, fifty-two abstracts, over three million in grant money."

"Corporate grants," Christina Pirelli said. "Not NIH grants."

Serkin puffed up his cheeks and nodded.

"He's been Director of Thoracic for two years," Kurtz pointed out.

"True," Moller said. "I vote to interview."

Serkin gave Moller a cool glance, then shrugged. Christina Pirelli reluctantly nodded. Moller looked around the table but nobody else spoke up. He turned to the secretary. "Get in touch with Dr. Kaplan," he said. "Let's bring him out here." He looked back down at the pile in front of him. "How about Thomas Henry Harris?"

"Extremely well qualified," Nash said.

"I certainly agree," put in Castillo.

Kurtz looked at Castillo in disbelief. Castillo was a PhD, a pharmacologist. He had never taken care of a patient in his life but still, Thomas Henry Harris was the very essence of a research clown: two hundred and thirty papers, eight million in NIH funding and no experience whatsoever in actually running anything outside of his lab.

Kurtz did not want to get a reputation as the odd man out, even if he was. The odd man out tended to be ignored, but Thomas Henry Harris, in Kurtz' opinion, was not the man for the job. Period. There was a long silence. Finally, steeling himself, Kurtz opened his mouth to speak, but before he could say anything, Todd Dunn spoke up. "This is a guy who, ten years ago, would have been a shoo-in, but today, I don't know."

"You don't know?" Castillo said. "What do you mean, you don't know?"

"The Dean specified a good clinical manager. Does this guy spend any time in the OR at all?"

Serkin looked at him. "He's a scholar. An eminent scholar. His CV is fantastic."

Dunn shrugged and sat back in his chair.

"Anybody else?" Moller said. Castillo shrugged and looked into space. Christina Pirelli doodled on a pad and seemed not to be following the conversation. "All right, let's vote on it," Moller said. "Stewart?"

"I vote to interview," Serkin said.

"John?"

"Interview."

Moller shrugged, wrote something on the applicant's folder, and looked up at George Linn, who said, "I think we should put him aside for the moment."

"What do you mean?" Castillo asked.

"Let's see who else applies. We have applications from highly regarded researchers who also have administrative experience. We can make the Dean happy and make ourselves happy, too. Why settle?"

Moller smiled at him. "I agree," he said.

Somewhat to Kurtz' surprise, this motion was adopted. Maybe, just maybe, Kurtz reflected, the Dean knew what he was doing when he picked this committee.

"Okay," Moller said. "How about"—he looked down at the pile of CV's—"David Leslie Johns?" Moller cocked his head at Christina Pirelli. "He's from Wake Forest, your old place. Anything you can tell us?"

"Forget it," Christina Pirelli said.

Castillo looked at her, surprised. "How come? He looks good."

"I used to sleep with him and he dumped me. He's an asshole."

"Oh," Castillo said. Nash looked up at the ceiling. Serkin gave another shrug.

Moller scratched his head. "Anybody else?" he asked. Nobody spoke. "Okay then, forget about David Leslie Johns," Moller said. "Timothy Fischer...?"

And so it went for another forty-five minutes. At the end, they had eliminated twelve applicants, tabled two and identified three who looked good enough to interview. Not bad, Kurtz thought. He glanced at his watch. Time for a little lunch before a gastric banding at 1:00 PM. A surgeon's life, he thought...a nice, routine, boring day, and nothing wrong with that.

Surgery, as every medical student soon comes to know, is fun. A chance to cut is a chance to cure. Everybody loves to operate. It's what goes along with operating that's the problem. You had to be able to put up with hours that were both long and unpredictable. You rarely had a weekend off. The work was physically demanding and emotionally draining.

Some get used to it. Some, even after years of practice, do not, and these are the ones who contribute most markedly to the notoriously high rates of alcoholism, divorce and suicide that go hand-in-hand with the profession.

Kurtz, after four years in practice, was used to it. He didn't necessarily love it, but he was used to it. Or so he told himself. It was harder to maintain his objectivity after forty hours of a forty-eight hour call shift.

Midnight. The witching hour. Kurtz did most of his cases at Easton but took call at Staunton at least twice a month, one of the

32

requirements for maintaining privileges at the school. He had finished a perforated diverticulum only twenty minutes before. He was sitting in the locker room, bone tired, thinking about getting dressed and heading back home, when the fire alarms went off. He winced. Hospital fire alarms were deliberately set on sensitive. They went off frequently, almost always for no particular reason, occasionally for something minor like too much smoke in the kitchens, and at least twice, that Kurtz could recall, from some idiot smoking in what was supposed to be a "smoke free" hospital. Then, of course, there was the case not too long ago when a neurosurgery patient's drapes caught on fire, set off by an electrocautery. Unfortunately, in that case, a nurse who wasn't thinking too clearly had sprayed a fire extinguisher into the patient's brain. The fire had gone out; so too, had the brain.

Fire alarms were annoyingly loud but usually stopped after a few seconds. Not this time. This time, as Kurtz put his pants back on, the faintest whiff of smoke came to his nostrils.

He felt a tingle in his fingertips. His tired muscles abruptly unwound. In a real fire, he reflected, the job of the surgical staff was to evacuate the OR and get all the patients out into the street. You closed every wound you could and packed the rest but one way or another, you got them out of there. Luckily, there were no patients in the OR at the moment, only the one post-op in recovery.

The fire alarms stopped. The scent of smoke did not, but neither did it seem to be getting worse. Gingerly, Kurtz poked his head out of the locker room and into the hall. The ER was at the other end of the hall. This was a standard arrangement; the OR and the ER should ideally be in close proximity, so that severely traumatized patients can first be worked up and stabilized, then wheeled quickly into the OR. A faint haze of smoke hung in the air of the corridor. Kurtz could hear shouting. Abruptly, the overhead paging system began to sound, "*Code M, Emergency Room. Code M, Emergency Room.*"

Code M. The "M" stood for manpower, hospital jargon for someone running amok, usually a patient undergoing a psychotic attack or out of their mind on drugs or delirious secondary to head trauma. Sometimes it turned out to be a relative or a friend whose only method of dealing with bad news was to start smashing things. When Security heard the page, they were supposed to come running.

The smoke was definitely beginning to dissipate. The shouting grew louder. Kurtz glanced at his watch as a slow smile spread across his face. The parking lot was outside the ER. He had to go through the ER to get out of the building. So why not see what was going on?

Anyway, Code M's were almost always entertaining.

The ER was divided into four segments: the administrative offices where physicians did their paper work and new patients were checked in, the lounge where family and friends could wait for news, the routine examining rooms, and the shock-trauma room, which was equipped just like a miniature ICU. The noise was coming from shock-trauma. Kurtz poked his head in through the door.

It looked like a hill, a hill composed of human bodies rippling and heaving and moving back and forth across the floor. Most of the bodies wore uniforms. One or two wore surgical scrubs, along with wide-eyed expressions as if they didn't quite know how they came to be down there on the floor and were sincerely regretting the impulse that had put them there. Occasionally, one of the bodies was shaken off the pile. When this happened, Kurtz could see that at the bottom lay a man who looked like a rogue biker. He must have been at least six and a half feet tall and about three hundred pounds. His head was shaved bald. He wore a sleeveless denim jacket without a shirt, black denim pants, and a gold skull on a gold chain around his neck. A constant torrent of curses and hoarse, incoherent screams came from his mouth.

A trickle of smoke still curled up from a wastebasket in the corner of the room.

Now, let's see...Kurtz had no desire to add to the pile-up. If he peeled off the top two layers, he might be able to get a hand on the guy, but this seemed a tad impractical. Suddenly, he saw it. The fire-hose. It was hanging inside a glass case set into the wall.

Yup. The fire hose. That should do it, all right.

A large hand fell upon his shoulder.

"Don't," a voice said.

Shit. "Don't what?" Kurtz said.

"Don't even think about it."

"Hey," Kurtz said, wounded.

"No hard feelings, Doc. Just don't." The man holding his shoulder was large and beefy. He had huge rolling shoulders, a huge rounded belly, a red hypertensive face and a brush haircut.

"So how are you, Patrick?" Kurtz asked.

Patrick O'Brien was the Assistant Head of Hospital Security, a retired New York City cop. Since the titular "Head" of hospital security was the hospital COO, who knew absolutely nothing about security, this meant that O'Brien was actually in charge. "I've been worse. I've been better," Patrick remarked, looking down at the pile of bodies with a disapproving expression. "I was hoping for a quiet night."

"Weren't we all?" Kurtz said.

Patrick grunted.

The biker's incoherent screams had turned into incoherent muttering. The pile wasn't moving quite so much. The biker's struggles had grown perhaps just a bit weaker.

"It may come as something of a surprise to you, Doc, but the forces of law and order are perfectly capable of handling this little problem," O'Brien said.

"Really?" Kurtz said. He peered doubtfully down at the pile.

"Really. We don't need you, doc. Time for the Lone Ranger to be home in bed, don't you think?"

Kurtz sighed. The fire hose looked *so* inviting. Of course, it might make a bit of a mess, but ER's were designed for that. They had drains in the floor so that blood and any other bodily fluids that happened to spray about could be neatly washed away. As if sensing Kurtz' thoughts, Patrick patted him on the shoulder. "He'll calm down soon. They got him with five hundred of ketamine in the rear end."

"Ah…"

"So no drastic measures will be required. Not tonight."

"I see," Kurtz said.

"Go home, Doc."

The biker was by this time lying on his back, spread-eagled, with two men sitting on each limb, his breathing harsh, his eyes glazed. "I guess you're right," Kurtz said reluctantly.

O'Brien grinned. "Have a good night, Doc."

Kurtz glanced at the clock, nearly one AM. He shook his head and sighed. "Good night, Patrick."

Chapter 5

He had never had difficulty sleeping, even during the worst of times. Sleep, in fact, had always been a refuge, but now, when his life held a brand new, golden, shining purpose, sleep was difficult to come by. There was so much more to do, so much to plan, so much to look forward to. He had so much *energy*. Life had taken on a kind of rosy glow.

He could feel himself changing. A new person, he reflected, with new standards: more discerning, more exacting, more demanding, both of himself and others. The easy way was no longer the best way. The standard now was perfection. Nothing less would do. Sitting by his chair was a cold tumbler containing Macallan Single Malt Scotch, 18 years old. He had bought it on an impulse. The hand holding the glass trembled, just a little. He ignored it and sipped his drink and let the dim light filter through the clear, crystal glass. *Perfection.*

Was it time?

Yes, he thought. It was. The initial ground work had been laid. It was time. It was time to move on to the next step in his campaign. *Soon*, he thought. The thought filled him with grim satisfaction.

Recently, the cafeteria at Easton had put in new coffee machines, which in addition to regular and decaf, dispensed French Vanilla, Hazelnut, Cappuccino, and hot cocoa. Kurtz was partial to the French Vanilla. He filled a medium sized styrofoam cup, picked out a container of chicken tenders and a cinnamon donut and took them over to a table by the window.

An almost new copy of the *Post* and a day-old copy of *US News and World Report* sat on the table. Kurtz picked up the *Post*, flipped it over and opened it to the back. Kurtz skipped the retrospective on the Jets' previous season and barely glanced at an analysis of the Knicks' prospects of reaching the playoffs. In Kurtz' opinion, the Knicks had no prospects whatsoever of reaching the playoffs.

"How's it going, Richard?"

Bill Werth, a psychiatrist and a friend of Kurtz' stood smiling down at him. Werth was slightly plump, with a wide, cheerful smile and curling black hair. Next to Werth stood a man who Kurtz did not know, tall, thin and stooped, holding a leather briefcase under one arm. Both men carried trays.

"Not bad," Kurtz said. "Have a seat."

The two men sat. Werth introduced Ted Burke, another psychiatrist. Burke shook hands limply and then proceeded to eat his lunch.

"How's Dina?" Kurtz asked.

"She's good." Werth smiled proudly. "She's up for full professor." Dina Werth taught English at NYU.

"That's great. Is there any doubt about it?"

Werth held his hand out and made a see-sawing motion. "Probably not. Her chairman wouldn't have put her up if he didn't think she was ready, but there's always politics."

Undoubtedly true, but Kurtz had no desire to hear about another institution's politics. He shrugged. "How about you?" he asked.

"How about me?"

"When are you up for promotion?"

Werth grimaced. "I'm on a lot of committees and the residents like me but I don't have much time to publish."

Kurtz had heard this lament before. He gave a sympathetic nod and took a bite out of a piece of chicken.

"The problem," Werth said, "is the social workers."

Kurtz looked at him. "Huh?"

Ted Burke, who had not appeared to be listening, grunted and nodded his head.

"Social workers?" Kurtz said.

"Yeah, social workers. Also, clinical psychologists, priests, rabbis, card readers, spiritualists and psychics. The competition. Anybody with a degree can set themselves up as a counselor these days. There are a lot of options besides seeing a psychiatrist. Social workers are a lot cheaper than psychiatrists."

"What does that have to do with you getting promoted?"

"I'm seeing more patients for less money, so there's less time to do all the other stuff."

"Ah," Kurtz said.

"We don't get paid like we used to," Werth said.

"Nobody does," Kurtz said.

"Nope." For a few minutes, all three men ate in silence, then Werth glanced at his watch and said, "Got to run. Patients to see."

Both men rose to their feet. "Nice meeting you," Burke said. They were the first words he had spoken.

"Sure," Kurtz said. "See you around."

Burke and Werth wandered off. Kurtz picked up the paper again, briefly glanced at an article on trout streams in Putnam County, and turned the page. A white piece of paper fell out and drifted to the floor. Kurtz picked it up. It was a sheet of typing paper, containing a crude drawing done in pen, the sort that a child might make, of a male figure, smiling, wielding a long knife and stabbing another figure, this one female, with huge, exaggerated breasts and an enormous pregnant belly, in the chest. Both figures wore white lab coats. Big drops of red blood dripped down to the floor. Kurtz grimaced. The paper contained no identifiable marks. Shrugging, he crumpled the drawing up and placed it on his tray. He had a gall bladder scheduled for after lunch, hopefully, an easy one.

"Doctor? Call for you on Line 2. It's Mrs. Kantor, from the Dean's office."

"Oh," Kurtz said. "Mrs. Kantor. From the Dean's office." He glanced at the clock and suppressed a sigh. "Put her on, thanks."

Mrs. Kantor had a bright, professional, cheery voice. "Dr. Kurtz? Dr. Kushner would appreciate it if you could drop by sometime this afternoon. He has something important to discuss with you."

Offhand, Kurtz couldn't see what the Dean would want to discuss with him, unless maybe he had a hernia. "Can you give me a clue?"

"I'm afraid not." Mrs. Kantor's voice grew hushed. "It's confidential."

Kurtz grimaced. He didn't have a lot of patients scheduled but the Dean's office was at Staunton, at least twenty blocks away from his own office at Easton and he had hoped to get home early. "How about three o'clock?"

"That would be fine."

The Dean stood up and smiled as Kurtz walked in, but the smile, Kurtz thought, appeared strained. "Dr. Kurtz," he said. "Sit down."

Kurtz sat. The Dean frowned and glanced down at his desk, then looked up again. "There's something that I need to discuss with you," he said. "It has to remain absolutely confidential."

Kurtz blinked. "Something surgical?"

"No," the Dean said. "It's more…administrative in nature."

"Administrative."

"Do I have your word?"

The Dean was a good-looking man, with dark hair touched with gray at the temples and a lean, athletic build. He wore a suit as if he had been born in it, which was almost a requirement for the position. At the moment, however, the suit appeared a bit rumpled and The Dean's face held a worried frown. Kurtz shrugged. "Sure," he said.

The Dean lightly touched a folder on his desk. "Take this," he said. "Look it over at your leisure, then get back to me."

A file full of notes, all of them hand written in crayon, except for the first two, which were written in pen: Christina Pirelli's best recollection of what they had said before she threw them in the garbage. Kurtz glanced through the file rapidly but they were all the same, tirades against the medical establishment, threats of bodily harm and formless declarations that 'Justice' would be done. Almost all had been directed at Christina, though recently, half a dozen had been received by assorted nurses on the Obstetrics floor and three had been received by the Dean.

Justice, Kurtz reflected…justice was such a slippery concept.

Each note had an attached sheet, presumably from Hospital Security, listing the recipient and the time and place that the note was received. There were twenty-six notes, dating back for almost two months. Seventeen of these had come by interoffice mail. Nine had arrived by the US postal service. All of these were still in their envelopes. The post marks showed that all had been mailed within a week of being read and all had been mailed from Manhattan, which meant nothing, really. Somebody living in the Bronx or Brooklyn or Connecticut could drop an envelope in a Manhattan mailbox and nobody would be the wiser. Smarter to do it that way, actually.

In addition, there was a single sheet documenting the dates and specifics—so far as they could be determined—of more than twenty harassing phone calls, again, the large majority to Christina Pirelli and all the rest to various members of her department.

The Dean, a man used to consulting experts in various fields, had decided that Richard Kurtz, MD, surgeon, was the right man for the job.

"As you will see, we've gone to the police. They haven't been helpful." The Dean shrugged. "They seem to feel that they have better things to do than investigate stupid notes and crank calls."

Kurtz was not surprised. Petty harassment was certainly a crime, but the police most often had more serious crimes to solve. "How about Security? Patrick O'Brien seems to know what he's doing."

The Dean raised an eyebrow. "Does he? I didn't realize that you knew him, but then, why shouldn't you know him?" The Dean sat back, his face grim. "The fact is that I don't know him. I'm glad to hear you express confidence. He was here before my arrival at the school and I've never had much to do with Security, before. I've never had to. You're one of us, a physician. I would appreciate your involvement in this case."

Kurtz looked at him, not allowing his face to express his doubts. "I'm not a cop. I've never been a cop. I'm a surgeon." A police surgeon, though, for almost a year, with the emphasis on *surgeon*. A police surgeon was employed by the police to oversee the care of wounded officers. A police surgeon, though he held the official rank of "Inspector," was definitely not a cop.

"So? I'm a pathologist. I'm also a coin collector. If we had a problem regarding a 1932 penny from the Philadelphia mint, I would feel myself perfectly capable of dealing with it." The Dean gave him a crooked smile. "You have a certain reputation around here. You may not be a policeman, but you have close contact with the police and somehow, you've managed to assist in solving three prominent crimes in the past two years."

True. Kurtz had managed to stumble and bumble his way through three murder investigations, in the course of which he had more than once been threatened, assaulted and nearly killed. "What exactly do you want from me, anyway?" Kurtz asked.

The Dean cocked his head to the side. "The motivation behind these incidents is unclear but they seem obviously designed to demoralize the staff of the Obstetrics unit, to intimidate a chairman, and possibly to damage both the reputation and the finances of the institution. So far, this has been confined to OB,"—he smiled ruefully—"plus myself, of course. We've managed to keep a lid on publicity, but I don't know how long we're going to be able to do that. The press isn't interested in a prank or two. I imagine that they would be considerably more interested in a clear pattern of intimidation."

"A little publicity might help," Kurtz said. "It would make it harder for the police to ignore the situation."

"Maybe. In the meantime, business would undoubtedly suffer. Columbia and Cornell offer the same services that we do. So do NYU and Montefiore and Mount Sinai. Nobody is obligated to come here.

"Please. I want you to look into this. Be a liaison between Security and my office. Deal with the police, if it should come to that." He shrugged. "Let's hope that it doesn't."

"Why don't you go the Pinkertons?" Kurtz said. "This is what they do."

"I wanted to. The Board of Trustees is unwilling to approve it. The Board is trying to pretend that this is a minor problem that is going to go away by itself. They may be right but I see no reason to assume so."

Kurtz frowned. "The Board, I suppose, knows nothing about me."

"Correct," the Dean said.

"And I suppose that in the event of discovery, you'll disavow any knowledge of my actions?"

"No," the Dean said. "I won't."

The Dean, or so Kurtz had heard, wasn't a bad guy. He was a good administrator, and, for a good administrator, reasonably honest. That was the word on the Dean.

"Give me the folder," Kurtz said. "I'll take a look at it."

"Thank you," the Dean said.

"I'm not making any promises," Kurtz said.

The Dean gave him a tired smile. "That's all I can ask."

The sky outside was cloudy. A seagull wheeled outside the picture window, then flew off, its wings steady against the wind. "You ever watch that show, *Diagnosis Murder?*" Barent asked. They were sitting in Kurtz' apartment, sipping coffee. A plate with two chocolate chip cookies was balanced on Barent's knee.

"The one with Dick van Dyke? No. I've never seen it."

"I have," Lenore said. "I like it."

"I've seen it a couple of times. Not what I would call true-to-life entertainment but I sometimes get a kick out of it."

"I thought you didn't like mysteries," Kurtz said.

"Usually I don't, but this one, I get a kick out of. I think of it more as a parody than a mystery. I suppose that it reminds me of you." Barent gave him a toothy grin.

"Oh, thanks," Kurtz said.

"This latest thing now, it's almost made for TV."

Kurtz looked at him. "Obscene phone calls and threatening letters? Seems a little trivial for TV. Anyway, you're on Homicide. Why do you care about petty harassment?"

"An excellent question." Barent grimaced. "After three murders involving Staunton and Easton, Harry and I are now considered the departmental gophers for all things medical."

Kurtz' lips quirked upward. "I don't know. Aren't crank calls below your pay grade?"

"You might think so, but actually, we're paid to do what we're told. They told us to investigate, so we'll investigate."

"Crank calls," Kurtz said.

"And threatening letters. Don't forget the threatening letters." Barent shrugged. "The guy who's doing it seems to know a lot of personal information about his victims. They're scared."

"Sounds as if they have reason to be," Lenore said.

Barent took a bite out of a cookie and thoughtfully chewed it. "Maybe they do, maybe they don't. Most crank calls and threatening letters turn out to be nothing."

"Are they all going to women?" Lenore asked.

"A few have gone to the Dean. All of the rest have gone to women," Kurtz said.

"Most crank calls do go to women, and most of the perps turn out to be men," Barent said.

"Figures," Lenore said. "All those dominance hormones."

"That's it exactly. Most of these guys have trouble with women. They resent women and they're angry about it. The administration has done their best to keep it quiet. Publicity of this sort is not designed to stimulate confidence in the security of the medical center."

"That's for sure," Kurtz said.

"It might, in fact, do considerable financial damage. There are a lot of hospitals in New York. Nobody has to go to Staunton. NYU and Columbia and Mount Sinai and a half a dozen others are perfectly viable choices."

The Dean, Kurtz pondered, had said much the same thing.

Lenore looked back and forth between Kurtz' frown and Barent's bland smile. She shook her head. "It also sounds," she said, "as if you don't have much to go on."

"This is true," Kurtz said.

Barent leaned forward, his face suddenly intent. "Whoever is doing this knows a lot about the medical center. Most likely, he works there."

Kurtz had already come to this conclusion. "Seems likely," he said.

"It could be anybody: a doctor, a lab tech, one of the cleanup staff, even somebody in Security."

"Even me."

"I'm willing to bet that it's not you."

Lenore gave a gentle, lady-like snort. Barent ignored her. "The Dean isn't wrong. We could use somebody on the inside, somebody who looks like he belongs there. A cop can't do that. We don't speak the language."

"A cop wouldn't have to pose as a doctor. As you said, one of the lab techs, even somebody in Security."

"Possible," Barent said. His voice was grudging. "But not optimal. We need somebody who has a legitimate excuse to be anywhere at any time, without arousing suspicion. Everybody else there has a specific job. They're part of a team. The nurses have an assigned station. The cleaning people have shifts and rotations. So does Security. You can't just wander around. Your co-workers get suspicious."

"Okay," Kurtz said, "but I can't just wander around, either, not when I'm in the OR and not when I'm seeing patients. So, what exactly do you want me to do?"

Lenore made a gagging sound. Kurtz looked at her. Lenore sipped her tea.

"Just what the Dean asked you to do," Barent said. "Ordinarily, we would resent a civilian butting in, but you've been useful before and you know not to step on our toes." He shrugged. "Keep your eyes open. Look into it. If you find something out, let us know."

"It sounds," Kurtz said, "as if you're not going to be devoting a lot of time to this very important case." Already, Kurtz reflected, Barent had shown more interest in the case than he had expected. "In fact, the Dean gave me the impression that the police weren't going to be involved at all."

Barent grinned. "Like you said, I'm a murder cop. I will be available to consult when needed and I'll be there if it seems necessary but Harry is taking point on this one—one of the advantages of seniority—but Harry also has bigger cases on his plate."

Barent took another bite out of his cookie and winked at Lenore. "I got a call from the Captain, who got a call from the Chief of Police, who got a call from somebody on the Board of Trustees. It's politics. They want it to stop. Okay. We all understand that. We even agree with it, but nobody in the NYPD is going to spend more time on this than they have to." He stolidly chewed the rest of his cookie, put down the cup of coffee and rose to his feet. "Hopefully, we can solve it quickly."

Kurtz sighed. "We can always hope."

Chapter 6

Vinnie Steinberg poked his head over the drapes and peered down at the incision. "How is the Search Committee going?" he asked.

Kurtz looked up. "Not bad. Why?"

"How are you getting along with Serkin?"

Ah, Serkin…from the look on Steinberg's face, he seemed not to believe that anybody, or at least not Kurtz, could get along with Serkin.

"Just fine," Kurtz said. Kurtz' hands kept moving. The case was an inguinal hernia in a healthy fifty-year old. They had perhaps twenty minutes left.

"Yeah?" Steinberg looked doubtful.

"I try to humor him," Kurtz said.

Steinberg's eyebrows rose. "Really?"

Kurtz shrugged. "He's not my chairman. I've found that he tends to be perfectly pleasant if you wipe the drool off his chin, pat him on the head and tell him he's a genius."

"You tell him he's a genius?"

"I was speaking metaphorically. Actually, I ignore him as much as possible."

"Oh. I see. That's probably just as well." Steinberg's face disappeared back down below the drapes. Kurtz could hear him fumbling with the blood pressure cuff. He popped back up a few minutes later. "He's asked me to be the Director here at Easton."

"Yeah? What happened to Patel?"

Mahendra Patel had been the Director of Anesthesiology at Easton for nearly ten years. He had been brought in by Gary Austin, the former Chairman of Anesthesiology. That, or so Kurtz had heard, had been a difficult time. The anesthesia staff at Easton used to be private. The Board of Trustees, seeking to make the place more 'academic,' had negotiated with Austin to take over the department. This naturally involved putting the anesthesiologists, who formerly billed for their services and kept what they billed, on salary, a considerably smaller salary than their previous private practice income.

Anesthesiologists were more vulnerable to this sort of thing than most other physicians since anesthesiologists were 'hospital-based.' Unlike surgeons, they didn't have their own offices, they didn't have to build up a practice and they didn't control patients who would just as likely as not go with them if the institution pissed them off enough to leave. The majority of academic institutions allowed private surgeons to operate, a mutually beneficial relationship. The surgeons were given a courtesy title like "voluntary" or "adjunct" assistant professor and the hospital received more patients. Very few such institutions, however, allowed private anesthesiologists.

The anesthesiologists at Easton had, of course, resisted these efforts. They had hired a lawyer and sued for anti-trust and restraint of trade and had, ultimately, lost. The administration at Easton was happy with the increased revenue. The fact that the department of anesthesiology did not become more academic, did not do more research or train more residents or advance the prestige of the institution in any way, somehow quickly ceased to be a concern.

"Serkin has asked Patel to resign," Steinberg said.

Patel, so far as Kurtz knew, was a good chief, an excellent clinician, easy to work with and responsive to problems. Kurtz had never heard anything bad about him. "Why? What's the matter with Patel?"

"In my opinion? Nothing. In Serkin's opinion?" Steinberg shrugged.

"What does Patel say?"

Steinberg looked around the room. The scrub nurse was peering down at the wound. The circulator was writing something in the patient's chart on the other side of the OR. Neither of them seemed to be listening, but Steinberg shook his head slowly. "You got a few minutes after the case?" he asked.

"Sure," Kurtz said.

"Let's get a cup of coffee."

Thirty minutes later, they arrived at Kurtz' office. Steinberg sat down on the couch, took the top off his coffee, blew on it and sipped. He looked surprised. "This isn't bad."

"I think they've changed vendors."

"They should have done it a long time ago."

"True," Kurtz said. Actually, it was pretty mediocre coffee, only marginally better than the old coffee. Except for the French Vanilla. Kurtz took a sip and smiled to himself. Now that they were in private, Steinberg seemed reluctant to talk. Kurtz got along fine with Steinberg in the OR but they had never socialized. Steinberg had a wife and four kids, wore a yarmulke, went to *Schul* every Saturday and possessed a stamp collection that consumed whatever was left of his passions after family and work. Not exactly a lifestyle that appealed to Kurtz. Steinberg was a good guy, though. He did a good job and had a keen sense of humor. Kurtz had always liked Steinberg, in a distant sort of way.

"You know about the situation with night coverage?" Steinberg said.

Offhand, Kurtz didn't. "What about it?"

"Serkin has decided that four residents in house is too many. He wants to cut it down."

"So?"

"The place is a trauma center. Sometimes we run all night long."

This, Kurtz knew. Sometimes he ran all night long, too. "That's what trauma centers do."

"Sure. But we also run an add-on list. Serkin wants to get rid of the add-on list."

"Add-ons are a problem," Kurtz said.

Steinberg rolled his eyes and gave a resigned sigh. "More for us than they are for you, believe me."

Add-ons were indeed a problem. Easton had sixteen operating rooms, and Staunton had twenty. Every one of those rooms, on an average day, was scheduled to finish at 4:00 PM. Unfortunately, what with late surgeons, sick calls, consent forms that failed to satisfy all the petty legalistic requirements and cases that simply took longer than expected, at least a third of those rooms ran late every day. Then there were the add-ons, theoretically urgent or emergent cases which, most of the time, were simply cases that the surgeon had not been able to fit into his elective time, and so they became 'emergencies.' A nice fat add-on list meant that at least a few of the nurses and anesthesia staff didn't get home until midnight. Kurtz,

48

who liked his evenings, had never booked an 'add-on' that was not a true emergency. "So, what's bothering you?" he asked. "You guys hate add-ons."

"Just pulling the residents isn't going to solve the problem. The surgeons are still going to book the add-ons and the nurses aren't cutting back on staff. They're still going to be able to run the same four rooms all night long and we aren't. The system is still going to be designed around add-ons, except for us. We're going to look bad."

"Oh," Kurtz said.

"Patel pointed this out to Serkin at the last Executive Committee meeting."

"Oh," Kurtz said again.

"So, a few days after the meeting, Serkin asks me to drop by his office and offers me the job. Patel, it seems, has pissed him off."

"Tough one."

"I think so."

"And what does Patel say about it?"

"I think he's relieved. Serkin is not the easiest guy in the world to work for."

"So, what are you going to do?"

Steinberg looked down at his coffee as if searching for enlightenment. He shrugged. "You know all those guys who were willing to manage the Yankees for George Steinbrenner? Sooner or later, they all got fired, but there was always another one waiting to step up to the plate and take a swing at it, willing to delude himself that this time, it would be different."

"So, you're going to turn it down?"

"Nope." Steinberg shrugged again, then looked up at Kurtz. "All those guys George Steinbrenner fired? They all went on to bigger and better things. Even if it doesn't work out, it's an opportunity—a chance to show what I can do—and besides, maybe this time, it really will be different."

"Ah," Kurtz said. "Well, I certainly wish you luck."

A hospital is its own little world, each specialized floor its own community, with its own unique character. The cancer wards were quiet, not necessarily grim, but there was always an undertone of tragedy floating through the air. The pediatric floors were happy places, more often than not, since kids tended to get better and go home. The OB wards were happier still, with nurses and new mothers and anxious fathers all milling about, looking forward to the future. The surgical floors were businesslike and organized, the psych wards chaotic and locked from the inside.

Kurtz knew all this but he rarely thought about it. He thought about it now, as he wandered from floor to floor, trying to see the place through the eyes of a potential terrorist. He shook his head. Despite the differences, all the floors shared certain characteristics. All of them had nurses bustling in and out of patients' rooms and gossiping at the nurses' station. All of them had housekeepers periodically mopping the floors and changing the linens. The pharmacy technicians pushed their carts down every hallway, re-stocking the PYXIS machines with medications, and all of them had doctors striding down the corridors, most of them wearing suits and ties, with stethoscopes draped around their necks like talismans of power. Another characteristic that they all shared, except for psych and maybe OB and pediatrics, both of which required you to call in before the door could be opened, was that they were easy to get into. At all the other floors, visitors were supposed to check in at the nursing station, and some of them did, at least the first time they arrived, but the place wasn't exactly security conscious. If you were there and you looked like you knew what you were doing, it was just casually assumed that you belonged. Anybody and his brother could waltz right through. Each floor had a bank of elevators in the middle and two stairways, one at each end. The stairways on peds, OB and psych were locked. The others were all open. This, Kurtz morosely reflected, was not going to be easy. He glanced at his watch and headed for the elevator. Ten minutes later, he was sitting at a table with Patrick O'Brien, cups of coffee at their elbows. "When did it start?" Kurtz asked.

Patrick O'Brian gave him a hurt look. Patrick was pouting. The Administration had made it quite clear that the forces of justice were to cooperate fully with the designated savior on the case, but Patrick still resented it, and Kurtz didn't blame him in the slightest. Kurtz had been a clerk for CID for a mere two years, which qualified him for exactly nothing. Patrick had put in twenty before retiring to a job as head of security. What made Kurtz better at this than Patrick or any of his men, for that matter?

Nothing. Patrick knew it and Kurtz knew it, too, but none of that made the slightest bit of difference because the Dean wanted Kurtz on the case and the Dean called the shots, at least until the Board of Trustees decided to wise up.

"We're not sure," Patrick said. "It could have been going on for months before anybody thought to report it." He shrugged. "The first one we know of was a little over two months ago, the second was two weeks later. After that..." Patrick puffed out his cheeks and let his unhappy gaze wander to the ceiling. "They seemed to come more often, maybe one every three or four days or so."

"Any breaks in the timing?"

Patrick shrugged. "The longest interval was a little over two weeks. The shortest was two days."

Two weeks could be significant. Two weeks offered plenty of time for a disgruntled employee to take a vacation; an assumption, of course, but considering how long this had been going on, the various locations in which the notes had been discovered and the incidents had taken place, an employee certainly seemed most likely. Then again, it was also possible that the notes had continued to arrive during the supposed hiatus, but that the recipients had chosen to ignore them rather than turn them in.

"You got a roster of all the employees?"

Patrick rolled his eyes and handed Kurtz a folder. The folder was over an inch thick. "You got the hard copy plus there's a CD with an excel spreadsheet. It's got all the employees, all the students, all the faculty, including the "voluntaries," and all patients who've been here continuously for the past three months."

"Many of those?"

"Some kids with congenital anomalies and a few gomers with chronic illness waiting for nursing home placement. Twelve in all."

Neither gomers nor kids, all of whom were seriously ill and bed ridden, or they wouldn't be living permanently in a hospital, seemed likely to be the bad guy.

"Any chance of getting vacation schedules?"

Patrick grinned and handed Kurtz another folder.

"Anybody with an obvious grievance?"

"It's a 600-bed hospital with a transplant program, a cardiac surgery program, multiple ICU's, a burn center and a trauma center. Approximately two patients die here every week and plenty of others are unhappy with what they perceive as their physicians' incompetence. I'm not an expert on the quality of medical care but when the physicians say that most people die from their diseases, not because anybody made a mistake, I've got no reason to believe otherwise; but sometimes the bereaved don't see it that way."

"Are you including Easton?"

Patrick narrowed his eyes. "They have their own Security. We have nothing to do with Easton."

"It's an affiliated hospital. At least half of the medical staff have privileges there, and I'll bet that plenty of the nurses and techs work part time at both places."

"So far as we know, none of the incidents have taken place at Easton."

Kurtz hesitated. He took a bite out of his sandwich, stolidly chewed, then spoke. "I'm not so sure about that," he said.

"Why? What do you mean?"

"A couple of weeks ago, I picked up a newspaper in the cafeteria. A drawing fell out. It was pretty ugly. A pregnant woman being stabbed by a man. It looked like something a kid would do. It was crayon, just like all the notes."

O'Brien sipped from his coke, looked out the window of the little diner. A mild drizzle was falling on the sidewalk. "You found it," he said.

"Yeah. In a newspaper, sitting on a table."

"It was never delivered."

"The drawing? No. I threw it out."

"None of them have been received at Easton. Not, at least, that we know of, but I think, if there were more than a couple, we would have been told by now. Somebody would have come forward."

Kurtz shrugged. "So how did the drawing get there?"

"Assuming it was done by the perpetrator, then the guy's job probably requires him to go back and forth between the two hospitals. Or else somebody at Staunton just happened to pick up the paper, brought it over to Easton and forgot about it. Or maybe it was delivered, and the person who got it stuffed it into a paper and left the paper in the cafeteria."

"You believe that?"

"Not really. No, you're probably right. Most likely, it was left there by the perp."

Kurtz grunted. "Do you have a list of the ones who've filed complaints?"

Patrick rolled his eyes to the ceiling and handed over another folder with another disk.

"Thanks," Kurtz said.

Patrick gave a barely audible sniff.

Serkin and Castillo were looking over papers. Dunn and Christina Pirelli whispered together in the back of the room, glancing occasionally at Serkin, who ignored them both. Moller walked in a couple of minutes later, accompanied by the latest interviewee, Richard Green, from Barnes, in St. Louis. "Sit down anywhere," Moller said.

They went around the room and introduced themselves, after which Moller rubbed his hands together, gave a sunny smile and said, "Why don't we begin…"

Richard Green, it quickly became apparent, was not going to get the job. For one thing, he twitched. Every one or two seconds a different part of his body would give a little jerk. Usually it was his eyes, sometimes his shoulders, sometimes his hands. This annoying mannerism might have been written off as an unfortunate neurological condition, but he also tended to wander around a point and not quite answer the question that was asked. It was a short interview. After a mere thirty minutes, Moller smiled brightly and said, "Thank you, Doctor Green. The secretary will conduct you to your first meeting. Have a nice day."

Green, seemingly oblivious to the undercurrents that he had created, smiled happily back and rose to his feet. "Let's hope that this is the start of a something exciting," he said.

"That would be nice," Moller answered.

Ten seconds later, Green was on his way. As soon as the door closed behind him, Moller smiled around the room. "Well?"

"He needs his lithium level checked," Dunn said.

"Not exactly what the job requires," said Nash.

"Anybody else?" Moller waited. Nobody else spoke. Moller shrugged his shoulders and made a note on his pad. "Scratch Richard Green," he said.

She had come to dread the daily trip to the mailbox. Gingerly, she opened the box, picked out the small pile of envelopes, walked back inside, hung her jacket on the back of a chair and looked over the stack. Sure enough, another letter had arrived. There was no stamp on the envelope. It was plain and white and unmarked, but she knew what she would find inside. She opened it, her hands trembling, and unfolded the single, white sheet:

> **You've always been stupid. Hard work alone isn't going to be enough. You also have to have brains and that's where you're lacking. Turner thinks you're an idiot. Go home before you flunk out. Go home before you waste any more of your father's money.**

She hated morning rounds. She didn't like speaking in front of her colleagues. She did know her patients, but when the attending and the residents and the other students were looking at her, the words, somehow, seemed to stick in her throat. Yesterday, she had nervously laughed, and Dr. Turner had made some obnoxious comment about laughing at her own ignorance. Turner was nobody's favorite attending but he seemed to take particular delight in abusing her.

She was far away from home and tired and alone. "Why do you want to do this, anyway?" her father had said. He had never tried to forbid her from pursuing a career but his disappointment in her was plain. She was the first generation to be born in this country and the first to go to college. Girls didn't become doctors back in Kosovo. They got married and had children and raised families.

Why did she want to do it? She hardly knew anymore. It wasn't what she had expected. It was hard and endlessly demanding and she was always tired and the hospital smelled bad. Her latest patient was five years old and dying from an undifferentiated sarcoma. He was sedated but there wasn't enough sedation in the world to overcome the pain he must be feeling. He whimpered constantly in his sleep and there was nothing that any of them could do for him but watch him suffer and wait for him to die.

Silently, she sat down at the table, put her head in her hands and began to cry.

Chapter 7

"Yaaah!" The scream was strictly by the book but Kurtz still felt stupid doing it. The idea was to distract the opponent, except that at this level of competition, everybody was good and nobody was going to be distracted by loud noises. The crowd expected it, though, and so did the judges. Style counted.

At one time, Kurtz had toyed with the idea of turning pro. He was good, but the idea of getting his head beaten in for a living seemed, in the end, to lack appeal. He had quit fighting for years until a couple of unexpected murders and a recent brush with an organized crime conspiracy (not to mention a few psychopaths) renewed his interest in the sport.

His opponent, a kid named Brian Marx, barely grinned as Kurtz cartwheeled in. Both of them ignored the noise. Marx abruptly stopped grinning when Kurtz reversed direction and swept his feet out from under him with a well-timed kick.

"Point," the referee said.

From the corner of his eye, Kurtz could see Lenore sitting in the stands with David Chao, Kurtz' partner, and Carrie Owens, David's small, blonde, newly announced fiancée. David, who usually gave the matches his total attention, was tonight gazing sappily into his lady love's clear blue eyes.

Marx rose to his feet, frowning. The referee held up his hand. Both men bowed. Marx immediately aimed a punch at Kurtz' face. Kurtz moved back by half an inch and the punch passed by his nose. Marx must really have been rattled. The back of his neck was wide open. Kurtz hit him with the edge of his hand.

"Point," the referee said.

One more point and Kurtz would have the match. Marx shook his head. He took a deep breath. Again, they bowed. This time, Marx circled warily, his hands open, his face impassive. Kurtz circled with him. Marx spread his arms wide, then took a sidewise step. Interesting, Kurtz thought. The white crane, a Tibetan style that looked good in movies but had one decisive practical weakness. The style emphasized evasive tactics and well-timed counterattacks.

Kurtz smiled to himself. With two points to his opponent' none, Kurtz did not have to attack. Sooner or later, Marx would have to come to him or he would lose the match by default.

They continued to circle. Marx' eyes flicked to the side, to the clock hanging on the wall. Suddenly, he screamed and lunged toward Kurtz' chest. He was fast. Kurtz barely avoided the lunge and had no time left to counter. Marx twisted, turned, aimed a kick at Kurtz' legs. Kurtz jumped, landed on the balls of his feet and barely managed to block a reverse kick at his abdomen.

The buzzer sounded. Marx drew a deep breath, sighed, then grinned. The two men bowed, then left the circle.

Peter Reinhardt was counting the days. Only seventy-three left. Seventy-three days until freedom. Funny, he didn't used to think of it that way. He was a physician, a surgeon, a *heart surgeon*. Heart surgeons were at the apex of the physicianly pecking order, the elite of the elite. Funny, how things changed. He had never realized how the responsibility weighed on him until he decided to lay it down. Now, he could hardly wait.

"Mount Sinai says they can do it for twelve," Alex Calderon said. Alex Calderon was the CFO of Staunton University Medical Center. He had an MBA from Harvard. His suit was expensive and fit him well. A *Phi Beta Kappa* key dangled from his vest. His hair was neat, his moustache a perfect black line on his upper lip. Peter Reinhardt couldn't stand him.

Twelve meant twelve thousand, as in dollars. Twelve thousand dollars per patient. This was what a chairman's job had come to. In the old days, a mere decade or so ago, they did a case, they charged for it. Oh, they might not get paid in full, but they got most of it. Today, they had to negotiate with every insurance company for a flat rate. Capitation, they called it. So much per head.

He sighed.

"If we want the contract," Calderon said, "we have to go better than twelve. Can we do that?"

Nice that they were asking him. Two years ago, the administration had seen fit to bid on a contract with Columbia-HFC for liver transplants. A total disaster. Nobody, including the chairman of surgery, had the faintest idea what their costs were

going   to   be.
But they knew that they couldn't let Downstate outbid them. It was a matter of pride. They got the contract, all right. And now they were stuck with it, losing at least three thousand a head on every case that came through the OR.

"Once you take out all of the overhead, twelve thousand means that my people would get paid about three hundred per case," Reinhardt said. "On average."

Calderon looked relieved. "You can do it, then," he said.

"That depends on what you mean by the word 'can'. Before you actually get a patient to the OR, you're talking a minimum of three hours of work, what with seeing the patient, reviewing the records, looking over the labs, talking with the cardiologist and then talking again with the patient and, usually, the patient's family. The case itself takes about five hours. That's if everything goes smoothly. The ICU stay averages about twenty hours but thankfully, we've got fellows, so the surgeon himself probably spends no more than a couple of hours there. Then you send the patient home and see him again a couple of times, say another two hours in total. Twelve hours of work, *minimum*, and that's for a case that has no complications. At three hundred bucks, that comes to twenty-five dollars an hour. Less than half of what a car mechanic would get. A lot less than a plumber."

"But you can do it," Calderon said. He was smiling.

"For twelve thousand? You said that Mount Sinai was bidding twelve thousand. What are we supposed to bid?"

Calderon looked at him carefully, weighing his words. "We were considering a bid of ten."

"Ten thousand."

Calderon gave a crisp nod.

"Do I have any choice?" Reinhardt asked.

"Of course, you have a choice," Calderon said. "You can say 'no.'"

"And if I say no, what happens then?"

"Then Mount Sinai gets the bid."

Reinhardt stared at him. "Don't offer ten," he said. "Offer eleven five. We might break even. Who knows? Maybe they'll go for it."

Calderon sniffed. "We have it on excellent authority that Mount Sinai is willing to go down to eleven."

"Eleven," Reinhardt said. "Right." His head was pounding. He looked at Calderon's blandly blank face. When did these guys come to own us? How did that happen?

"I will not accept responsibility for ten thousand," Reinhardt said. "Not even for eleven."

Calderon frowned. "Your department might take a loss, but we feel that the institution as a whole would do better than break even, and we would be willing to supplement your budget from the general revenue."

Clearly, this guy was delusional. It *always* cost more than you expected. That was a law of the Universe. Reinhardt closed his eyes and swallowed. "As I said, I will not accept responsibility for that bid."

"But you won't say no."

Reinhardt smiled. He felt like his face was cracking. "No," he said, "I won't say no."

Seventy-three days, and counting.

Henry Tolliver was forty-six years old, a little on the young side to be applying for chairmanships, but he had eighty-seven peer-reviewed papers to his credit, nearly three million in NIH grants, and a full professorship at Hopkins. He had a round, ruddy face, a dignified pot-belly and prematurely gray, curling hair. He looked around the table and beamed, as if there were no place on earth that he would rather be at that instant. Moller had already introduced the committee and they had spent a few minutes on casual chit-chat when Christina Pirelli asked the first significant question. "Tell me, Doctor Tolliver, what is your vision of the sort of department you would like to run?"

The chairmen on the committee tended to use the word 'vision.' 'Vision' meant that they saw things that the ordinary mortal did not. It was very important that a chairman have vision.

Tolliver nodded wisely. "Patient care must come first and foremost. The second priority is that the residents and fellows be properly trained, but make no mistake, I want to run an academic department, which means an environment where scholarly work is not only encouraged but rewarded."

Encouragement could mean so many things, Kurtz thought: a raise, a bonus…a flogging.

Serkin, however, nodded. So did Nash and Castillo. Moller looked doubtful. "How do you plan on accomplishing this?"

"By aligning the incentives properly. Reward people for their productivity. I would give salary increases for research productivity but reserve a bonus for those who are most clinically productive. That way, everybody has something to work for."

"How much experience do you have with managing a budget?" Moller asked.

Tolliver gave a minute frown. "My father was a businessman, and I've taken two management courses at Harvard. I'm aware of the principle that the money coming in has to equal the money going out."

In other words, none. Tolliver was Associate Chief of Thoracic Surgery, which sounded good but which meant almost nothing. Tolliver had no budgetary experience whatsoever, but this did not necessarily disqualify him for the position. Obviously, Tolliver was a smart man, which might be enough to carry him through if he was also a hard-headed and practical man. You didn't need an MBA to be a chairman, though these days, a lot of people who were aiming for chairmanships decided to get one. Nevertheless, a little experience would have been reassuring, to Kurtz at least, and presumably to Moller as well.

"Tell me," Serkin said, "do you plan on continuing your research once you're a chairman?" It was a question with no good answer. There had been considerable turnover among the cardiac surgeons in the past few years. One of the reasons cited had been the lack of opportunity to do research. A chairman was expected to give his people a reason to stay, an opportunity to develop a career. On the other hand, a chairman who did research himself might not have the time for the numerous other tasks required of a chairman.

Tolliver looked faintly surprised at the question. "Of course," he said.

Serkin, to Kurtz' surprise, frowned at this. "Chairman," he said, "is, in essence, an administrative position. If the demands of the position turn out to be such that you have no time available for research, would you then be willing to give up your research?" Or not too surprisingly, now that Kurtz thought about it. Serkin, he recalled, had abandoned his own research as soon as he arrived at Staunton, and apparently without a qualm. No research, no clinical work. Serkin spent his days in a business suit. Very nice suits, Kurtz noted. They looked like Armani.

"I will do whatever turns out to be necessary to be successful in the position." Tolliver looked like he meant it. Serkin nodded his head and sat back in his chair.

"However," Tolliver went on, "I do have funding. I would expect to bring along my research assistant, who is quite capable of carrying on the work without my direct participation. I am certain that I could find some time to give guidance." The work, according to Tolliver's CV, was on the exact mechanisms of cellular damage in association with brain injury after cardiopulmonary bypass, a very hot topic these days.

Christina Pirelli grunted. Castillo and Nash exchanged glances. Funding was an important asset. Funding bought equipment and space and personnel, and in an emergency, might be used to surreptitiously hire another surgeon or two on a 'research line.' Nobody gave up funding unless they had to.

Christina Pirelli looked at Moller and gave a tiny nod. Moller smiled at Tolliver and asked, "What can we tell you about Staunton?"

Tolliver leaned forward, his face intent. "First of all, what is the size of your support staff?"

And so it went. Fifteen minutes later, Henry Tolliver was on his way to see Peter Reinhardt. After that, he would talk to the Dean, then somebody in hospital administration, then the head nurse in cardiac and at least two of the cardiac surgeons. He would spend a full day, by the end of which, Henry Tolliver would presumably have a good working knowledge of the ins and outs of the institution and the institution would have a good working knowledge of Henry Tolliver.

On the whole, Kurtz approved. He liked the way Moller was running the committee. He even liked the people they were bringing in for interviews, most of them. He smiled to himself at the thought.

The process was seductive. He had developed an appreciation for research—if not for the research clowns—that he hadn't had in the beginning. Research was the glue that held an academic department—and an academic institution—together. The trick was to have balance. You couldn't let yourself be blinded by the number of papers. You had to insist that the guy also be rational. God knows, a number of the applicants obviously were not. One former chairman who had had the gall to send in a CV—an otherwise amazingly impressive CV—was known to have been asked to resign because he had been having an affair with one of his junior residents. This would not usually have resulted in a firing, but the affair was a homosexual one and the resident had felt 'pressured' to go along. Also, the resident's wife had made quite a stink.

But Tolliver, at least, seemed normal. Not bad, Kurtz thought, not bad at all.

"I've seen you naked. You're really ugly when you're naked. Your tits hang down to your waist and the fat on your ass jiggles when you walk. Did anybody ever tell you that?" The voice on the phone held a pleasant, lilting tone.

Christina Pirelli ground her teeth together. Christina had had a long day, first surgery, then a joint practice meeting with pediatrics to discuss complications in the neonatal ICU, then a meeting with the obstetrical nursing staff. The nurses were upset. Gee. Wonder why.

"I know all about you," the voice said. "I've watched you when you're naked. I've watched you masturbate in the shower. I've watched you sucking off your boyfriends. Would you like to do it right now? Would you like to suck me off? Does my voice turn you on?"

Not really, she thought. Mostly, it grossed her out, which, she supposed, was the point. The voice was obviously filtered through some sort of device, with a deep mechanical vibration. It sounded inhuman. This wasn't about sex, or even sexual titillation, it was about power, the power to make her react. The voice annoyed her, and also frightened her, just a little, but still...

"Answer me, you bitch," the voice said.

Okay, more than a little. She had had caller ID installed on her home phone but the guy seemed to have a scrambler of some sort. The numbers that it reported were random. The police had so far been able to do nothing.

If she put the phone down, the SOB would only call back. If she took it off the hook, then nobody else would be able to reach her. She looked at the clock on the wall, considering. She wasn't on call and she did have her beeper and her cell phone, though she never quite trusted the cell phone. In Christina's experience, cell phones tended to have dead zones, though dead zones were much rarer than they used to be, particularly here in the city. Mirthlessly smiling, she hung up the phone, waited five seconds, then picked it up again and listened. Good. A dial-tone. She put the ear-piece down next to the cradle and checked to see that the cell phone and the battery in her beeper were fully charged.

She went into her den and tried to go over the income projections for next year. However, after ten minutes of reading the same two lines she realized that her mind just wasn't in it. That phone call…there had been at least a dozen of them, and Christina wasn't the only one who was getting them. Most of the nurses on the obstetrical unit were also being harassed. For all she knew, half the women in the hospital were getting the same disgusting treatment. It wasn't the sort of thing you liked to talk about. Grimly putting down the flow chart, she looked at her watch. She had a hysterectomy scheduled for the morning, as well as two post-due patients coming in for induction of labor. Damn it, she really didn't need this.

And besides, her tits did not hang down to her waist and the fat on her ass did not jiggle, not more than a little, and that little, she had it on good authority, was a definite turn-on. She did masturbate in the shower, now and then, but there was no way the pervert could have seen that.

Shaking her head, she rose to her feet and padded into the bedroom. Obviously, she wasn't going to be able to concentrate on income projections. She might as well try to get some sleep.

Maybe, now that she thought about it, she'd take a shower first, a nice, long, hot one. It would calm her down.

Chapter 8

The monthly meeting of the OR Committee at Easton was scheduled for 8:00 AM the next morning. Kurtz rarely missed an OR committee meeting. Not that they ever accomplished very much but he was expected to go, and you just weren't one of the boys if you didn't participate in the group dynamic, even if every single member of the committee knew that it was a waste of time. He often regretted having accepted membership when Moller offered it to him. Kurtz' problem, he often thought, was an exaggerated sense of civic responsibility. A more boring and basically dysfunctional organization would be difficult to imagine. For one thing, the majority of the members were the surgical chairmen at Staunton, a bunch of strutting bulls if ever there was one. Aside from the surgical chairmen, membership consisted of the head OR nurse, the Chief of Anesthesia, the OR administrator and two ad hoc members appointed by the chairman, in this case Kurtz and John Watkins, a gynecologist who wasn't a bad guy but who hardly ever opened his mouth.

Kurtz was on time. The majority, as usual, wandered in late. Most went over to the coffee pot on the side table and fixed themselves a cup before sitting down. Vinnie Steinberg arrived, hesitated, then found a seat next to Kurtz. He looked grim. Kurtz didn't blame him. This was Steinberg's first meeting as Chief and Patel had been popular. "Relax," Kurtz said. "What can they do to you?"

"Eat me alive?"

"Hey, don't worry. They'll cook you first. The pain won't last more than twenty minutes, thirty at the most."

"What a relief." Steinberg grimaced.

Moller, perched serenely at the end of the table, gave Steinberg an encouraging smile, then called out, "Let's get going, people." He waited a few moments for everybody to sit down and stop talking, then said, "First of all, does everybody accept the minutes from last month's meeting?"

Ralph Akins, the Chairman of Orthopedics, big, fat and balding, raised a lackadaisical hand. "Motion to accept."

Reese Stephens, Chairman of Urology, thin, beady-eyed and also balding, said, "Seconded."

Moller looked around the table. Nobody spoke. "Minutes accepted as written," Moller said. Then he smiled, "As our second order of business, I would like to welcome Dr. Steinberg to the committee."

Everybody stared at Steinberg. Steinberg gave a weak smile back.

"Okay," Moller said, "next item is the OR statistics for last month. Irene?"

The rest of the business was routine until the open forum at the end. Moller glanced at the clock and said, "There's one more item that we need to discuss." He looked at Steinberg. "An important item, I'm afraid. The Department of Anesthesiology is changing their system of night coverage. I would like to hear from Dr. Steinberg exactly what this is going to mean for us."

Steinberg looked glum but he nodded resolutely. "Basically, night coverage is expensive. For the past few years, we've had an attending anesthesiologist and four residents in-house, and on most nights, there aren't enough cases to justify these numbers. From now on, there's going to be only one resident in the OR and we're only going to do life threatening emergencies after 8:00 PM."

Evidently, most of the dignitaries assembled around the table had already heard this news. They stared at Steinberg, looking grim.

"That's insane," Akins said flatly. "Sure, some nights there are no cases at all, but some nights there are three or four at once. What happens then?"

"The sickest patient will go first. The others will have to wait."

"And what if they can't wait?"

"If a case really can't wait, then we'll call someone in from home. Like I said, we're only going to do life threatening emergencies."

Many cases were not life threatening, not immediately at least, but they couldn't wait forever. They were urgent. A broken hip, a hot appendix, for instance. Such cases could wait for a few hours but they certainly could not wait for a slot to open up in the elective schedule, which could take days.

Kyle Lerner, the OR administrator, rose to his feet. Lerner had black, neatly groomed hair and a brush moustache. Kurtz had never seen him look harried or disheveled or without a smile on his face. He had started out as an operating room nurse and was known to be ambitious. "I was speaking with Dr. Serkin just yesterday," Lerner said. "He assured me that all urgent cases would be done."

Steinberg stared at him. "That's not the policy," he said.

Lerner stared back. "Maybe you misunderstood."

"I don't think so."

Moller interrupted. "Obviously, there's some confusion. I'm going to ask Dr. Steinberg to clarify his department's position and get back to us by next month's meeting."

"When is this new policy supposed to take effect?" Stephens asked.

"The first of the month," Steinberg said.

Which was only a week away. Stephens shook his head. "Next month's meeting will be too late."

"All right," Moller said. "I'll ask Dr. Steinberg to talk to his chairman and get back to me, personally, by Friday. How's that?"

Stephens shrugged. Nobody else spoke.

"Any other business?" Moller said. "No? Then the meeting's adjourned."

"Sponge," Kurtz said.

The scrub nurse handed him a long clamp with a rounded end. A folded piece of gauze was held at the tip. Gingerly, Kurtz inserted the sponge into the wound and tried not to gag. Theoretically, this should have been an easy case, the debridement of a decubitus ulcer on an old man, bedridden with Alzheimer's. The wound, unfortunately, was necrotic all the way down to his sacrum, and what was almost as bad, nobody had known, not the nurses who were supposedly taking care of him, not the residents who were supposedly changing his dressing every other day.

"You have an explanation for this?" Kurtz asked.

Levine's face was pale. His hands, as they held a retractor, trembled slightly. "It didn't look this bad, yesterday," he said.

Part of Levine's distress may have been guilt, for somehow or other not noticing the extent of the patient's condition. Part may have been revulsion for the truly awful smell of rotting flesh mixed with feces arising from the patient's rear end.

Sandra Jafari stood to the side, holding a retractor. She swayed a little. Her face was green, her hand barely trembling. Kurtz hoped she didn't faint. "Sandra, why don't you go sit down?" he said.

She nodded, cleared her throat but said nothing, handed the retractor over to a nurse. She stripped off her gloves and surgical gown and left the room. Levine gazed after her and frowned.

Kurtz wasn't feeling too good, himself. He grunted. The old guy was going to die, if not from this, then from pneumonia or a stroke or an MI. Kurtz knew the signs. Impossible to make a tragic mistake in a case like this. Death, in fact, would be relief to all concerned, but that wasn't the point. The point was that a serious complication had gone unnoticed and he was pissed off.

Kurtz's hands worked steadily, cutting away the dead tissue, irrigating the open wound with gallons of antibiotic infused saline, then packing it with iodophor gauze.

"Get him a bed in the ICU," Kurtz said. "He's going to need it."

Levine glumly nodded.

"To be perfectly honest," Lenore said, "I don't know these people. I would rather be going to a movie."

"To be perfectly honest," Kurtz replied. "So would I."

"Hard to argue with a man who agrees with you," Lenore observed.

"Only one of the many reasons why you adore me and can't live without me."

She gave him a distant clinical look, rolled her eyes and coughed. "How do I look?" she asked.

She looked gorgeous, but then, she always did. She was wearing a black blouse with green and pink highlights and a matching green skirt. "Good," he said.

"Then let's get going."

They were going to Paul Moller's for a party, cocktails plus a dinner buffet. Informal, supposedly. Ordinarily, Kurtz would have looked forward to it, since he liked Moller, and Moller's wife, Sara, was a great cook. However, what with the Search Committee and the Dean's unconventional request, Kurtz was not in a mood to be reminded of business. He was uncomfortably aware that new and potentially more serious crimes could be committed at any moment, and, quite frankly, he still had little idea of how to track down the culprit.

He had reviewed the data that Patrick O'Brien provided, which included cross-checking and correlating the various spreadsheets. Patrick knew his job. Nobody who had taken vacation matched up with the gaps in the delivery of the notes, and neither did anybody on the list of employees who had filed grievances of one sort or another. Basically, they were nowhere.

The party, however, proved to be entertaining. Christina Pirelli was there. Christina, as Kurtz had heard, liked to party. She looked good. Her hair was piled on top of her head in thick black ringlets and she was dressed in a plunging blue dress, her impressive décolletage threatening to burst out of the front with every deep breath. A slim, balding man, middle-aged and at least three inches shorter than Christina's own imposing height stood by her side, saying nothing, looking up at her with bemusement as she cracked off-color jokes and related long and involved anecdotes, most of them regarding her own sexual misadventures. "I was at a meeting to discuss the new monitors we're getting for OB and somebody started talking about the contract negotiations. They said that I got everything out of the Dean but his pants. Well, I guess I was a little distracted at the moment and so I said, 'Gee, whiz, if I could've gotten his pants, I would have traded away all the rest of it.' Suddenly, they're all giving me disapproving looks, but I ask you, have you ever seen a sexier man than the Dean?" She smiled benignly down at the bald head by her side. "He's almost as sexy as you, Snookums."

"Who is that?" Lenore asked.

"Christina Pirelli, the Chairperson of Ob-Gyn."

Lenore looked at Christina Pirelli for a long moment, then grinned. "So, tell me, have you ever seen a sexier man than the Dean? Aside from Snookums?"

Kurtz scratched his head, thinking about it. "I guess the Dean just isn't my type," he said. "Come on, I'll introduce you."

Lenore, somewhat to Kurtz' surprise, seemed to get along just fine with Christina Pirelli. Not more than ten minutes had passed before the two of them were ensconced in a corner of the room with glasses of white wine, their heads together, giggling. A few lowered glances were cast in Kurtz' direction, followed by more giggling, which made Kurtz vaguely uncomfortable. A few minutes later, three other women who Christina seemed to know sat down and joined the conversation.

With Lenore apparently having a good time without him, Kurtz decided to leave her to it. He said hello to Moller and mixed himself a Bloody Mary, which he sipped contentedly while watching a Knicks game on the TV in Moller's den. Two other men who Kurtz did not know but recognized from the hospital were already there. After a few minutes, Snookums wandered in, sat down and began to watch along with the rest.

Nobody said anything until halftime. The Knicks were down by seventeen. All the men except for Snookums and Kurtz rose to their feet, shaking their heads in sad resignation, and left the room. Snookums looked at Kurtz, smiled and held out his hand. "I'm John Crane," he said.

"Richard Kurtz."

"I know. Christina told me about you."

"Yeah?" Kurtz said.

"She likes you. She said you're not a stuffed shirt."

Kurtz sipped his drink. "Christina is okay," he said.

John Crane grinned, looking suddenly like a lovestruck puppy, and said, "Oh, yeah."

Kurtz grinned back. "Known her long?"

"About a month. I met her up on the OB floor. I'm a neonatologist." Crane looked suddenly uncomfortable. "Some strange things are happening up on OB."

Kurtz looked at him. "Oh?" he said.

"Strange things," Crane said again. He frowned at the TV. A group of good-looking women in cheerleading costumes were performing a dance routine. "I probably shouldn't talk about it," he said.

"No," Kurtz said, "I imagine you shouldn't."

Crane gave a tired grin. "Except that Christina tells me you already know."

Kurtz sighed. "Maybe I do," he said, "and maybe I don't. 'Strange things' can mean anything at all. Why don't you tell me about it?"

"Somebody is making crank phone calls to the obstetrics floor."

"Okay, that I do know," Kurtz said.

Crane frowned at him then shrugged. "She won't talk about the details, not to me, but I know they bother her." Crane stared down at his drink with a grim expression.

So far, aside from keeping himself apprised of the situation and examining the data, Kurtz had stayed away from direct involvement. He was a consultant, not the lead detective on the case, which would presumably be Patrick O'Brien, or maybe Harry Moran. On the other hand, not much had happened so far to make it all go away. Maybe the time for reticence was over. "I'll talk to Christina," Kurtz said.

Crane looked up at him, sudden hope in his eyes. "Would you do that?"

Kurtz cracked a smile. "Yeah," he said. "I guess I better."

Joseph Banks was fifty-two, tall, lean and balding. He had a thin smile and knowing eyes. He looked around the room at the members of the committee and waited calmly for the first question. "Dr. Banks," Serkin said, "what particular expertise would you bring to the position? What do you have to offer that sets you apart?"

Banks smiled. And why shouldn't he? Kurtz thought. An easy pitch like that one fairly begged to be hit out of the ballpark. Banks had a hundred and fifteen papers, with nearly four million in grants from the NIH.

Serkin had expressed great enthusiasm for Bank's application. Kurtz had been ambivalent. Director of Cardiac Surgery at University of Alabama for nearly ten years, his books were balanced, his surgical expertise universally acknowledged. If anybody was ready for a chairmanship, it should have been Banks, but Banks had a problem, at least to Kurtz' way of thinking. He was, according to reports, arrogant, overbearing and obnoxious.

"It's not his job to be liked," Serkin had said. "It's his job to make the Department run better, to train the residents and fellows, to take care of his patients and to advance scientific knowledge."

"I know the academic mission," Kurtz said. He felt like uttering an obligatory *Sieg Heil*. The academic mission was like the Holy Grail, the Bible or the Torah, to be brought out, admired and meditated upon, on occasions both special and routine. The academic mission, after all, was what distinguished them all from the mundane world of private practice.

Serkin had looked at him and sniffed.

In the end, Kurtz had gone along. The guy did have an impressive CV, and despite any personal failings, he also had an impressive record of accomplishment. Might as well interview him. And so here he sat, looking down, or so Kurtz imagined, upon them all.

"I have ten years of experience in organizing a service," Banks said. "I've trained over thirty fellows and I've more than doubled the departmental research funding. I look at things from a systems approach. No one individual can effectuate change, not all by himself. Everything we do in medicine involves a system. If you want to make things better, then you have to change the system, and that requires cooperation and consensus."

That actually sounded intelligent. Kurtz gave Banks a long, level look. Maybe he had misjudged the guy. Maybe Serkin was right all along.

Serkin smiled. Moller nodded his head. Nash leaned forward and asked, "Tell me about your research."

And so it went. An hour on the hot seat and then off to see the Dean.

Tolliver, and now Banks, and at least five more to go. Kurtz glanced at his watch. In fifteen minutes, he was due in the OR.

Chapter 9

Was there an undercurrent of fear when he walked the floors? Perhaps he imagined it, but he thought that there was. The voices were not as loud as they used to be. The staff seemed to look at each other with quick, side long glances, wondering…or perhaps not. Perhaps this was only his imagination, but he liked to think that they did. Everybody, even those who had not received a letter or a phone call, seemed to sense that something was up.

He smiled. Yes, he thought, things were coming along nicely. The work had taken on a life of its own, aside from the original cause, the target and the justice of his motives. Art for art's sake. Beauty needs no other justification. It simply is. Was this a conceit? If so, it was one that artists all throughout history would have recognized.

An artist of mayhem. He smiled at the thought. He liked that idea. He liked it a lot.

Jonas Saltzman said all of the right things. He talked about the rewards of the academic life, the joys of patient care, teaching and research, and the dismal requirements of dealing with HMO's. Nevertheless, the committee was not impressed with Jonas Saltzman. He had a slow, languid way of speaking. His eyes barely moved. The same half smile stayed fixed on his face. He looked, talked and acted as if he were sleep-walking through the interview. Chairman is a leadership position and a necessary part of leadership is the ability to inspire the troops. Jonas Saltzman was more likely to put them to sleep. Forget Jonas Saltzman.

Maurice Sexton, on the other hand, was tall, slim and good-looking, with iron gray hair and deep green eyes. His voice was animated, his gestures fluid and arresting. Maurice Sexton looked good and he sounded good. The Committee added Maurice Sexton to the A-list.

Vivian Connelly had an impressive CV. She was personable and pleasant. She seemed to know her stuff and she said the right things. The Committee liked her and so did the Dean. Unfortunately, Vivian

Connelly had obvious reservations. New York was crowded. It was cold in the Winter. Vivian Connelly had lived most of her life in Southern California and pined for blue skies and sunny days. It wasn't entirely clear why she had bothered to interview but she wanted a Chair and Staunton was offering one. In the end, it seemed apparent that Vivian Connelly was destined to go somewhere else.

Dennis Cole was a problem. Vice-Chairman of the Department, Peter Reinhardt's prize import, he was the obvious heir apparent. Unfortunately, his vision was not compatible with that of the institution. Dennis Cole wanted a "Cardiac Center," with himself as its head, an integrated institute combining cardiology, cardiac surgery and invasive radiology, with his own building housing his own operating rooms, cath labs, MRI's, CAT scans and bed floors, with a commitment to expand Cardiac Surgery from its present six surgeons to at least ten. Dennis Cole was thinking big. Too big.

"Dennis Cole is too expensive," the Dean said.

Moller had asked the Dean to come to their next meeting, just to discuss Dennis Cole. "I'd hate to lose him," Moller said. "He's a top-notch surgeon, a gifted researcher and an excellent administrator. But we can't give him what he wants."

"He'll probably leave if we don't," Serkin said.

The Dean looked grim but he shrugged. "Then he'll leave. No one man is bigger than the institution. Let him find a place that can afford him."

So much for Dennis Cole.

George Ames. Thomas Alan Dean. Niles Schobin. Lester Washington. Francis Xavier Jenson. William Harold Schapiro. After a while they began to blur together in Kurtz' memory. And finally, mercifully, they were done.

"So, we're agreed?" Moller asked. The question was rhetorical. They had considered every candidate, dissected every interview and arrived at a short list of the very top candidates. Henry Tolliver, Maurice Sexton, Francis Xavier Jensen. A good list, Kurtz thought. All of them were top notch, or at least they seemed to be. It was always possible to be fooled. Nevertheless, the references were glowing and unqualified. In the end, they had not needed to compromise. These three names had it all, research, administrative experience, clinical competence, glowing personalities, cool heads.

Now, it was up to the Dean.

Natalie Ward was seven months pregnant and very pissed off. "Is it true, Doctor Jones, that in the last three years, you have been sued five times for malpractice?"

Conrad Jones was an obstetrician, a hard-working obstetrician, a good obstetrician. But like all obstetricians in New York State, he paid more than a hundred thousand dollars a year in malpractice insurance, precisely because obstetricians do get sued. They get sued a lot. These were not the good old days, the days when people trusted their physicians, meekly accepted fate, and put their faith in God. Nope. People came into the hospital to have a baby and they expected top of the line service, a happy experience and an A-one product. They were paying for it (well, their insurance companies were, but so what?) and they expected to get what they paid for. The simple reality was, however, that the large majority of congenital anomalies and pre-natal accidents were both unpredictable and unavoidable. You can't detect them and you can't prevent them, but unhappy parents and duly aggrieved lawyers do not necessarily care about reality. To a lawyer, reality is whatever he can talk a judge and jury into believing.

Sure, Conrad Jones had been sued five times in the past three years. Name an obstetrician who hadn't?

He had nothing to feel guilty about, damn it. Still, it was almost impossible to escape the nagging doubt, the suspicion that things might have turned out differently if he had just done...something. Even if he couldn't for the life of him figure out what that something might have been. "Mrs. Ward, I'm not going to lie to you. I have been sued a number of times. Most obstetricians do get sued. I'm sorry about that but there's nothing I can do about it."

She looked at him, her expression radiating contempt. "Baloney," she said.

Conrad Jones shrugged. "I'm sorry you feel that way." After a moment, he asked, "Where did you get this information from?"

"I received a phone call."

"A phone call..."

She gave a curt nod.

"And from whom did you receive this phone call?"

74

For the first time, Natalie Ward seemed uncertain. She looked away and frowned. "I don't know. It was a man. He told me that he wanted to warn me that my physician was a malpracticing quack."

"And you believed him."

"Why shouldn't I? It's true, isn't it?"

He opened his mouth, then closed it.

She looked at him again, her expression radiating contempt. "When I've selected a new obstetrician, I'll have him contact your office for a copy of my records.

"Goodbye, Doctor."

"Aren't the records sealed?" Moran asked. Harry Moran was in his early forties, a tall, husky guy who evidently cared about his appearance. His hair was slicked back. He wore suspenders instead of a belt over a shirt of Italian linen and his suit looked expensive. Kurtz had worked with Moran and Lew Barent before and he counted both of them among his friends.

"Not exactly," Kurtz said.

They were sitting in a diner a few blocks from Easton. Moran had a tuna fish sandwich on whole wheat toast sitting in front of him. Occasionally, he poked at it with a finger, frowning unconsciously down at the plate. He had yet to take a bite.

"It's not going to poison you," Kurtz said.

Moran snorted. "I hate tuna fish."

"So why did you order it?"

"The lesser of all the evils. My cholesterol is high. If my doctor had his way, I'd live on bread, celery and carrot sticks."

"A fine, healthy diet," Kurtz said. Kurtz was eating a hamburger, with a side order of fries. Moran looked at the fries, naked longing in his eyes.

"Oh, for Christ's sake, take some," Kurtz said.

"Well, maybe just a few." Moran slid more than half the fries onto his own plate, dipped one into some ketchup, popped it into his mouth and closed his eyes in ecstasy. "Thanks," he said. "I needed that."

"I think it was better for you than it was for me."

"So," Moran said, "tell me about the medical records."

"Okay. Most of the charts are kept in a file room. It looks like a library, with the charts arranged alphabetically in stacks. Normally, any physician on staff can request any medical record. You have to put in a written request and sign for the ones you want, but nobody is going to say no and nobody is going to question your motives."

"You're saying that the guy is a doctor."

"Not necessarily. He has to have a doctor's ID to get access to the charts but it wouldn't be too difficult to forge one."

"I'm surprised your records aren't computerized."

"We're moving in that direction. Probably another couple of years."

"So, if somebody signed for these particular charts, then there should be something in writing."

"Yes. But the only reason they have people sign is so they know who to go after if the chart doesn't come back. It's not a log, it's just a written request slip, and once they have the chart back, the request slips get thrown out. Also, I said that most of the records are handled this way. The ones where lawsuits are either threatened or actually filed are sequestered. They're kept in a separate room under lock and key. A physician who wants to see them can still sign for them, but they can't be taken out of the locked room. You have to look at them up there."

"Interesting," Moran said. "The Ward woman knew that Jones had five suits against him but she didn't mention the names of the plaintiffs."

"The guy may not have known the names."

"But maybe he did know the names. The people who work up in medical records, they must have a list of patients who are suing. Who would have access to that list?"

Kurtz shrugged. "I don't know. I guess I'll ask them."

Moran nodded his head and gave Kurtz a wolfish smile. "Good idea," he said. "But you may be barking up the wrong tree. Information regarding civil lawsuits is not confidential. He may have gotten it from a simple search of the court's website." Moran cocked his head to the side and smiled. "Then, of course, there's the fact that all successful professional liability suits get reported to the National Physicians Data Bank, which is also public information."

"Not exactly true," Kurtz said shortly. "You have to have authorization to access the data." Kurtz, along with every other physician in America, despised the National Physicians Data Bank with a fiery passion.

Moran shrugged. "Easy enough to work around. So, you have no evidence at all that he got his information from the hospital."

Kurtz sighed. "We have to start somewhere."

"Well, then," Moran said. He crooked a finger at the waitress, who walked over to the table. "Bring me a hamburger," Moran said. "Medium." He glanced at Kurtz. "And some more fries."

"The list is computerized." Lillian Mayberry looked like a stereotype of the village librarian. She was short, thin and middle-aged, with dyed blonde hair and round, frameless glasses. She had a small office with glass walls, through which she could see the activity in the stacks of medical records in the opposite room. The walls were covered with light brown blinds, which she could pull closed if she wanted privacy. At the moment, the blinds were open. "The file containing the names of patients considered to represent potential liability is protected by a password," Lillian Mayberry said.

Too bad. Kurtz had been hoping for something a little more old-fashioned, like say a hand-written list kept under lock and key in a location, something that might have represented a clue. "Who has access to this computer?"

"Everybody. It's not just one computer. You can access our website from any computer in the hospital. You can even get in from outside, so long as you have a password and ID." Lillian Mayberry said this with evident pride. A fine modern system, all the latest and greatest in modern computer technology. Kurtz was hardly an expert in computer security, but he was fairly certain that such a system was about as secure as a sieve.

"The file that we were talking about, the one containing the names of patients who, as you say, represent potential liability, you can access that file, too?"

"Only if you know the password."

"And what does that mean, 'represent potential liability?'"

"A suit has actually been filed, an intent-to-sue form has been received, or we get an inquiry from a lawyer in a case where we know that there's has been a poor outcome."

"How many of the 'intent-to-sues' and 'poor outcomes' actually result in a lawsuit?"

Lillian Mayberry puffed her cheeks out. She appeared to think about it. "Certainly less than half."

"How long do you wait before you return the chart to the regular file room?"

"If a suit is actually in progress, we leave the chart locked up until the case is over. For the others, we wait one year."

Kurtz grunted. Passwords, even passwords composed of random numbers could be hacked. Not by himself, of course, but he knew enough about the modern world of computer crime to know that anything stored on a hard drive was fair game to the right people.

Still, this wasn't narrowing down their options, not one bit. The perpetrator could have known what he was doing with computers to the extent of infiltrating the system, or, as Harry Moran had suggested, he could have gotten the information from the other end of the process: the courtroom.

"Any hard copies of these passwords lying about?"

She blinked at him. "In my desk," she said.

"And who might have access to your desk?"

"Nobody. It's locked up at night."

The desk was a simple office desk, the lock a simple sliver of metal turned on or off by a simple, steel key.

"Does anybody else have a key?"

"Only my secretary."

Offhand, Kurtz could think of half-a-dozen ways of obtaining copies, from temporarily lifting the original to purchasing one from the company. He shook his head and rose ponderously to his feet. "Thanks," he said.

For the first time, Lillian Mayberry displayed uncertainty. "What's this all about?" she asked.

Kurtz forced himself to smile. "A routine investigation," he said. "Strictly routine."

Chapter 10

The next morning, Kurtz had just begun a laparoscopic ventral hernia repair when the trochar hit the patient's inferior epigastric artery and bisected it. In retrospect, this was not a surprise. The patient had had previous abdominal surgery. Her belly was covered with scars and the normal anatomy was obviously distorted. The trochar was placed in the midline, specifically in order to avoid any delicate and easily damaged structures. It was simply bad luck that in this patient, an artery that was usually situated lateral to the rectus abdominus had been pulled into the midline by scarring.

The first warning that Kurtz had was when Levine looked through the scope, frowned, and said, "It's red."

Just then, the anesthesiologist, a woman named Sylvia Waite, poked her head over the drapes and said, "Her pressure's dropping."

Hurriedly, Kurtz looked through the scope. Levine was right. Red. It wasn't supposed to be red. Red meant…

"We've got to get into her," Kurtz said.

Levine looked at him in bewilderment, then he seemed to suddenly get it because he gave an abrupt nod, pulled the trochar and the scope out in one smooth motion, turned to the scrub nurse and said. "Give me a knife."

Within seconds, the patient had an eight-inch vertical incision and they could see what was inside.

"Suction," Kurtz said. The circulator, who was scurrying around the room, opening up a laparotomy tray, hurriedly threw the suction tubing up onto the field. The scrub nurse pushed a big suction catheter onto one end of the tubing and handed it to Kurtz. Kurtz popped it into the abdomen and within seconds the suction canisters began to fill with blood.

Where was it coming from? The trochar had been inserted below the umbilicus, too low to have hit either the liver or the spleen. The inferior mesenteric artery could have done it but blood seemed to be dripping from the abdominal wall. Spurting, rather. "Give me a Kelly," Kurtz said. "And a lap pad."

The scrub nurse handed him a large clamp with a slight curve on the end and a large white pad. He wiped the clotted blood from the peritoneum with the pad. Instantly, they saw it, gushing from the hole where the trochar had been, a spurt of blood with every heart beat. Kurtz took the clamp and placed it around the bleeder, then ratcheted it tight. The spurting stopped.

"How is she?" Kurtz asked.

The anesthesiologist answered from the other side of the drapes. "Pressure's seventy over thirty. I've called for the blood."

"It should be okay, now," Kurtz said. "I think I've got it." He hoped. He peered back inside the abdomen, saw no more blood and breathed a relieved sigh.

"Good." The anesthesiologist sounded distracted. She was working at the patient's left arm, starting a second IV.

"How much do you think she lost?" Kurtz asked.

"There's almost two liters in the suction bottles."

Two liters. More than a third of her blood volume.

"Shit," Kurtz muttered.

Levine smiled wanly. Disgusted, Kurtz shook his head. "Two-O Proline," he said to the scrub nurse. She handed him the suture and Kurtz placed it around the base of the clamp and pulled it tight. They spent a few minutes making certain that nothing else was bleeding. By the time they had finished, two units of blood were dripping steadily through the IV lines and the patient's pressure was almost back to normal.

"Now what?" Levine asked.

Kurtz shrugged. "No reason not to finish the operation. She still needs her hernia fixed and we've already opened her up."

"Sure," Levine said.

An hour later, the patient was safely in recovery. Kurtz had a headache. He glanced at the clock. An hour to grab some lunch, then office hours.

The first patient of the afternoon was named Shirley Bannon, a small woman with light brown hair, blue eyes and a beaten down look. Her husband was tall and skinny, dressed in a three-piece suit with a real watch chain across the vest. She had gallstones. He had attitude. "I want you to know that if anything goes wrong with this operation, you'll regret it," he said.

Kurtz knew without having to be told that he would regret it if anything went wrong with this or any other operation. The guy seemed to mean it a little differently than usual. "How so?" Kurtz asked.

The guy's eyes narrowed. "I'll let you figure it out."

Kurtz tapped his pen on the desk, considering. The surgery was elective. If she had come into the emergency room, Kurtz could not have turned her away, this being Federal Law in the United States of America, but they were sitting in his office after a routine evaluation. "How about we do it this way," Kurtz said, "turn around, go away, and find yourself another surgeon."

They both looked startled. "What do you mean?" the guy said.

"I mean that I don't do surgery on people who threaten me. It's a little quirk of mine."

The guy's face was suddenly ugly. "You can't do that," he said.

"Sure, I can," Kurtz said.

"I'll get you," the guy said. His breath came suddenly faster and he leaned forward across the desk. "Don't think that I won't."

The woman looked at her husband, shook her head and sighed.

Kurtz picked up the phone and punched in his secretary's number. She picked up after one ring. "Mrs. Schapiro?" Kurtz said. "Please call the police."

Suddenly, the guy looked concerned. "Now wait a minute," he said. "We can work something out here."

"The only think we're going to work out," Kurtz said, "is how long it's going to take for you to get out of my office."

They guy seemed about to say something when the woman put her hand on his arm. "Jimmy, for Christ's sake, forget it," she said. She looked at Kurtz sadly and for a moment he almost changed his mind. "Let's go," she said. "There are plenty of other fish in the sea."

Evidently, the woman knew her husband. Within a minute she had hustled him out through the door. After they had gone, Kurtz put his head in his hands and rubbed his temples. His headache, having temporarily abated, was threatening once again to pound a spike into his skull. He glanced at the clock. Two thirty. Four patients to go.

Thank God, he had the evening off. He needed a hot shower and a cold drink.

Oh, well, he consoled himself, these things happen. He just wished that they would happen to somebody besides him.

At seven fifteen in the evening, they called an emergency Caesarian section on a woman named Cecelia DeJesus. It wasn't an emergency in the sense that anything was wrong with the baby. It was an emergency because she had been in labor for fifteen hours, was only four centimeters dilated and was evidently not making any progress. Enough, in the opinion of her obstetrician, was enough. Time to get the baby out, call it a night, and go home.

At seven thirty-five, the spinal was in, the patient was numb from the sternum down and the surgeon was poised to begin. A nurse on the opposite side of the OR opened a pack of instruments and something wet and very red plopped out onto the floor. The nurse gave a little shriek, quickly stifled. The surgeon glared at her. "Did you stub your toe?" The surgeon nodded toward the end of the table, where Cecelia DeJesus' head was concealed by the drapes, and raised his eyebrows. The nurse closed her eyes, drew a deep breath and visibly shuddered. The neonatologist, John Crane, who had been standing toward the side of the operating table, waiting for the new baby to make its appearance, looked down at what was sitting on the floor and pursed his lips. "Better get a new pack," he said. "This one's contaminated; and when the case is finished, call Security. And don't touch this or the rest of the pack that it came in. It's evidence."

Harry Moran appreciated the thought but quickly realized that murder was not the correct word for it. The blob on the floor turned out to be a dead baby, which was exactly what it had appeared to be, but the baby was dead from natural causes. Every once in a while, for reasons that could only be surmised, a full-term infant died in utero. The theory was that the umbilical cord wrapped around the infant's neck or otherwise became compressed and the infant died from lack of oxygen. The previous evening, a lady named Amanda Thomasson had given birth to just such a stillborn infant. Mrs.

Thomasson was resting under sedation on the Fifteenth Floor and the dead infant had been taken to pathology.

Somebody, evidently, had removed the infant from pathology.

"Pretty sick joke," Kurtz said. When Kurtz had first appeared on the OB floor, Moran had ignored him. Kurtz did not take offense at this. He did not delude himself that his status as the Dean's personal investigator extended to investigating a murder, despite the previous three murders that Kurtz, Barent and Moran had investigated. Once it became apparent that the crime was more in the nature of a practical joke, Moran had deigned to talk to him.

Glumly, Harry agreed. "But not murder."

Patrick O'Brien, who had given Kurtz the call and who was standing silently by while the NYPD took point, looked at him and silently shook his head.

"Still a crime, though," Kurtz said.

"Not much of one." Moran shrugged. "So, who had access to the pathology lab?"

"Probably everybody," O'Brien said.

"You're probably right. Let's find out."

It wasn't quite everybody, but near enough. The lab was kept locked at night, but almost anybody could wander through during the day. Everybody who worked there, the pathologists, the lab techs, the cleaning staff, all had keys. Security had never been a consideration. And why should it be? Most people avoided the place. Not only might you run into something gross like a disembodied brain, an eviscerated liver or a dead baby, but the place smelled bad. A faint undercurrent of decay mixed with phenol was ineffably present.

"Anybody see anybody unusual?" Harry asked.

Bob Josephs was the Chief Pathologist, a lean guy with thick, brown hair, pale skin and a ready smile. At the moment, he was not smiling. He puffed up his cheeks and gave Kurtz a gloomy look, evidently wondering what Kurtz was doing there but too polite to ask. "How should I know?"

Good question, Kurtz thought.

"Let me rephrase that," Moran said, "did you, personally, see or hear about anything unusual?"

"No."

Of course not. A bull elephant wandering through might be considered unusual. An ordinary person who looked as if he had some business there? Forget it. But propriety demanded that the forces of justice at least pretend to take it all seriously. Harry Moran sighed. He had more important things to do, but he was already on the scene. Might as well go through the motions. "I'm going to have to talk to your people," he said.

"Is that absolutely necessary?"

"I'm afraid that it is."

Josephs shrugged.

They started with the seven pathologists, went on to the fifteen lab techs and then the six cleaning staff. Nobody knew anything. Nobody saw anything. Nobody heard anything.

Oh, well.

The surgical storage area was a bit more fruitful. Surgical packs were prepared in a locked area on the fourteenth floor. The instruments were cleaned, gathered together according to the type of surgery intended, wrapped and then sterilized. The sterilized packs were stored on shelves and sent up on a dumbwaiter when requested, either to obstetrics or to the OR.

"Yeah, I saw somebody." Irene Garcia was a plump, middle-aged Hispanic lady with a grumpy attitude and an excellent work record. She looked at Kurtz with evident suspicion but at least seemed inclined to cooperate.

Moran raised an eyebrow. "Tell me about it," he said.

"It was yesterday afternoon. Some guy dressed in scrubs. I'd never seen him before. He was wandering around in the storage room."

"What did you do?"

"I asked him who he was. He said that he was a new OR tech and he wanted to see how the instruments were processed."

"Did that sound reasonable to you?"

"It was unusual but it wasn't nuts. I mean, the man works here. It's only natural to be curious." Irene Garcia shrugged. "I told him that nobody was allowed in without authorization and he better leave."

"What happened then?"

"He left."

"Okay," Harry said. He rubbed his hands together in satisfaction. Maybe they were finally getting somewhere. "What did he look like?"

"Sort of on the tall side, I guess. Slim. He was white, I could tell that much."

Harry looked at her. "What do you mean? Wasn't that obvious?"

"He had scrubs on, including an OR cap and a mask."

"Is that usual?"

"In the store room? Yeah. The instruments are sterile. You're not supposed to breathe on them."

"So you couldn't see his face?"

"Not all of it."

"Okay, what could you see?"

Irene Garcia gave a tiny shrug, as if she hadn't really noticed and didn't really care. "He had brown hair."

Kurtz wrote *white, above average height, slim, brown hair* in his notebook. "Fine. What shade of brown: light, medium or dark? Was it curly or was it straight?"

She frowned. "I don't know," she said. "It was brown. Medium, I guess. I couldn't tell if it was straight or curly. Most of it was tucked under the cap."

"How about his eyebrows? Same color as the hair?"

Irene Garcia frowned. "Probably. I didn't notice."

"How about his eyes? Did you notice the color."

She looked at him as if he were an idiot. "No," she said.

"How about his skin. Dark? Pale?"

"Sort of pale. He had some freckles on his arms."

"Arms? You could see his arms and not his face?"

"Surgical scrubs have short sleeves. I told you he was wearing surgical scrubs."

"Yes, you did," Harry said. "That's great. Did you notice anything else? Scars? Tattoos? Anything?"

"Not that I noticed, no."

"How about his voice? Anything distinctive? Was it deep? How about an accent?"

"It was a voice. It wasn't deep. I didn't notice any accent."

"And after he left, did you report the incident?"

"No." Irene Garcia shook her head. "It's not as if we have drugs in here. I mean, there's nothing worth stealing. I didn't think it was important."

"Well, thank you," Harry said. "You've been a big help."

"I have? How?"

Harry smiled at her. "I can't tell you," he said. "It's confidential."

Irene Garcia sniffed and walked off.

"He's escalating," Kurtz said.

Harry shrugged. "It's still petty harassment and I have real crimes on my plate." He did sound a bit hesitant, though, which Kurtz noted with some satisfaction.

"It's petty harassment, so far, but it's escalating. You want to bet that it will stay petty harassment?"

Moran grunted. "True," he said grudgingly. Then he gave a half-hearted grin. "Lucky for us we have two guys with your experience permanently on the scene." O'Brien made a gagging motion behind his hand.

"Thanks," Kurtz said. "Thanks a lot."

Kurtz sipped his coffee, surreptitiously glanced at the clock hanging on the cafeteria wall and wondered when he had become Steinberg's psychiatrist. It seemed that Steinberg had spoken with Stewart Serkin yesterday regarding the new call arrangements. To Steinberg's chagrin, it turned out that Kyle Lerner had been correct. There had never been any intention to restrict night cases to life threatening emergencies. Of *course*, urgent cases were also going to be done. How could there have been any doubt?

"Except that he specifically called me the day before the OR Committee," Steinberg said. "He told me what the policy was and he ordered me to present it exactly the way I did." Steinberg stared down at his coffee. His eyes were wide, his hands trembling.

Serkin, in the interim between instructing Steinberg to promote and defend the new policy, and the morning of the OR Committee meeting, had conveniently decided to amend the policy, and had neglected to inform Steinberg of this fact. This, at least was Steinberg's interpretation. Serkin's interpretation, the official interpretation, was that Steinberg had misunderstood the new policy from the beginning. The scary thing about Serkin was that he actually seemed to believe his own bullshit. And at this point, even Steinberg was uncertain of what had really happened. "One week on the job and already I look like a goddamn idiot. I'm damned sure certain of that, at least." He shook his head. "Jesus."

"Has it occurred to you that maybe that was the plan?" Kurtz asked.

Steinberg drew a deep breath and gave a wan smile. "I think it was Napoleon who said, 'Do not readily attribute to malice what can be explained by stupidity.' So deliberately making me look like an idiot was probably not Serkin's plan."

"Probably," Kurtz said.

"Yeah," Steinberg said. "Probably."

"Or probably not."

Steinberg frowned. "Now you're confusing me," he said.

Kurtz smiled. "That was the plan."

Maurice Sexton arrived back for his second interview on the following Monday. This time, he was scheduled to meet with the hospital director, the CFO, the departmental administrator, the chief of professional billing, the chief of cardiology and all of the surgical chairmen. Now, it was time to get serious.

Mrs. Sexton came along with him, as well as the oldest Sexton child, a boy of fifteen. If Maurice Sexton became chairman, the family would have to move from Cleveland to New York. It was a big decision, a decision that involved the entire Sexton family. The Dean's administrative assistant, a sharp-eyed woman named Marcia Cohen, was assigned to show Mrs. Sexton the available housing, the choicest neighborhoods and the best schools.

Maurice Sexton was as affable as he had been on his previous visit, but it quickly became apparent that Maurice Sexton was a mistake. He had apparently not bothered to read the packet of information that he had been sent, which outlined the departmental budget, the administrative organization, the list of HMO contracts, the NIH grants and the biographies of the departmental staff. He claimed, in an easy, almost bored tone of voice, that he had never received it. This might have been chalked up to a postal error, except that Mrs. Sexton, apparently not realizing the implications of what she was saying, told Marcia Cohen that the information packet had been received at the Sexton household the week before. Maurice Sexton nodded politely when he was spoken to but was quite obviously just going through the motions. He had no plans, no ideas, and no questions beyond the obvious.

"The guy is a jerk," the Dean declared.

"He doesn't want the job," Marcia Cohen said. She had dropped Mrs. Sexton off at their hotel an hour before and come back to report to her boss.

"Then why did he interview for it? He's wasting everybody's time, including his own."

"This isn't the only chair he's looking at. He's probably already negotiating with Duke or Harvard or UCSF."

The Dean glared at her. "So, we're a negotiating chip? I want a chairman who's interested in us."

"We'll get one," Marcia Cohen said. "Don't worry."

"Right," the Dean said, and glumly nodded.

Chapter 11

"My mother has bought herself a computer," Lenore said.

"Uh-oh," Kurtz said.

Lenore nodded. "An iMac G5. Aunt Sylvia insisted. A successful real estate agent has to stay connected to the market." Lenore's face was grim. "It wouldn't be too bad if she just used it for business, but she's discovered online shopping."

Kurtz shook his head. "Tough one. Let's hope she doesn't stumble on the porn."

Lenore winced. "Did you know that there are web sites devoted to planning weddings?"

"I never thought about it." Kurtz shrugged. "It doesn't surprise me."

"She's been bombarding me with phone calls." Lenore shook her head. "I keep telling her; it's a small wedding. One of the photographers in my office does weddings on the side. I've already asked him. One of my friends from college, Jennifer Schaefer, runs a catering business. I've already booked her. It's true that we haven't registered our patterns and I don't have a dress, yet, but she's hyperventilating."

"Patterns? What patterns?"

"Dishes, silverware, cutlery, tablecloths. We're supposed to register our patterns so people will know what to give us."

"Oh." They didn't register patterns where Kurtz came from, West Virginia being a bit less formal than Brooklyn. Then again, maybe they did. Kurtz was not exactly an expert on the etiquette of a modern, up-to-date wedding.

Kurtz scratched his head. "The rabbi seems nice."

Rabbi Shmuel Levy, Congregation Beth Shalom. They had met with him in his office two weeks previous. The rabbi had smiled benignly at them both and said to Lenore, "Your mother gave me a call the other day. An interesting woman."

Lenore made a small distressed sound. Kurtz suppressed a chuckle. Lenore glowered at him.

"In your mother's opinion," the Rabbi said, "Reform Judaism is a perversion of the natural order, just this side of Unitarianism."

"Wasn't Thomas Jefferson a Unitarian?" Kurtz said.

The Rabbi shrugged. "Beats me. Anyway, I did my best to reassure her that the Lord will nevertheless smile on your nuptials." The Rabbi grinned. "I get the impression that she actually likes you but she doesn't want to say so, you being of a scandalously un-Jewish persuasion. She has to maintain her status in the neighborhood."

The neighborhood, again. "Nothing I can do about it," Kurtz said.

"It seems you like to beat up Nazis. She approves of beating up Nazis."

In the course of the three murder investigations that Kurtz had been dragged into, he had indeed beaten up a few career criminals and one rogue martial artist. "They weren't Nazis," Kurtz said.

Lenore sighed. "Can we get back to the point?"

"Sure," the Rabbi said. "What's the point?"

"You're supposed to counsel us. Isn't that so?"

"Oh." The Rabbi scratched his head. "Here goes…" He smiled. "The secret to a good marriage is communication."

Would never have guessed that, Kurtz thought.

Lenore looked doubtful. "You think that's obvious?" the Rabbi said. "It's not. You two, for instance, you both listen when the other one talks. You treat each other with respect. You communicate. I'm not worried about you two. Trust me, I've married thousands of couples. You can always tell the ones that are going to make it."

"That's it?" Kurtz said.

"Pretty much. Be thankful that we're past the days when a wise, elderly lady of the congregation was appointed to inform a tremulous young bride all about the birds and the bees, just in case her mother had neglected to do so."

Lenore shuddered. "Yes, let's be thankful."

The Rabbi smiled. "And I imagine you won't be needing any information on the Family Purity Laws?"

"Huh?" Kurtz said.

Lenore frowned at him. "The times of the month when we are allowed, or rather, not allowed, to do certain things, according to traditional Jewish law."

"Oh," Kurtz said.

"No," Lenore said to the Rabbi, "we won't."

"Excellent," the Rabbi said. "I wouldn't think so, this being the Twenty-First Century, but a conscientious rabbi should never make assumptions."

Lenore shrugged. Kurtz pretended to look around the room. The Rabbi grinned. "So, I'll see you in a few months. Call me if you have any questions and don't let your mother get you down. She means well."

"The road to hell," Lenore said.

The rabbi smiled again and they left...

"Yes," Lenore said. "I do like the rabbi."

"So, when are you going to get a dress?" Kurtz said.

"I have an appointment next Tuesday. I'm not expecting it to be a problem."

"And this pattern stuff? You want to do that?"

"Frankly? I couldn't care less, but the guests will expect it."

"So, everything is taken care of," Kurtz said.

"Pretty much."

"Then what's bothering her?"

"Nothing, really. She just wants to feel involved." Lenore smiled. "I'll take her with me when I shop for the dress. She actually has good taste and it'll make her happy." Lenore gave a small laugh.

"What?"

"Among the Orthodox, it's a tradition that a mother accompany her daughter to purchase lingerie for the wedding night."

"You're kidding me."

"Nope."

"That might be awkward," Kurtz said.

"Yep. Luckily, I already have all the lingerie that I need."

"Is there such a thing as 'enough lingerie?' Maybe you should get some more."

Lenore smiled. "Maybe. But I'll leave my mother at home."

Eight o'clock the next morning found Kurtz sitting in Christina Pirelli's office, a large room, brightly lit, with colorful abstract art hanging on the walls, a plush, blue carpet on the floor, bleached oak furniture and wide picture windows giving a view of the Hudson River and New Jersey off in the distance. "Coffee?" she asked Kurtz. "Tea?"

"No, thanks," Kurtz said. "I've got surgery in an hour but I needed to talk to you." He leaned forward. "Tell me about the phone calls."

She gave him a quizzical look. "The Dean told me that you knew about them."

"Apparently, not enough. Give me the details."

Christina picked up her tea, took a sip and then carefully placed the mug back down on her desk. "They started a couple of months ago. Only a few, at first. Lately, there have been more."

"Mostly here, or at home?"

"A few here, but mostly at home."

"I assume your phone number is unlisted?"

"Yes, but the hospital switchboard has it and it's posted on the OB floor. You never know when a patient is going to get into trouble. They may need to reach me in a hurry."

"Tell me," Kurtz said, "do you have any enemies?"

"Enemies?"

"Somebody has a reason for doing this," he said.

Christina shrugged. "I suppose, but 'enemies' sounds so melodramatic." She leaned back in her chair and stared off into space. "I'm successful," she said finally. "I'm a chairman. There are always issues and you can't make everybody happy. It's just the way it is. Enemies...? I suppose the people I beat out for the job might be enemies, but most of them aren't in New York and none of them are at Staunton."

"Why assume that it's business? It's just as likely to be personal."

"I have a daughter in her freshman year at Swarthmore and two ex-husbands." She shrugged. "The first one died from alcoholic liver disease five years after we divorced. The second happily married his former secretary, less than a year after the breakup." She gave a wry smile. "Life goes on."

"I'm sorry to hear that. Were these divorces amicable?"

Christina raised an eyebrow. "Are they ever? The first one was an adolescent mistake. I was in college and thought I was in love. Then I got pregnant." She leaned back in her chair and stared into space. "Maybe I was in love, for awhile. The second was a disaster from the beginning. He was a neurosurgeon who worked long hours. When he came home, he wanted his dinner and his blow job." Christina shrugged and smiled wanly. Kurtz, who also worked long hours and appreciated his dinner and his blow job, tried not to wince. "Basically, his idea of marriage consisted of me waiting on him hand and foot. Since I was an OB resident when we met, and I also had a daughter to raise, he was obviously deluding himself. It lasted three years and we were both happy to call it quits."

"Any other family?"

Christina smiled with genuine fondness. "I have one sister, Elizabeth. She and her husband are biogenetic farmers. They have three kids. They're coming next week for a visit. Lydia is looking forward to it. She and my sister are old friends. They're both theater buffs. We're going to see *Les Mis* and then *Macbeth*."

"Lydia?"

"Lydia Cho: my research associate. I've known her since High School. She came with me from Wake Forest."

Kurtz nodded. "What exactly is a biogenetic farmer?"

"Elizabeth and her husband raise aquaponic food. They also manufacture and sell the equipment."

Kurtz scratched his head. "What is aquaponic food?"

Christina rolled her eyes. "You sure you want to hear this?" Kurtz wasn't, but you never knew what might turn out to be relevant. He pasted an interested look on his face and said nothing. Christina shrugged and went on. "Most hydroponic systems are not considered organic because the nutrient solutions that they use to feed the plants aren't organically derived. In order to be classified as organic, living things like fungi, micro-organisms and actual manure are required." Christina smiled. "Or so my sister tells me. I'll admit, it sounds like BS to me. With aquaponics, they also grow fish and re-circulate the fish water through the tanks where the plants are growing. The fish supply all the natural fertilizer that the system needs. Then it's organic."

Probably more information than he needed, Kurtz thought. "They make money this way?"

"Amazing, isn't it? It seems that a lot of people are interested in growing their own food. With aquaponics, the yields are higher, the insects are fewer and it takes up a lot less space than growing crops in soil. And in cities, if there's no room for an actual fish pond, you can set up a tank, and if you don't care about making it "organic," a simple hydroponic system is even easier. They're getting rich."

Good for them, Kurtz reflected, but nope, hard to see how any of this might be relevant.

"Have you ever fired anybody?"

"No," Christina shook her head. "It's a good, solid staff. I made sure of that before I came here."

"How about before you came here?"

"No. I never had to."

"Have you cut any salaries?"

"I have two people whose research productivity didn't warrant the amount of academic time they were receiving. I cut their academic time." She shrugged. "They've had to see more patients but their salaries have gone up, since they now participate in the clinical bonus."

"But they wanted an academic career, and you've disappointed them."

"They can still have an academic career. All they have to do is get off their butts, do some solid research and publish some papers. If they do that, they'll get the academic time back. In the meantime, they can take care of patients."

"Are they angry about this?"

"Frankly, they both seem relieved. Neither of them really liked research. They like teaching and they like clinical care. Research turned out not to be for them."

Kurtz understood that, completely. "Why don't they leave? They can take care of patients in private practice and make more money."

"They probably will, sooner or later. Most do."

True, Kurtz thought. Sooner or later, well over eighty per-cent of 'academic' physicians left for private practice, when they realized that they had no interest in research, were doing exactly the same job as their friends in private practice and were making half the money. "Did you bring anyone else with you when you came here?"

"Aside from Lydia, just Jenny Suarez. Jenny was the Chief Resident at Pritzker and then a junior attending at Wake Forest." Christina smiled. "She always wanted to live in New York."

"She still feel that way?"

"You'll have to ask her."

He smiled wanly. "I guess I will. I'll have to talk to both of them."

"Why do men like oral sex so much?"

"Huh?" Kurtz said.

"I was reading an article in Cosmo. It said that thirty-eight per-cent of all men prefer oral sex to the regular way. Why is that?"

Kurtz and Lenore were sitting on the couch, sipping Chardonnay and watching the sun set over the river. Copland's *Third Symphony* was playing on the stereo. Kurtz had the results of his computer search open on his lap.

Crank calls and anonymous notes rarely left a lot of clues behind, not if the perp was careful, and the motive, more often than not, was simply boredom. Most crank calls were committed by young males, usually teenagers. Most of the victims were picked at random. Actual threats were rare. More often, they were hang-up calls in the middle of the night, or simple heavy breathing, which teenage nitwits tended to think humorous.

These crank calls, quite obviously, did not fit the pattern.

They had begun over two months ago, as the information given to him by the Dean had indicated, and as Christina Pirelli had confirmed, only a few at first but swiftly increasing in frequency. The targets were mostly, but not all, women. Five of these calls, so far, had been received by the Dean, threatening nameless destruction unless the school stopped its ungodly ways. Exactly which activities might qualify as ungodly were not specified. And of course, the threats just might be for real. The women getting them were scared. They had reason to be, Kurtz thought. So far, it was all talk, but the talk was escalating. Sooner or later, talk might not be enough to satisfy whatever perverse urges were driving the guy.

And let's not forget the dead infant so humorously removed from the morgue.

The exact times of nearly half the calls had been pinpointed, not so for the notes, which could have been sitting in an inbox for days before being noticed. While the majority of people could slip away for a few minutes and make a phone call, many could not. OR personnel, in particular, once scrubbed, were stuck there. Somebody involved in surgery at the time of a phone call could not have made it. The OR records were exact. They had been able to eliminate nearly half of the nurses, scrub techs and anesthesiologists, as well as many of the surgeons.

The timing of the calls might be revealing. Most of them were at night, between the hours of seven and ten. Only five had come during the day. Most likely, the guy waited until he was off work and had eaten his dinner before comfortably sitting down for a pleasant evening of harassment. On the other hand, maybe he worked the night shift and just didn't want to leave a record from his own phone.

It was hard to make crank phone calls when people were around. Wives tend to notice when hubby is on the phone a lot, and they tend to get upset when hubby does naughty things. Most likely, the perp was unmarried. But then again, maybe he was married. A wife wouldn't be around if he was calling from the job. Still, probably not. The odds said not. The guy had a grudge against women, or at least he had a grudge against Christina Pirelli, that was for sure. Of course, maybe he was married and just didn't like his wife.

He pursed his lips as he looked over the case notes from the cops who had responded, mostly to Christina Pirelli's complaints. Not too much there. The responding officers had given the usual reassurances. The majority of such callers tend to get tired of it after awhile. Ignore him. Hang up as soon as you know it's him. Jot down the times and anything distinctive about the voice, which she had done. Male, supposedly, not deep, no accent, which at least jibed with what Irene Garcia had told them. Almost undoubtedly the guy came from the Northeastern United States, because everybody on Earth has an accent and the only people who think you don't are people who talk just like you. Aside from that, nothing. Up to this point, the cops hadn't taken the whole thing seriously, but Kurtz, and also the Dean and Harry Moran, neither of whom were dummies, were concerned about the escalation. The notes and calls were coming more frequently. The dead baby in the surgical pack was grotesque and outrageous and a definite step up on the scale of harassment. He wants something, Kurtz thought, and sooner or later, he's going to get what he wants or he's going to crack.

Over five-hundred physicians had privileges at the medical school. Over five-hundred nurses worked there. Ancillary personnel including technicians, clerks, administrators, support staff, etc. numbered another thousand or so.

A preliminary attempt to narrow down a suspect list had proven marginally useful. Forget the phone calls. The phone calls could have been made from anywhere, and even people supposedly away on vacation might have hung around to commit some casual mayhem. About half of the two-thousand were female and could at least tentatively be eliminated. Ditto the African-Americans, about a fifth of the males. They had decided to keep all the Asians on the list, since a Chinese or Japanese could easily look Caucasian behind a surgical mask, and older guys with bald heads or graying hair were kept on, since the brown hair that Irene Garcia reported might have been a wig. That still left over five-hundred people in the suspect pool. He had been here for at least two months, assuming he was an employee of the medical center, which seemed likely but not certain. He had a legitimate ID or he had access to a fake one and at least knew enough to pass. None of this rested upon assumptions. None of it was firm, but tentatively, at least, they could cross out another three-hundred or so, just by the fact that they had started work too recently or their jobs were nowhere near OB, pathology or the OR.

His specific grievance was unclear, but seemed to center around women, the medical school rather than the hospital *per se*, and the department of OB-GYN. Christina Pirelli, certainly, had been personally harassed.

And he was smart, that much was clear. None of the notes had fingerprints on them. All had been written with children's crayons in block letters. The spelling was perfect. No handwriting that could ever be identified. The phone calls, what the recipients could recall of them, revealed no pattern at all. No background sounds, no extraneous noises. The guy knew how to cover his tracks.

A good scientist (and a good cop) was leery to indulge in too much speculation. A little speculation, that was okay. A little speculation, solidly extrapolated from what they actually knew, that was the way forward. Too much speculation was likely to lead them down blind alleys.

Stick to what they knew, or at least stick to what they were reasonably certain was the truth. So, they had a few things to go on, and now that they did, how could they narrow it down further…?

"I don't know," Kurtz said. "I guess men just like seeing a woman on her knees."

"Yeah?" A little smile played around Lenore's lips.

"You know, the old submissive, dominant thing."

"Ah," Lenore said, "the old submissive, dominant thing. Of course."

"That's my theory, at least."

"Well, you are a man. You ought to know."

Kurtz smiled modestly. "Also, a surgeon. Surgeons have special insight into these issues."

"I didn't know that. Do they teach you all about oral sex during your residency?"

"No. They teach us all about submission and dominance. Speaking of which, and now that you've brought the subject up…"

Lenore smiled at him, a faint, speculative smile. "Cosmo says that fifty-seven per-cent of men like to switch roles now and then."

Kurtz raised an eyebrow.

"You could say I'm a Cosmo girl," Lenore said. "Modern, sophisticated…"

"You must have inherited that from your mother."

Lenore frowned. "Leave my mother out of this."

Kurtz grinned. "Come here," he said.

"Okay," Lenore said, "I mean, since you asked me so nicely."

Francis Xavier Jensen came across well. He had read the information packet. He asked reasonable questions. He could speak with insight regarding networking, cost containment and faculty development. He had good ideas and stated a definite interest in the job. The only problem was his wife. The Jensens currently lived outside Atlanta, where they owned a large house on four acres that had cost them a little over two hundred thousand. For two hundred thousand anywhere within reasonable commuting distance of Manhattan, you might get a small cottage with a front lawn about the size of a postage stamp.

Marcia Cohen did her best, pointing out the museums, the art galleries, the theatres, the restaurants and all the myriad attractions that made New York the greatest city in the world. Mrs. Jensen did acknowledge that these were attractions, but she seemed, in the end, unconvinced.

"I don't know," Marcia Cohen said.

The Dean looked glum. "The husband won't be happy if the wife doesn't want to live here."

Marcia Cohen gave an expansive, eloquent shrug.

"Well," the Dean said, "we're not going to write him off, at least not yet. I like him, and he is interested."

"See what Henry Tolliver is like."

The Dean smiled reluctantly. "You think the third time will be the charm?"

"Could be. If none of them work out, the Search Committee will have to reconvene."

"Peter Reinhardt," the Dean said, "is going to retire, whether we have a replacement or not. He wants to play golf and he's tired of waiting."

"Let's look on the bright side," Marcia Cohen said. "I have a good feeling about Henry Tolliver."

"I hope you're right," said the Dean.

That evening, Sandra Jafari brewed a cup of tea. When the tea was strong enough for her purpose, she put in two teaspoons of sugar, hesitated, then put in a third. She sipped, nodded her head, and opened a small medicine bottle, from which she extracted twenty capsules. Carefully, she pried apart each capsule and emptied them into her tea. She stirred the tea until all the powder had dissolved, then sat down on a couch and drank the tea. By the time she had finished, she felt herself growing sleepy. She suppressed a sniffle, angrily wiped a tear from the corner of her eye, then lay down upon the couch and closed her eyes.

Within minutes she was unconscious. Minutes later, the front door of the small apartment opened and Jennifer Wu, Sandra Jafari's roommate and best friend, returned home early from a date. "Sandy?" Jennifer called.

There was no response. Frowning, Jennifer Wu walked over to her friend and peered down at her. "Sandy?" she said again. Jennifer saw the medicine bottle, still open on the table. Her eyes widened. "Oh, my god," she whispered, then she grabbed her cell phone and dialed 911.

Chapter 12

"It was Valium," Moran said. "She had a prescription for it."

Kurtz gave a morose, sour grunt. Kurtz was angry. Kurtz knew Sandra Jafari. Kurtz liked Sandra Jafari. Like all medical students, Sandra Jafari worked very, very hard. She was bright, highly motivated and earnest, even if she didn't have much talent for surgery.

"I understand she was a student of yours," Moran said.

"Yeah."

"The roommate says she's been depressed lately," Moran said.

"I hadn't noticed."

"What had you noticed?"

Kurtz shook his head. "Nothing. The students spend most of their time with the residents and the other students. I saw her on rounds, a couple of times in surgery. It wasn't social." Kurtz shrugged and scowled out the window. "She didn't laugh much. I guess I noticed that. I figured she was the serious sort." Kurtz was not happy. Was any of this was his fault? Should he have suspected that something was going on? "She asked intelligent questions," Kurtz said. "She did her work."

"That's all?"

"Yeah."

"Not too much to go on."

"Valium is for anxiety, not depression," Kurtz said. "In fact, it's contraindicated in depression. Valium can make depression worse."

"So they tell me." Moran shrugged. "She had also been anxious."

"About what?"

Moran peered down at his notepad. "According to her internist, nothing too specific. She was studying too hard. Her parents are from the old country and wanted her to get married and have kids. They were never supportive of her goal to become a doctor. She felt like the world was closing in on her, or some bullshit like that. He referred to it as 'formless anxiety.' Frankly, when I talked to him, he seemed less interested in his patient's current condition than he was in justifying the fact that he gave her the stuff."

"Can you blame him?" Kurtz asked. "He's feeling guilty. *I'm* feeling guilty."

Moran shrugged and gave a thin smile. "Her anxiety wasn't quite as formless as the old boy thought. Her roommate found these in her bedroom, sitting out on the desk." He waved a manila folder in Kurtz' direction.

The folder contained letters, nine of them, printed in black crayon on white paper with no return address. The first was typical:

> **Doctor Kurtz was talking about you in the cafeteria. He was laughing. He said that he never had a more clumsy student. You're not doing well in Surgery. A doctor has to be able to draw blood without spilling it. Too bad...**

The author of the letters seemed to know Sandra Jafari quite well, well enough, at least, to have stimulated the poor girl's anxiety. All of the letters were similar. They named names and specific incidents. A wave of anger swept over him. "That son of a bitch," he muttered.

"Any truth to this stuff?" asked Moran.

"I never spoke about her in the cafeteria. I never spoke about her at all. It's true that she wasn't the best medical student I've ever had, but she was nowhere near the worst. Frankly, she *was* clumsy. She wasn't stupid, though. She wasn't going to get Honors in the rotation but she was in no danger of failing. She just wasn't cut out for surgery. One of the more cerebral specialties, medicine maybe, or psychiatry, one that doesn't emphasize procedures." He shrugged. "That son of a bitch," he said again.

"We're analyzing the paper," Moran said, "and the crayon. Maybe we'll come up with something."

"Fat chance," Kurtz said.

"Don't take it so hard. She's going to be all right."

"This one," Kurtz said. "This time. Maybe not the next time. That's what's really bothering me. This lunatic is still out there."

"Yeah," Moran said. He stared down at his notepad. "I know." He grinned at Kurtz, a hard, mirthless grin. "He knows your name, though. I wonder if you know his."

Henry Tolliver came to town with his wife and youngest son. The older son was a junior at Columbia, a definite plus. The family already knew the city, had a reason to bond quickly and to feel committed. From the beginning, things went well. Tolliver had read the information packet. He asked intelligent questions. He seemed eager. Within hours, he was on a first name basis with the Dean and the surgical chairs. Mrs. Tolliver, it turned out, came from Long Island and loved New York. She was a theater and opera buff.

"Okay," the Dean said with satisfaction, and rubbed his hands together. "This is a live one."

"Didn't I tell you?" Marcia Cohen said. "The third time's the charm." She glanced at the clock. "Where are you taking them?"

"*Le Bernardin*. They like seafood."

"Perfect. They're already on the hook. Now all you have to do is reel them in."

The Dean looked at her and grimaced. "Ouch," he said.

"What's the matter? You don't like my sense of humor?"

"Forget it," the Dean said. "I'll do my best. We need a chairman. Peter Reinhardt is not going to wait forever."

Jenny Suarez was tiny, barely five feet tall, with black hair, high cheekbones and deep brown eyes. Despite her size, she radiated confidence. "Christina told me you were going to stop by. What can I do for you?"

"Tell me about yourself," Kurtz said.

"I'm from Dearborn, Michigan. I like my job. I'm single." She gave Kurtz an appraising glance, which unaccountably cheered him up.

"How do you know Christina?"

"She was my Chief at Wake Forest. When she got this job, I asked to come along."

"Why?"

"Wake Forest is in Winston-Salem, North Carolina. You ever been to Winston-Salem, North Carolina?"

"Can't say that I have."

"You weren't missing much. It's boring."

"Christina said you wanted to live in New York."

"Why wouldn't I?"

Kurtz knew of a few possible reasons but decided not to mention them. "You know about the letters and the crank phone calls?"

Jenny Suarez pursed her lips and looked momentarily annoyed. "Oh, yeah," she said.

"Any ideas?"

She frowned. "You mean who's doing it?"

"Who's doing it? Why they're doing it...?" Kurtz shrugged.

"Nope."

Helpful, Kurtz thought. *Very helpful*. "Does anybody not like Christina?"

"Not that I know of."

"Does anybody not like you?"

She grinned. "A few ex-boyfriends, maybe."

"Did you dump them or did they dump you?"

Her smile grew wider. "Generally, I'm the one doing the dumping."

"Any of these ex-boyfriends live around here?"

"So far as I know? No."

Lydia Cho had long, black hair, a round face, very pale skin and a white lab coat. She seemed to have a perpetually quizzical look.

"Sorry to bother you," Kurtz said.

"That's fine. Christina said you would come by."

"I understand that you know about the phone calls and the letters."

Lydia Cho nodded but said nothing.

"What do you think?"

She pursed her lips and let her eyes wander around the room. It wasn't as if she was bored with the subject, not exactly. More like she was determined not to think about it. "Some lunatic," she said. "It has nothing to do with me."

Probably not, Kurtz thought, but it was way too soon to reach that conclusion. "But what do you think? You must have some ideas."

"No, actually, I don't. I'm a scientist. I try not to speculate when I have no data."

Ouch, Kurtz thought. "In police work, getting the data is most of it."

"What do you mean? Aren't you a surgeon?"

"I am, yes, but the Dean has asked me to look into it." He frowned. Even to his own ears, this sounded absurd. "I've had experience with these things," he said. "More than I wanted to."

She peered at him with a little more interest but still said nothing.

"Does Dr. Pirelli have any enemies that you know of?" Kurtz asked.

Lydia Cho looked taken aback. "No."

And so it went. Lydia Cho had been pre-med, an old friend of both Christina and Christina's sister, Elizabeth, but Lydia Cho found that she liked research. She had started out in the MD-PhD program at Northwestern but had dropped the MD part after her first year. Patients were too...she squinted and rocked her hand back and forth in a see-saw motion. "Imprecise, I guess. There's too much in medicine that never does add up. Patients get sick. Mostly, they get better. I was shocked at how often you never do figure out exactly what's wrong. I liked research better." Her particular interest was in the hormonal changes affecting blood chemistry during pregnancy. She and Christina were co-investigators on three NIH grants totaling nearly five million dollars and were co-authors on over forty papers. She was happy doing what she was doing. "There's more money in being an MD," she said, "but then you always have a chairman hovering over you, looking at the bottom line. They like it when you publish but they also want you to take care of patients. You have to be good at both in order to be successful and I just didn't feel like taking care of patients. This way, I can do what I want."

Kurtz glanced at his watch. He was scheduled to be in the OR in less than twenty minutes. "Yeah," he said, "I know what you mean. It's nice if you get to do what you want." He rose to his feet. "Thanks for your time."

Lydia Cho nodded. "Don't mention it. I'll give you a call if I think of anything that might help."

Not likely, thought Kurtz. "Excellent," he said. "Please do."

Vinnie Steinberg felt as if the walls were closing in on him. He had been Director of Anesthesiology at Easton Medical Center for a little over a month and he had already realized that this time was not going to be different. Not one iota. Patel, at least, had had experience. Patel had been Director for ten years. Patel knew how to recognize a lunatic masquerading as an administrator. Steinberg did not. Or had not, rather; he certainly did now.

"This"—Serkin waved a sheet of paper at him—"is unacceptable. I can't have this."

"You can't have what?" Steinberg asked. His voice, he noted absently, was squeaking. He cleared his throat and said it again. "What?"

"You wrote a policy for discharging patients from the recovery room."

"Yes?" Steinberg asked tentatively.

Serkin's nostrils flared. His face was turning red. "Are you trying to deny it?"

"No, no." Steinberg felt faint. He blinked and attempted to focus his eyes on Serkin's face. "I mean, yes, I did. The head nurse and I wrote it together. We needed a set of standard orders. The staff had to write the orders out by hand. Now you just check off the ones you want. It saves time."

"Did it occur to you that the Department covers three different sites? And that the staff rotates among those sites? I absolutely require that policies and procedures be identical at all of those sites. It's the only way to be efficient. We cannot have a policy that applies to only one site. Nobody authorized you to write policies."

"But we do things differently at all three sites now." Speaking of efficiency. Efficiency wasn't really the point, Steinberg had come to realize. The point was control. Serkin was the ultimate control freak, which might have been bearable if Serkin himself had realized it. As it was, he wouldn't let you do anything and then he criticized you for supposedly not being able to make decisions. "Two of the sites already have a discharge policy," Steinberg said.

"Yes, and now we have *three* discharge policies. I don't want three. I want *one* discharge policy. Understand?" Serkin's face was red. He was trembling.

"Yes," Steinberg said. "Absolutely."

"Get out of here," Serkin said.

"Right," Steinberg said. "You bet."

"You want to do what?" the Dean asked.

"Take a sabbatical," Peter Reinhardt said.

"A sabbatical…" The Dean had been working in administration for a very long time and he had wondered if something like this might happen. He had hoped not but hope, of course, was cheap, unlike paying a former chairman his usual very high salary while he took a sabbatical.

"I'm a full professor with tenure. I'm entitled to a sabbatical. I've never taken one."

Technically, this was true. The system entitled a faculty member with tenure to take a sabbatical one year out of every seven. One year at half pay or half a year at full pay. However, you were supposed to do something with your sabbatical. Study the way they did heart surgery in Mozambique, come up with a new device for shunting blood through the brain. Something. It wasn't supposed to be a vacation. And then you were supposed to come back to your parent institution and contribute the benefits of your new-found knowledge. You weren't supposed to take a sabbatical and then retire. Unfortunately, there were already three semi-retired chairmen—urology, pediatrics and dermatology—who, rather than quietly leave when their time was up, had decided to hang around, 'take care of a few patients,' and draw a salary that they did almost nothing to earn. That was the problem with the tenure system. Once a man had it, you couldn't touch him. You tried, and he sued you.

"What do you plan on doing with a sabbatical?" the Dean asked.

"Write a textbook," Reinhardt said.

"A textbook," the Dean muttered. "Of course." You could write a textbook while sitting at home in your study, and if somehow the textbook didn't get written, or even if it did get written but never got published, the sabbatical would already be over, the money already spent. Clever, the Dean thought. Very clever.

"What?" Reinhardt asked.

"Nothing," the Dean said. "Nothing at all."

"Amazon, I'm telling you." John Norris nodded wisely and said it again. "Amazon. It's the investment of the decade."

Kurtz listened quietly to the conversation but felt no urge to get involved. Norris was a neurosurgeon. Norris, like all neurosurgeons, made a lot of money. The average neurosurgeon in the United States brought in close to $500,000 per year. The average neurosurgeon in

New York City made probably twice that amount. The residency for a neurosurgeon was seven years, the longest of any specialty. Neurosurgeons were highly trained, highly intelligent experts. Experts, unfortunately, have a tendency to regard their expertise as extending to all sorts of fields other than their own. Like investing.

"Amazon," Chuck Weisberg said, "was the investment of the last decade." Weisberg was a pediatrician. Pediatricians were at the bottom of the physicianly pecking order, averaging a mere $200,000 or so. Weisberg, however, did not seem to feel cowed by the presence of medical royalty.

John Norris reared his head back and gave him a scathing look. "Baloney," he snorted.

Kurtz took a bite out of his sandwich and wished they would all shut up.

"If you had put ten thousand dollars into Amazon when the company first went public, you would have over a million today," Norris said. "Think about it."

Weisberg shrugged. "That was then. This is now. Amazon is a big company. Big companies can't grow as fast as small companies. Amazon's best days are behind it. Sooner or later, Amazon is going to crash. It's inevitable."

Over the years, Amazon had already crashed more than once, but the stock had always, sooner or later, stabilized and moved back up, fueled by rosy projections and steadily increasing revenues, if not always a profitable bottom line. About two years ago, Kurtz had put a few thousand into Amazon. Amazon had gone up. Kurtz had sold out with a 40% gain and considered himself lucky. Weisberg, he thought, made sense, but then so did Norris. In Kurtz' opinion, the stock market was inherently unpredictable. Putting money into the stock market was not so different from betting it on the horses. This didn't bother Kurtz. Kurtz liked to gamble, now and then, but he tried not to confuse good luck with genius.

He yawned. He hadn't slept well last night. Somewhere, a lunatic was stalking his next victim. Somewhere, a new atrocity was about to take place. He yawned again, slowly finished the last few bites of his sandwich and rose to his feet. "See you later," he said. Norris looked at him. Weisberg absently nodded. The others ignored him.

Half an hour later, he was operating on a hernia. The hernia was a tough one, the patient fat, the wound deep. Loops of bowel intermittently popped up into the incision. After stuffing bowel back into the abdomen for the third time, Kurtz turned to the head of the table and said, "Can't you keep him relaxed?"

The anesthesiologist poked her head up over the drapes. "He is relaxed," she said. "He's just fat."

Kurtz restrained himself from saying anything he might later regret and decided to ignore her. He knew the patient was fat. He also knew that he was having a hard time with what should have been a routine case.

Calm, he told himself. *Stay calm.* He placed a new retractor and continued. An hour later, bowel tucked neatly into the abdomen, abdominal wall sutured nice and tight, they dropped the still sleeping patient off in the recovery room. Kurtz dictated his operative note, changed into a jacket and tie and took the elevator up to the Fifteenth Floor. Night had already fallen. He shook his head sadly. He had hoped to be home before sundown and he still had to make rounds, maybe another hour of work to do.

His first patient was a woman named Cloris Right. Kurtz had removed her diseased gallbladder the day before. She lay in bed, watching television. "How are you today, Mrs. Right?" Kurtz asked.

"Fine," she said. She gave him a half-hearted smile. "When can I go home? It's impossible to sleep here. The nurses are yakking away all night long."

Kurtz looked at the chart. No temperature, vital signs stable. "Let me see your incision," he said. The incision was white, the edges tightly closed. From the looks of the bandage, the drainage had stopped. "How about tomorrow morning?"

Her smile grew wider. "Thanks," she said.

"I'll see you in my office in a week. Okay?"

"You bet."

Kurtz had barely walked out of the room when there came a shriek from down the hall and an alarm began to blare. A nurse poked her head out of a patient's room, yelled, "Call a Code!" at the secretary sitting at the nursing station. The nurse's head vanished back into the room.

Jesus, what now? Kurtz thought. Then he ran.

A withered old man lay on the bed. An intern stood at the head, squeezing an Ambu bag, while the nurse pumped rhythmically on the patient's chest. Two other nurses rolled in a code cart. "Give me some scissors," Kurtz said. A nurse handed him the scissors and he slit the patient's gown off his chest, slapped some ECG leads on and looked up at the monitor. Nothing. "Epinephrine," he said. A nurse handed him an amp and he injected it into the IV, then turned the drip up as fast as it would go. The flat line began to waver slightly. Fine v-fib. Not good but better than nothing. "Give me the paddles," he said.

"Ready," the nurse said.

Kurtz touched the two metal paddles onto either side of the patient's chest, said, "Everybody off." The intern looked up, realized what was about to happen and scrambled off the bed. Kurtz pressed the button. A snapping sound came from the machine and the patient's body jumped into the air, then fell heavily back. The ECG showed the same fine, quivering line. "Again," Kurtz said. The patient jumped again.

The body, Kurtz noticed, wasn't stiff but was completely unresponsive, the skin waxen and cool, the eyes fixed and dilated. This was not going to work. The old guy must have been dead for a half an hour at least when the nurse happened to notice him. But you had to give it an honest try, even when you knew it was hopeless.

"Give me another epi," Kurtz said. "And an amp of bicarb." Bicarb was no longer part of the advanced life support algorithm, but this guy was cold and undoubtedly acidotic. Epinephrine doesn't work if there's too much acid in the system.

They worked on him for another twenty minutes before Kurtz finally said, "That's enough, people. Let's call it."

The intern looked at him uncertainly. "Isn't there anything else we can do?"

"No," Kurtz said. "He's dead. He's going to stay dead."

"Oh," the intern said. He sat down in a chair, staring at the body, his face white.

"Your patient?" Kurtz asked.

"Yeah."

"I'm sorry," Kurtz said.

The intern drew a deep breath. "What am I going to tell his family?" he asked.

Kurtz scratched his head. They gave the new interns lectures in how to break such news to the family but they somehow weren't much help when you had to do it for real. "Tell them we did everything we could. It's the truth."

"I suppose." The intern looked up at Kurtz with bewildered eyes. "I've never lost a patient before."

It won't be the last, Kurtz thought, but looking at the intern's pale face and trembling lips, he knew better than to say it. "I'm sorry," he said again.

Chapter 13

"I wanted you to know that I've accepted a position at Stanford," Dennis Cole said. His tone was casual, almost bored, as if his chairman's reaction was a matter of no concern to him at all, which was probably the case.

"I'm sorry to hear that." Peter Reinhardt was sorry, but not at all surprised. The institution had calculated the pros and the cons and had made a deliberate decision not to give Dennis Cole what he wanted.

Dennis Cole was big and beefy. He looked more like a truck driver than a surgeon and he tended to loom over the people he was talking to, which he realized and used to his advantage. He had come here, years ago, with certain goals and expectations. Those goals and expectations had largely been fulfilled. His research was respected, even cutting edge, his clinical acumen beyond dispute. It was time for him to go on to the next level, if not here, then somewhere else. It was too bad, but inevitable. Academics in all fields tended to be transient, following the next opportunity to a new university, a new town, sometimes a new state or even a new country.

"When will you be leaving?" Reinhardt asked.

"Four months. That will give me time to wind down my current projects and get my new lab set up."

"I'm sorry it's worked out this way," Reinhardt said.

"So am I," Cole said, "but that's life."

The Executive Committee of the Department of Anesthesiology met twice monthly. Two weeks prior, Vinnie Steinberg had been stuck with a difficult case and had not been able to make it to what would have been his first such meeting after being appointed Clinical Director at Easton.

Sitting around the table were the Clinical Directors at Staunton and St. Agnes, as well as all of the various Division Directors: Cardiac, Regional, Neuro, General, Pediatric and Obstetrical Anesthesia, Intensive Care and Pain Management. Steinberg had met all of them before but the only one he had ever exchanged more than a few words with was Jerry Hernandez, big, overweight and balding, who was both the Director of Neuro and the Clinical Director at Staunton. Steinberg settled back in his seat, happy to finally be one of the movers and shakers of the Department of Anesthesiology but his happy feeling faded quickly as he soon discovered that nothing was moving and nothing was shaking. Serkin talked for over an hour, giving an update on various departmental initiatives, research projects and institutional imperatives. He spent about half this time pointing out the various ways in which Staunton was superior to Columbia, Cornell and NYU, ways that struck Steinberg as at least mildly delusional, such as a higher state rating on cardiac surgery mortality. Steinberg happened to know that Peter Reinhardt, who naturally took the lion's share of credit for this particular statistic, referred out his most difficult cases to Mount Sinai. Finally, at the end of the monologue, Serkin looked around the room. "Anything else?" he asked.

Everybody smiled. Nobody spoke. Finally, tentatively, Steinberg raised his hand.

Serkin frowned at him. "Yes?" he said.

"What about the Discharge Policy?"

Serkin nodded. "I've appointed a sub-committee to come up with a unified policy. It will be headed by Susan Greene."

Susan Greene was the Director of Pediatric Anesthesia. She had recently been recruited (if that was the right word) from Virginia, where she had kept a low profile and had no accomplishments of any sort to her credit. Susan looked at Serkin, pursed her lips and said nothing.

"Oh," Steinberg said. "Well, then, so long as it's being taken care of." Objectively, Steinberg knew that the whole discharge policy issue was not exactly Earth shaking. What was more important, from Steinberg's point of view, was that the Departmental decision-making body quite obviously was not allowed to make any decisions.

"See you in two weeks," Serkin said.

"Right," Steinberg said. They all filed out. None of them said a word as they trooped down the hallway and into the elevator but as they went their separate ways in the lobby, Jerry Hernandez, who had no doubt been through this many times before, gave him a sad, knowing smile and a sympathetic shake of his head.

Go home, Steinberg thought, put his feet up, have a nice drink…on second thought, maybe a double. Eat dinner, then boot up the old computer and make sure his CV was up to date. The thought cheered him. He left the building with a little bounce to his step.

"Sure, we have surveillance cameras," Patrick O'Brien said.

Kurtz looked at him, surprised. He had asked the question as a matter of routine but had expected a different answer. "Where are they?" Kurtz asked.

"No cameras allowed in any of the patient areas," Patrick O'Brien said. "That would be a HIPAA violation. The entrances to the building are pretty well covered, including the ER. Also, the parking lots."

"How long do you keep the data?"

Patrick shrugged. "We keep it for a year."

"Okay," Kurtz said, "I've got an idea…"

Over the next week, two messages were received on the obstetrics floor, one obscene phone call was made to Christina Pirelli's home and one other to the Dean's secretary, Mrs. Kaplan. The messages on obstetrics came, as most of the messages had, by interoffice mail. Both, as most of them had, threatened nameless destruction for unspecified sins. One was addressed to the head nurse during the morning shift, the other to the unit secretary. Both women called Security when they arrived and then put the messages from their minds. By now, obscene messages had become part of the background noise of their jobs.

All together, this made over thirty messages (so far as they knew) that had been mailed in the hospital. Interoffice mail was picked up and delivered twice each day. All of the messages had been received in the morning, which meant that most, perhaps all, had been mailed the prior afternoon.

Staunton offered three weeks of vacation to all of its non-medical employees, four weeks to the physicians. By correlating vacation schedules and recorded sick days with the known times of letter delivery and cases of sabotage, and by correlating surveillance data with the vacation schedules, they were able to confirm that the majority of possible suspects did not enter the hospital on at least one day when a message would have been delivered. Within a week, they had narrowed down their suspect list to eight men who fit the demographic criteria and who could be seen coming to work on all thirty or so days when one of the messages could have been mailed, and also on the evening when the dead fetus had been stolen from the pathology lab.

Kurtz neither knew nor had ever heard of any of them. One was a pediatrician, one was a PhD in biomechanics who worked for the department of orthopedics, designing prosthetic joints, one was a technician in the Pathology Lab, two were housekeepers, one was an ex-marine who worked for Security, one was an OR tech and the last worked in the cafeteria. Some possibilities seemed more likely than others. The guy in pathology would have ready access to the dead infant. The OR tech would have had some familiarity with surgical packs. Security had ready access to keys, could easily get into locked rooms and could presumably nose around the whole institution without exciting suspicion, though people do tend to remember a uniform. If it was the Security guy, he was probably wearing plainclothes, Kurtz reflected. The others seemed less likely. The cafeteria worker's job was relatively restricted and the housekeepers were assigned to the tenth and eleventh floors. On the surface, at least, these three would have less freedom to roam.

"This isn't bad," Lew Barent said.

Barent had been on vacation in Los Angeles for a week, visiting his oldest daughter and her new baby. He had arrived back home two days earlier and had already spoken with Harry Moran. This was the first time he and Kurtz had gotten together since his return. He looked tanned and well-rested. They were sitting in a booth at the diner a few blocks from Easton. Kurtz was eating a turkey club and Barent had a bowl of chili with a side order of potato salad. Patrick O'Brien nursed a cup of coffee. Moran, sitting next to Barent, smiled down at his sandwich, a chicken cutlet with Swiss cheese and sauerkraut on rye bread, slathered with mayonnaise.

"I thought you were eating healthy," Kurtz said.

Moran smiled wider. "It's chicken. Chicken is healthy."

"Ah," Kurtz said. "Of course. I knew that." He turned toward Barent. "So, any chance of getting search warrants?"

Barent looked briefly amused. "What, are you kidding?"

Kurtz shrugged. He was kidding, actually. No judge in America was going to issue a search warrant on data as speculative and flimsy as this.

Moran glanced at O'Brien. "You have enough people to keep an eye on these guys?"

"None of their offices are in patient care areas." O'Brien grinned. "We're going to put a few cameras where they'll be useful."

"Excellent."

Kurtz sat back in his chair. This was good, he thought. Very good. Finally, they seemed to be getting somewhere.

James Rosen and Mary Lustig were the two faculty members whose non-clinical time had been reduced by Christina Pirelli. Kurtz spoke to both of them and found out nothing useful. Rosen had a wife who liked expensive furniture and wanted a "cottage" in the country. The hand writing was already on the wall where Rosen was concerned.

"Yeah, my CV is out." Rosen smiled apologetically. "Teaching is okay but research leaves me cold. I like taking care of patients. Might as well take care of patients and get paid for it."

"What do you think of Christina?" Kurtz asked.

"Christina is okay. She's an academic. She wants an academic department." He shrugged. "I don't fit in. It's nobody's fault. Good that I discovered it."

Mary Lustig's story was just as unhelpful. Her husband was an investment banker. He brought in far more money than either of them could ever spend. Unlike James Rosen, Mary Lustig was not interested in more money. "I'm going part time," she said. She patted her abdomen, which was noticeably rounded. Kurtz estimated about five months along. "When I was a resident, one of my attendings once said to me that he would like his job a lot more if he could do it a little less." Mary Lustig looked around her office and smiled. "I'm lucky. I can afford to do what I want."

A week later, it was apparent that they had gotten nowhere. All eight men arrived at work on time and spent their days doing exactly what they were supposed to do. Nothing suspicious was picked up by any of the cameras. Five of the eight placed memos in the outbox in their departmental offices. All five memos were examined in the mailroom before being delivered to their intended recipients. They were all innocuous. During that week, two more messages were received, one by the Dean and one by a secretary in the Department of Obstetrics and Gynecology. Both were written in crayon. Both threatened nameless destruction. Both came by interoffice mail.

On Wednesday morning, a veterinary technician in the medical school arrived at work to find that all of the cages in the animal lab had been opened during the night. Rats, mice and four dogs looked up as the door opened, then scattered.

"Shit!" The technician had enough presence of mind to immediately close the door behind him, then, cursing under his breath, he picked up the phone and called, first his immediate supervisor, then Security.

In the end, none of the animals escaped (so far as they could tell) but ten mice and four rats were never found. The dogs, presumably, had eaten them. And since one mouse looks much like another, all of the ongoing experiments were ruined.

On a table in the center of the room was a note.

You can't stop me. You can't find me.

"We don't have cameras on the entrances to the school," O'Brien said. "Just the hospital."

"The only previous incident of actual sabotage was in the hospital," Kurtz said. "The stolen fetus."

O'Brien frowned, looked out the window and across the street to where the medical school and the research pavilion seemed to be jeering at them. "And the school connects to the hospital by a tunnel under the street, which, somehow, we didn't think significant."

Kurtz glumly nodded. "Okay, so we're idiots."

"It could be anybody," O'Brien said. "I'm having cameras placed in the tunnels, but the horses are already out of the barn."

"Maybe they'll come back," Kurtz said.

O'Brien shrugged. "Oh, sure," he said. "If they do, they'll probably be disguised."

Two days later, they got a break. A teenager named DeMarcus Landry walked down an aisle of the hospital gift shop, casually picked up two CD's, slipped them into his pocket, proceeded to the checkout counter and paid for a package of mints. As he was leaving the gift shop, a bored security guard in plainclothes named Luis Rodriguez walked up to him. "Forget something?" Luis Rodriguez asked.

The teenager gave him a cool look. "No," he said. "Why do you ask?"

Rodriguez smiled at him. "You better come with me," he said.

"Wait a minute." Suddenly, the teenager looked concerned.

Rodriguez shook his head. "You're not too bright, are you?"

For a moment, the kid tensed up and looked like he was about to bolt, then he noticed the three other security guards in uniforms standing nearby. His shoulders seemed to slump. "Shit," he said sadly.

"Where did you get this?" Patrick O'Brien said.

When asked if he would object to being searched, DeMarcus Landry had appeared for a moment to be contemplating rebellion. Then he shrugged, and said in a bored voice, "Why should I?"

A note, written in crayon, neatly folded in two, inside an institutional mailing envelope, was found in the inside pocket of DeMarcus Landry's black leather jacket. When Luis Rodriguez saw the note, he gave DeMarcus a sharp look, sat down at his desk, picked up the phone and dialed Patrick O'Brien's number. "I think you better come up here," Patrick said. "Bring the kid." Then he dialed Harry Moran.

DeMarcus Landry looked at the note in Patrick O'Brien's hand without particular interest. "A guy gave it to me," he said.

"A guy," Patrick O'Brien said. He grinned and raised an eyebrow at Moran, who was standing in a corner with his arms crossed and a bored look on his face. Moran shrugged.

"A white guy," De Marcus said.

"Well, that's helpful. What did he look like, this white guy? Aside from being white, I mean."

"Hard to say. You white guys all look alike." DeMarcus smiled.

Patrick did not smile back. "In a way, DeMarcus, you're a very lucky young man. Shoplifting is not considered a major crime in this city and if we choose to press charges, you would in the normal course of things most likely get off with a warning, maybe a little community service." Now Patrick smiled. "Unless, of course, you have a record, in which case, it may go worse for you, particularly since you have—all unwittingly, I have no doubt—gotten involved in a major crime spree. You don't have a record, do you, DeMarcus?"

"Huh?" DeMarcus said.

"A major crime spree," Patrick said again.

"What you talking about?" DeMarcus said in an aggrieved voice.

"Let me be blunt, DeMarcus. Let me lay my cards right out on the table. Tell us everything you know about that letter, that envelope, and the guy who gave it to you, and you may get to walk out of here. No harm, no foul, no further questions asked."

DeMarcus looked from O'Brien's smiling face to Rodriguez' impassive one to Moran's bored one. "No reward?" he said.

O'Brien smiled wider. "Now you're playing with me." He turned toward Moran. "What does the NYPD think about this situation?"

Moran shrugged. "A little jail time might help him remember."

"No, no," DeMarcus said. "Let's not be hasty. Hmm…" His face screwed up in thought. "I met him in Riverside Park, near the Church…"

Chapter 14

You're going to get exactly what you deserve. It's fate. You're going to die a miserable coward's death, just as you deserve

He liked that one. It had just the right touch, a nice, all around non-specific threat, enough to inspire fear but not enough to let the bitch prepare for anything in particular. *I'm coming for you*, he thought. *Oh, yes, I am.* Happy with his work, he folded it up and popped it an envelope. *Soon.*

"You're leaving?"

"Afraid so." Jeremy Wang was young, only two years out of his residency and a good, solid anesthesiologist. He shook his head sadly. "Serkin is cutting the vacation reimbursement, also the expense account money. Fuck him."

"Fuck him," Kurtz muttered. His hands moved almost automatically as he sewed up an umbilical hernia, an operation he had performed so many times before that he could almost do it in his sleep. "Where are you going?" he asked.

"Roosevelt and St. Luke's. The Chairman there doesn't screw with his staff."

"How can he cut vacations? Don't you have a contract?"

"Sure, we do. He isn't cutting the vacation time. He's cutting the amount that the Department reimburses for vacation time that isn't used. We get twenty days per year. If you don't take them all, they rollover into the following year. The contract says you can only accumulate twenty extra days but they've always paid the equivalent amount of money if you happen to go over. Serkin has decided not to pay. Some of the old-timers have accumulated fifty or sixty days extra. They're royally pissed."

"Anyone else thinking of leaving?" Kurtz asked.

Wang gave a thin, feral smile. "Almost everyone," he said.

"Riverside Park," Patrick O'Brien said. "Near the Church."

Riverside Church lies at 120th Street and Riverside Drive, on the upper West Side of Manhattan. A neo-gothic cathedral, Riverside is the tallest house of worship in the United States and one of the largest in the world. In most cities, it would be a major tourist attraction, but in New York City, it tends to be overshadowed by other, more famous landmarks. "When?" Kurtz asked.

"That's the problem. We don't know when. DeMarcus is obviously not the only mule that this guy is using. He made his initial contact on the street and since then, he contacts him by cell phone whenever he has a message that he wants delivered. DeMarcus has delivered five messages. He comes into the school, looking like a student, comes through the tunnels into the hospital, finds an empty office and places the envelope in the out-bin. No fuss, no muss."

"And is DeMarcus going to let us know when the guy gets in touch?"

O'Brien smiled. "Oh, yeah. He knows what will happen to him if he doesn't."

"What happens if the guy never calls him?"

O'Brien shrugged. "Too bad for DeMarcus. A little time at Rikers should teach him the error of his ways."

"So, we wait," Kurtz said.

"Not much else to do."

"I hate waiting."

O'Brien looked at him. "Tough," he said.

As Harry Moran had said, DeMarcus Landry knew enough to know when to cooperate. Moran had a police artist drop by O'Brien's office, where DeMarcus did his best. The result may have been better than nothing, but may also have been worse. "That moustache looks fake," Kurtz said.

"No way to tell," O'Brien said.

The shape of the face was probably accurate, thin, with hollow cheekbones. The eyes were sunken, a vivid green, but the color could have been due to contact lenses.

"We'll give them out to Security," O'Brien said. "Maybe they'll help."

Patrick O'Brien had no authority whatsoever outside the confines of the Medical Center. Harry Moran did. Five cops in plainclothes wandered the streets around Riverside Church as they waited for the perp to show up.

DeMarcus Landry had called only a few hours before. The next delivery was set for this evening, near sundown. DeMarcus was leaning against the side of the Church, looking, Kurtz thought, nervous.

"Jackass," he muttered to himself.

Kurtz had finished with his last patient in the office nearly an hour before. He and Patrick O'Brien had been invited along as a courtesy but had been told to stay out of the way. That was fine with both of them. They were looking out through the window of a grocery store across the street from the Church.

O'Brien smiled. "Yeah, but he's our jackass."

"For the moment."

"Look." O'Brien pointed. Across the street, a tall, thin white guy strolled up to DeMarcus. He had dark brown hair, a thin face and a brown moustache. He wore a baseball cap and a jacket with a Mets logo over the pocket. He stopped, said something to DeMarcus and handed him what looked like a manila envelope. DeMarcus glanced down at it, nodded and took a step back. At that instant, three large cops converged on DeMarcus and the white guy. The white guy looked up, seemed startled, but against Kurtz' expectations, remained completely calm. He frowned once, shrugged, and went along without protest as he was arrested.

"His name is John Glover," Moran said. "A plumber's assistant." He smiled.

"Huh?" Kurtz said.

"Also, he has an IQ of about 70. This guy is not your criminal mastermind, to say the least."

"Then what is he?" O'Brien asked.

"A go-between."

"Oh, shit," Kurtz said.

"How many are there?" O'Brien asked.

"Go-betweens?" Moran shrugged. "We don't know that."

"Ten? Twenty?"

122

Moran suppressed a grin. "Probably less."

"And is John Glover going to cooperate?"

"Why not? In point of fact, he's done nothing illegal. Some guy that he can't identify paid him to get in contact with five kids from the neighborhood, give them some envelopes—none of which contain drugs or any illicit substance—and pay them to put them in the mail."

"Threatening letters are definitely harassment," Kurtz said. "Harassment is illegal."

Moran shrugged. "So is opening an envelope that isn't addressed to you. He claims he didn't know what was in them. He's probably telling the truth and we have no way of proving otherwise. If we try to press a case against John Glover, we'll look like idiots. And anyway, he is willing to cooperate."

Kurtz glanced at O'Brien. "Mind if we sit in?"

Moran grinned. "Not at all."

John Glover sat at a table, drinking a cup of coffee. He had a placid expression on his face, as if wondering what all the fuss was about. Moran, Kurtz and Patrick O'Brien pulled up chairs and sat down. Glover gave them a vague smile. "So, John," Moran said. "Run it all by me again."

"I already told you," Glover said.

"My friends would like to hear it, too. Tell us again."

"Okay," Glover sipped his coffee. "I got a phone call from some guy, asking me if I would like to earn some easy money. I said, 'Sure. What do I have to do?' The guy says to meet him at the corner of 110th and Broadway, he'll give me a bunch of envelopes and all I have to do is pay some kids to take them into the school and drop them."

Moran looked at Kurtz and O'Brien. He raised an eyebrow. Kurtz leaned forward. "What did the guy look like?"

"White, brown hair, nothing special."

"Thin? Fat? Young? Old?"

Glover frowned, evidently mulling this over. "Sort of in the middle," he said. "He was on the tall side."

"How often did you meet this character?"

Glover hesitated. He stared into the distance. "Five times?" he said.

"Five times," Kurtz said.

"Maybe six?"

Kurtz glanced at O'Brien and Moran. Moran shook his head and smiled. O'Brien looked glum. "When did it start?" Kurtz asked.

"Probably around the end of the summer…"

"Probably?"

Glover looked troubled. "I don't really remember."

"He called you."

"Yeah."

"How did he get your number?"

Glover looked puzzled. "I don't know."

"How does he pay you?"

"Are you kidding? Cash. What else?"

Kurtz looked at O'Brien and Moran. "I was hoping for a check, maybe a credit card." Moran suppressed a laugh. Patrick O'Brien snorted.

"You think I'm an idiot? Cash."

Idiot was just about right. Kurtz stifled the urge to say so.

"When does he call?" Moran asked.

"You mean what time of day? It's always at night, not too late."

"Did he ever say anything to lead you to believe that you're not the only one?"

Glover frowned, seemed to think about the question. Then he shrugged. "No," he said.

"Okay." Moran leaned forward. "Now, the next time he calls you, you're going to call us. Understand?"

Kurtz rolled his eyes.

"Sure, but I don't think there's going to be a next time."

"Why not?"

"This last time? He gave me a little extra and told me that I had done a good job. I got the impression that maybe this was the end."

"The end…" Moran sat back and shook his head. "Well, if he ever does call you again, get in touch."

"Sure, man." Glover shrugged again. "Why not?"

"Dr. Kushner?"

"Dr. Tolliver, what can I do for you?" The negotiations so far were going well. Henry Tolliver seemed satisfied with the current state of the department. His expectations were realistic. His demands made sense. The Dean had a good feeling about all of it.

"I just received a rather interesting letter in the mail. I thought you should be aware of it."

The Dean stared at the phone. He cleared his throat. "A letter…" he said.

"A rather unpleasant letter. It's written in crayon. It tells me that I'll regret it if I accept a position at Staunton. Beyond that, it doesn't go into a lot of details. The postmark is from Manhattan."

"Oh," the Dean said.

Chapter 15

A gallbladder: routine, boring and predictable. Kurtz had long since learned to enjoy mornings like this. One thing everybody who works in an operating room for any length of time comes to realize is that there's a lot to be said for routine and boring. Boring means that everything is going smoothly. If you're not bored, then you're in trouble, and nobody wants trouble.

"Patient okay?" he asked.

"Yup." Vinnie Steinberg sounded depressed.

Kurtz suppressed a smile. "You okay?"

Steinberg gave a small, disgusted snort. "You notice any new faces around here lately?"

"You mean anesthesiologists?" Kurtz's hands moved with smooth precision as he manipulated the scope. The gallbladder had been peeled away from the liver and was dangling freely in the abdomen. Kurtz moved a plastic bag beneath it as he prepared to cut the gallbladder off at the base.

"Who else would I mean?"

"I don't know. Nurses?"

"Hell," Steinberg muttered. "Serkin is rotating the staff. If you haven't noticed any difference, then that's all to the good; but it hasn't been easy on my end, I'll tell you that."

"Why is he rotating the staff?"

"The department covers three different hospitals. It's more efficient if everybody can work at all three sites."

Kurtz glanced up at Steinberg out of the corner of his eye. "Can't argue with that. So, what's the problem?"

"Look, surgeons are used to working at different places. You give the nurses your preference cards and they know what you want for every case. You stand there, hold out your hand and say 'scalpel' and the nurse gives you a scalpel. It's different for us. If we want an endotracheal tube, we have to get it for ourselves. The problem is that all three sites are different. The start times are different. The surgeons are different. One surgeon takes an hour to do a case and he likes his patient to have a spinal, another might take two hours to do the same case and he prefers general anesthesia. St. Agnes uses Siemens anesthesia machines. The school uses Dragers and we have Ohmedas. They all work a little differently. The carts have the same basic stuff but it's in different places and some of it is made by different manufacturers and it doesn't all work exactly the same. You have to orient the new guys or they'll fumble around like morons."

"Okay, so orient them."

"I've been trying. Last week, I called a staff meeting to go over the basics. Two days later, Serkin calls me up and says, 'I hear you held a meeting.' I say, 'Yeah, it was a staff meeting.' He says, 'But you don't have a staff.'" Steinberg shook his head. "He doesn't want me to have meetings."

"I don't get it," Kurtz said. "Why not?"

Steinberg grinned wanly. "Because it's not my staff. It's his staff."

"But you said you have to orient them."

"Apparently having a meeting might lead some of them to think that I have some authority, that maybe I'm authorized to make a few decisions."

"Aren't you?"

Steinberg frowned. "Apparently not."

Kurtz pulled the bag containing the gallbladder through the small hole in the abdominal wall, took a quick look around for any bleeders and proceeded to close. "Tough one," he said.

Steinberg shook his head and didn't answer.

"He's got a method that's been working. He'll probably continue with it," Moran said. He looked over at the coffee pot in the corner of the room and raised an eyebrow.

"Coffee?" O'Brien asked.

"Sure," Moran said. He smiled. "Black."

O'Brien looked at Kurtz. "You?"

"Cream," Kurtz said. "Two sugars."

O'Brien placed two mugs of coffee on the table then leaned back in his chair. "Do you think he knows we're on to him?"

"It might be too much to say that we're on to him. We've figured out a little of how he's doing it. We're not much closer to figuring out who, or even why."

"Henry Tolliver is not pleased," Kurtz said. The Dean had called him as soon as he got off the phone with his newest prized recruit.

Moran shrugged. "A chairman has to be able to deal with minor frustrations."

"Maybe the guy didn't get tenure," O'Brien said.

"Most don't. It's not usually that big a deal," Kurtz said.

"Not for you," Moran said. "You're a surgeon. You can take care of patients and make a lot of money. What if the guy had nothing else to fall back on?"

"I suppose he might be pissed."

"Something to look into," O'Brien said.

Kurtz puffed his cheeks out in thought. "The Chairman of the Promotion and Tenure Committee is George Ryan. I'll give him a call."

Moran peered down into his cup. "Crappy coffee," he said.

"Too bad," O'Brien said. "Next time, you can bring your own."

"Ours is worse," Moran said.

"Penny for your thoughts?"

Lenore was wearing a dress that showed an elegant hint of cleavage, just enough to draw the eye, not enough to be slutty.

"Why am I wearing a tie?" Kurtz said.

"So, you can see and be seen?"

"I don't think anyone can see me." They were eating at Bouley, a dimly lit temple to fine dining in downtown Manhattan. Half of the customers wore suits and dresses. The other half looked ready to jog down the street. "Surgeons are expected to wear a tie," Kurtz said. "It's like a uniform, but I never actually liked wearing a tie."

"Have you ever seen those old pictures from the 1940's? People used to dress up all the time. They dressed up to go to baseball games."

"Times have changed," Kurtz said. He grinned, took off his tie, folded it and put it in the pocket of his jacket.

"Lucky you," Lenore said. She grinned. "Maybe I should slip off my pantyhose."

Kurtz grinned back. "Fine by me."

"Maybe later," Lenore said.

The waiter appeared with their appetizers, two pieces of poached lobster with lemon foam and caviar for Lenore, foie gras with cinnamon and apricot sauce for Kurtz. Both of them ate carefully, giving the food their full attention. When the waiter had taken the plates away, Kurtz said, "Has it ever occurred to you that everything is changing?"

Lenore narrowed her eyes. "Often. Do you have something specific in mind?"

"Suits and ties are vestiges from a more formal time. It might have been uncomfortable but everybody knew the rules and what they were supposed to do, and generally, they did it. Not anymore."

Lenore nodded. "Okay...I read an article a few days ago on social disruption. Supposedly, according to this article, the French Revolution and the fall of the Soviet Union were actually decades in the making, but in the end, they took almost everybody by surprise. The system goes on and on and on, and all of a sudden, it collapses." She smiled. "So, what's your point, exactly?"

"I'm talking about our stalker. What motivates the guy? Did he get kicked out of a residency program? Did he think he was following the rules and the system somehow blew up in his face? What did the school ever do to him? There's real hatred here. There's real resentment. And when you think about it, the system is broken. The guys who want an academic career don't have much chance of getting it, not unless they want to sacrifice a ton of money and also work hours that are inhuman and ought to be illegal. The game is rigged."

"More wine, Madame? Monsieur, another beer?" The waiter was tall, dark and thin. He had fashionably spiky hair and a severe face and wore a tuxedo.

"Yes, please," Lenore said.

"I'll have another," Kurtz said. He was drinking Duvel.

"You think he ever wears a tuxedo when he's not at work?" Kurtz said.

"Why should he?"

"My point exactly. At least the guy has a job but they don't give college degrees in waitering. He was probably a Sociology major, or

129

maybe English. Bill Werth was telling me that there are openings for four assistant professors in Dina's department. They've got twelve hundred applications. Why do all these kids major in English, anyway? Where do they think the jobs are?"

Lenore shrugged. "I started out as an English major with a minor in Dance. Then I switched to graphic arts."

Kurtz made a rude noise. "What a scam. The academic beast needs an endless supply of fresh victims. Even the professions aren't immune. I read somewhere that sixty percent of law school graduates in this country are not employed as lawyers."

Lenore nodded and took a sip of her wine. "In the old days, college was primarily for the rich. They already had money so getting a job wasn't a consideration. A liberal education was supposed to teach you to think, or at least, that was the claim. It was supposed to make you a better human being. The only actual job that a degree in English qualifies you for is teaching English."

"Academic medicine has a safety net, at least. You can always say fuck it and go out and be a doctor."

"This is true," Lenore said, "but getting back to your original point, I think you're jumping to conclusions that are not warranted by the evidence. The motivations of lunatics frequently make no sense to anybody but themselves and aside from generalities like 'resentment' and 'hatred' you have no real idea what motivates your stalker. And even hatred and resentment may be incorrect. Who knows, maybe the guy is just bored? Maybe this is the way he gets his kicks." Lenore smiled gently. "Anyway, it's Friday night," she said. "We're eating a nice meal and we have a nice weekend ahead of us. Why don't we try to relax?"

Kurtz drew a deep breath. "Okay. Fine. I suppose you're right." He reluctantly smiled. "What do we have to complain about? Most people can't afford to eat at Bouley."

"Exactly," Lenore said. "Let them eat cake."

Kurtz winced. "Ouch."

Chapter 16

George Ryan was the Chairman of the Appointment, Promotions and Tenure Committee, an MD, PhD in the Department of Radiation Oncology, with the rank of Professor. He was tall, middle aged and thin, with a few wisps of graying hair combed over his otherwise bald head. It was not, Kurtz thought, a good look. Nevertheless, Ryan smiled pleasantly, shook Kurtz' hand and invited him to sit. "What can I do for you?" Ryan asked.

"I was interested in the work that your Committee does," Kurtz said.

Ryan gave him a sharp look. "Why?" he asked.

"The Dean has asked me to look into something. I'm not at liberty to discuss the details, but the Promotions Committee may have some bearing."

Ryan looked at him doubtfully then shrugged. "All right," he said. "What do you want to know?"

"Anything you can tell me."

Ryan frowned. "Well, to start with, when a new faculty member joins the institution, his Chairman proposes an academic rank. For people just out of training, or newly graduated PhD's, the rank is always Assistant Professor. The Committee has to approve these but it's almost always pro forma. Once we approve, the Dean signs off on it, and that's it. The real work comes with promotion, or with bringing people on board who are already senior." Ryan barely smiled. "That can be contentious."

"How so?"

"There are three academic ranks, Assistant Professor, Associate Professor and Professor, with two tracks for each: tenure and non-tenure. Academics tend to be transient. Let's say a man has built up a good reputation but he wants to move up the ranks and his own institution doesn't have an opening. We do, and we hire him. He expects a promotion. Why leave your old job and come to a new job if there is no promotion? His Chairman has promised him a promotion, but his Chairman can't dictate to the Committee. Sometimes he's an Associate Professor and he's expecting to be a

Full Professor here, but even though the system is supposed to be pretty much the same all over the country, standards do differ. An Associate Professor here might be an Assistant at Harvard, or even a Full Professor at some place in the boonies. The guy has to meet our standard or he doesn't get the rank." Ryan shrugged. "Presumably his Chairman has discussed all this with the Dean before hiring the guy, and hopefully they've run it by me, just to make sure there won't be any trouble, but sometimes..." Ryan shrugged. "The internal promotions work the same. A guy has been here for five or six years, he's done some research, he's got maybe a dozen papers, he wants to get promoted. His Chairman proposes him and then the Committee has to evaluate his CV and vote. Does he have any Service, which includes committee work, clinical work, et cetera? Does he have an administrative position? Is he a good teacher? Has he fostered any innovative programs? All this stuff comes into play."

"How about tenure?"

"Tenure includes all of the above plus grant money. If somebody has tenure, the institution is obligated to pay his salary for as long as he wants to work and can't fire him except for moral turpitude. It's a lifetime commitment. You have to show that your research can generate enough money to fund at least a good part of your salary, plus pay for a lab which includes supporting the salaries of your techs and your post-docs. It's not easy."

"How often do you turn somebody down?"

Ryan cocked his head to the side and frowned. "Not often. If he's smart, a chairman won't send somebody up until he's ready. For a physician, it's complex. The standard is much easier to define for the basic sciences: biochemistry, physiology...the PhD's.

"Our former Dean once described the institution as a 'trade school.' It wasn't a popular comment, believe me, but there's a kernel of truth in it. Medicine is, in its essence, the taking care of patients. We've grafted this profession, this trade, if you will, onto an academic system with which it is not necessarily, and certainly not entirely, compatible."

"Research," Kurtz said. "Advancing the science."

"Exactly," Ryan said. "The purpose of medical education is to train physicians. The purpose of the physician is to take care of patients. The purpose of the academic establishment is to expand and perpetuate a body of knowledge. These goals often exist in an uneasy alliance. Sometimes, they conflict."

Kurtz barely smiled. "Actually taking care of patients doesn't matter to your committee at all, does it?"

"Better to say that being an excellent physician is only a part of what we consider. But, there is some truth to what you've said; it's entirely possible to advance up the ranks without taking care of patients."

"Some people might consider that a kick in the teeth," Kurtz said.

"Yes," Ryan said, "they might."

He sat in his chair after dinner and listened to something slow and mournful on the stereo. His campaign so far had reaped predictable benefits. Satisfying, he reflected, but he was getting a little tired of halfway measures, frustrated even. The zing that sending messages gave him, that making phone calls, that came from a little creative mayhem, was getting...old? Boring? Yes, that was it. It was getting boring.

How shall my hatred be shown? Simple. Only your blood will satisfy me.

It wasn't a bad note, he reflected, but how many notes can a person receive before she stops taking them seriously? He sat, chewed his very expensive, very excellent steak and pondered. Yes, he decided, he would send the note. No reason not to, after all, but it was definitely time to up the ante.

"Do you like gardenias?" Lenore asked.

"Huh?" Kurtz looked up from the latest edition of *JAMA* that he had been trying, with minimal success, to get through. Lately, he was having a bit of difficulty in concentrating on work. Gee. Wonder why. Gardenias...they were tall, weren't they? "Are those the ones on stalks?"

"No," Lenore said. "You're thinking of gladiolus. Gardenias look more like camellias."

Kurtz sighed. "You have pictures?"

Lenore shook her head. "Flowers for the wedding. Why do I even give a damn? Am I turning into my mother?"

133

Lenore's mother was five foot one, plump, with a round face and a mouth like a raisin. Lenore was almost six feet tall, with straight blonde hair and had done some modelling work during college. "No," he said, "you're definitely not turning into your mother." Kurtz put down the journal and looked at her. "I thought that everything was under control."

"I thought so, too, but somehow, picking out flowers seems to be a bridge too far." She frowned. "It might help if you could show a little interest," she said.

He raised an eyebrow. "I can't help it if I don't know the difference between a camellia and a gladiola. Anyway, the problem isn't my lack of interest. The problem is *your* lack of interest."

She gave a reluctant grin. "I thought you surgeons were supposed to be control freaks. Make some decisions. Take me away from all this."

"The only thing I care about here is that you're happy. You should have the sort of wedding that you want."

She sighed again, glanced down at the catalogue in her lap and closed it. "Gardenias," she said, and stretched out on the couch, tickling Kurtz' thigh with her big toe. "Let's go to bed."

"You're such a control freak," Kurtz said.

She smiled. "Yeah," she said. "In the end, none of us can deny our nature. I have big plans for you tonight."

He sighed. "Oh, well," he said. "Duty calls."

"Superior mesenteric artery? Are you sure?"

Jason Lee frowned down at the cadaver and idly poked at the swollen, purple blood vessel with a metal probe. "I think so," he said.

Linda Drake said, "It's not supposed to look like this."

It was not uncommon for medical students to work on their cadavers at night. There were ten classrooms that doubled as labs. Each room held four cadavers and sixteen desks, four students per cadaver, sixteen students per classroom. Dissection typically began early in September, started on the head and worked its way down. By the end of the school year, there was not much left of the cadavers. It was nine o'clock at night and the anatomy midterm was scheduled for early next week.

Kyle Stockton frowned down at a textbook propped open on the table. "I think it's an anomaly. The inferior mesenteric is coming off the superior mesenteric. It's supposed to come off the aorta. That's why it looks so weird."

"Maybe," Jason Lee said. He sounded doubtful.

Danny Rosen, the fourth member of their anatomy group, frowned down at the offending structure but said nothing.

A small metal can flew into the classroom, bounced once on the floor and came to rest against the wall, clear liquid spraying from its opened top. The door to the classroom gently closed. All three students glanced over at the door, then down at the can. A flowery smell began to fill the room.

"What the hell?" Kyle Stockton said.

They stared at the can for a few seconds as a small puddle spread out onto the floor. "I'm getting dizzy," Linda Drake said.

"Fuck!" Danny Rosen ran to the door and grasped the knob. It refused to turn. "It's locked."

Jason Lee picked up the can and ran to the sink. He turned on the water and poured the remaining liquid into the drain. By the time the can was empty, Jason was barely conscious. "Someone call the police," he whispered, and slumped down to the floor, his head between his knees.

Danny Rosen crawled over to the air vent and took some deep breaths. Kyle Stockton fumbled with his cell phone, punched in 911 with numb fingers, and spoke into the phone. "They're coming," he said.

Linda Drake appeared to be unconscious, but she was breathing. Slowly, the sickly sweet smell began to dissipate.

"What was that stuff" Jason Lee asked.

Danny shook his head. "I don't know."

"Ether," Lew Barent said. "It was ether."

Harry Moran had taken a couple of days off and was in New Jersey visiting his wife's family. Barent was by himself.

"We don't use ether anymore," Patrick O'Brien said. "Where did he get it?"

"We don't use it for surgery," Kurtz said. "It has a tendency to explode. They still use it in the animal lab. It's the easiest way to anesthetize small animals."

"Yeah?" O'Brien sounded doubtful. "How do you know that?"

"When I was a student, we anesthetized a rat, then we tied off the ureter and injected it with bacteria. The rat got pyelonephritis. A week later, we killed it and examined the kidney under a microscope." He shrugged.

"That's a mean thing to do," O'Brien said. He sounded offended.

"It was a rat. People don't like rats. It's not like it was a dog."

Barent frowned at them both. "We'll examine the can for prints but I doubt that we'll find anything. This guy hasn't been stupid so far." He looked at Patrick O'Brien. "Let's take a look at the tapes." He shook his head, "Whoever it was is probably home by now, enjoying a cold one."

The tapes showed a man with dark glasses, a light brown beard, a moustache and a baseball cap coming in the front door of the lab building. Ten minutes later, he left. He was about six feet tall and lean. He carried a small paper bag. As he passed by the camera, supposedly hidden inside a lighting frame, he held up the bag to the camera and winked.

"Well, the son of a bitch is certainly enjoying himself," Patrick said.

Barent frowned and sat back. "The beard and maybe the moustache are probably fake." He reached out and touched the screen. "Look at his nose."

"What about it?" Kurtz said.

"Notice the size of his nostrils? The way they flare?" Barent shook his head. "Nose putty. His real nose will look different. This guy is no dummy."

"We already knew that," Kurtz said.

"His height is probably real," O'Brien said. "Those don't look like lifts in his shoes. Also, his body habitus. You can't make a fat guy look lean."

Barent grunted. "We already knew that, too. We're not exactly narrowing things down here."

"We'll just have to try harder," Kurtz said.

Barent gave him a cold look. "Right," he said.

He wasn't enjoying a cold one. He was sipping *Cardinal Mendoza Carta Real* from a brandy snifter, about two hundred bucks a bottle, but a successful urban terrorist deserved to celebrate with the best.

God, that had been fun. He could just imagine the looks on the little shits' faces. He hadn't intended to kill them. There wasn't enough ether in the bottle for that, just scare them a little, and by extension, the school administration.

Let them know who they were dealing with. *Be afraid*, he thought. *Be very afraid.*

It was going well. So far, he was satisfied, but he knew that the forces of justice were mobilizing against him.

Kurtz, he thought. Richard Kurtz had a certain reputation. Macho. A bull in a china shop, but a bull who managed to get things done. Kurtz was peripheral to his own campaign but Kurtz, at the request of the Dean, had managed to turn himself into an impediment.

Kurtz would serve as an excellent distraction, and besides, Kurtz wasn't the only one with a macho reputation. Far from it. He sipped his brandy as he pondered. Yes…he nodded to himself. He would enjoy taking Richard Kurtz down a peg.

He smiled at the lights of the city as he plotted his next move.

Chapter 17

Stewart Serkin frowned at the paper on his desk. It was a resignation letter from a junior but highly regarded attending.

Serkin was of two minds about resignations. On the one hand, the department was clearly overstaffed. He had three full professors with tenure who spent two days a week in the OR but who hadn't had a grant in ten years or more. He had five associate professors who worked in the OR three days per week and spent two days in the lab. Each of them had a couple of grants but the grants didn't come close to paying two days-worth of salary. He had a residency director and an assistant residency director, each of whom had three non-clinical days per week, supposedly required for the endless administrative burdens of running the program. He had a director of preoperative services whose job was marginally necessary but whose position brought in no money, preoperative evaluation being considered part of the anesthesia and bundled into the global fee for each case. On top of that, every junior attending felt that they deserved a non-clinical day each week, even if they weren't doing any non-clinical work. And on top of that, every dollar the department collected was shaved a cool seventeen percent, seven for the billing service, five for the Dean's tax, three for the President's fund and two for the reserve fund. They got some of that back in salaries for nurse anesthetists and anesthesia techs but not all of it. For accounting purposes, each department was considered an independent entity with an independent budget, and his department was losing money, only one of the things he had been hired to fix.

On the other hand, he could find it in himself to resent a physician so ungrateful as not to appreciate all that Serkin was doing here. A prophet was without honor in his own country, that was for damned sure. By the time his plans came to fruition, this department would be a well-oiled machine, efficient and responsive. Staunton would be a Mecca for modern operational simplicity, a model for the academic department in the brave new world of health care reform.

And if they didn't want to be a part of that, then fuck 'em.

Still annoyed, he opened the next letter in the stack. It was a single sheet of white paper. Written with blue crayon, in block letters, it read:

> **Your department is a running joke. Your attendings despise you. The other chairmen are laughing at you and the administration thinks you're a fool. Enjoy it while it lasts. It won't last long.**

"I've been told that Serkin is not very popular," Kurtz said.

The Dean frowned. "He's still new. He'll come around."

"Any truth to this?" Kurtz waved the letter at the Dean.

"The administration does not regard Dr. Serkin as a fool."

Kurtz raised his eyebrows. "Misguided perhaps? Maybe even deluded? His attendings, from what I've been told, do, in fact, despise him."

The Dean looked away. After a moment, he said, "He has some issues."

"You know," Kurtz said, "you can't do surgery without anesthesia. If this guy drives away half of his department, we're not going to be doing a lot of cases around here."

The Dean gave a glum smile. "That point has been made prior to this conversation, by more than one individual. I am aware of the problem."

Moran, who was looking bored, said, "Can we get back to the issue?"

The Dean raised an eyebrow. "Which is?"

"You've got a lunatic running around loose, and that's unfortunate, but what makes this letter different from any of the forty or so others that you've received?"

The Dean sniffed. Patrick O'Brien suppressed a smile.

Moran leaned forward and said, "Why am I here?"

"Oh, I don't know," the Dean said. "Possibly because you investigate crimes and this is a crime?"

"Actually, it probably isn't. There is nothing criminal in informing Dr. Serkin that he's a fool and that his department despises him. That bit about it 'not lasting long' might be construed as a threat but could just as easily be taken as an observation that he's doing a lousy job and is likely to be fired. What this is, is a waste of my time. Most criminals are stupid, and most of them are caught, when they are caught, because they make mistakes. This guy is not stupid and so far, he hasn't made any mistakes. The NYPD is happy to help in any way that we can but I could not care less about a chairman with a bruised ego. Tell Dr. Serkin that we sympathize with his feelings and will do everything we can to apprehend the perpetrator. And don't bother me again with bullshit."

Moran turned on his heel and walked out of the office.

"Hmm," the Dean said. "Didn't that go well?"

"I think he's taking it personally," O'Brien said.

Harry Moran's wife was pregnant again. The baby was due in less than a month. Both of them, according to Barent, were getting grumpy.

"No matter what happens," the Dean said, "Detective Moran will go home at the end of the day and sleep soundly. The future of his institution is not on the line. I wish that I could say the same for mine."

Kurtz frowned. Patrick looked grim. The Dean sighed. "Go away, gentlemen. Do something useful."

"Right," Kurtz said. "You bet."

"We've got him," O'Brien said.

Kurtz stared at the phone. "Where?" he said. "How?"

"I'm looking at one of the surveillance screens. Our boy has just walked into the front entrance to the school. When he comes out, we're going to grab him. You want to be there?"

Kurtz glanced at the clock. He had a patient scheduled in an hour but his office was twenty blocks away from Staunton. "Sure, but don't wait for me. I'll try to get there," he said.

Twenty minutes later, Kurtz stood next to O'Brien in the Security Control Center, basically a room with monitors providing views of every corner of the school and every non-patient area of the medical center, now including the tunnels connecting the hospital to the school and all of the entrances to both.

"Look at him," O'Brien said. "Cheeky as hell."

He was tall and lean, with a moustache, a light brown beard and a high, arched nose. He wandered down the aisles of the medical school bookstore, stopping to peer at a coffee mug with the school's logo on the side then examining a display of recent bestsellers along a far wall.

"What's he doing?" Kurtz muttered.

"Shopping?" O'Brien said.

The guy stared into a display case containing gold pens, felt the material on a school sweatshirt, wandered down an aisle full of medical textbooks and finally stopped before the section on medical oncology. He seemed to study them for a few moments, then pulled one from the shelf, tucked it under his arm and walked across the store to the checkout counter.

"Cash is anonymous," Patrick muttered. "I'll bet he pays cash."

He didn't pay cash. He placed the textbook down on the checkout counter, pulled a wallet out of his back pocket and took out a credit card, which he handed to the clerk. He hesitated for a second, selected a chocolate bar from a candy rack next to the cash register and placed it on top of the book. The transaction took only a few moments. He signed the credit card slip. The clerk placed the book and the candy into a plastic bag. The guy tucked the bag under his arm and wandered out the door.

"Here," O'Brien said. He pointed to a different screen, this one focused on the hallway outside the bookstore entrance.

O'Brien wore a thin, wraparound microphone around his neck. He pressed a button on the console and said into the microphone, "Tail him. Let's see where he goes."

The target walked down the hallway, followed at a reasonable distance by two large men who Kurtz assumed were O'Brien's. One of them had black hair, a stocky build and an eager look on his face. The other was thin and blond and looked bored.

As he reached the end of the hallway, the target vanished from one screen and appeared on the screen next to it. He continued down the hallway as if he hadn't a care. A double glass door leading out to the sidewalk stood at the end of the hallway. The target went out the door and turned left. "Now," O'Brien said into the microphone.

The two big guys sped up. "Sir?" one of them said to the target.

The target turned around, took one look at their faces and began to run.

"Stop!" Both security guards began to run after him. A cop stood in the middle of the street, directing traffic. The target ran up to the cop, pointed behind himself at the security guards and said something to the cop. The cop drew his gun and pointed it at the guards. The target peered out from behind the cop's shoulder and smiled at the security guards. "Down on the ground," the cop said. The security guards hesitated. "Now!"

"Shit," one of the guards said. They looked at the target's smiling face and the cop's grim one and did as they were told.

In the Security Office, Patrick O'Brien sighed. "Well," he said, "a nice little clusterfuck all around." He picked up the phone and dialed 911.

"His name is Ronald Sterling," Moran said. "He's an assistant professor of neuroanatomy." Kurtz, Moran, O'Brien and Lew Barent sat in O'Brien's office. They were all big guys and the office was crowded.

"Oh," Kurtz said. O'Brien nodded. He looked glum.

"Aside from a superficial resemblance to the guy who threw the ether into the classroom, there is nothing to link him to any criminal behavior whatsoever. He got a parking ticket back in 1998; no other record." Moran smiled at them. "He's cooperated fully. He's not the guy."

"He looks like the guy," O'Brien said.

"Presumably, the resemblance was deliberate," Barent said. He put down his coffee and leaned back in his chair, which gave an ominous creak. "The real bad guy likes playing jokes. We already knew that."

"Shit," O'Brien said mournfully. Kurtz shook his head.

That afternoon, a letter arrived in the Security Office, addressed to Patrick O'Brien. It said:

You can't find me. You can't stop me. I know that you're wondering what I'll do next. Keep on wondering. You'll find out soon.

The parking lot was well lit but deserted. Still a lot of cars, though, since hospitals never entirely went dormant. He parked on the ground floor, as close to the front entrance as he could get. Kurtz always felt just a bit uncomfortable walking through the place in the

142

middle of the night but the neighborhood used to be worse. About twenty years before, a senior surgery resident had been stabbed while walking the half block between the garage and the ER entrance. Luckily, he had survived. Security had been increased after that but it was still spotty, a two man patrol that wandered through on an irregular schedule.

It was 2 AM. Kurtz was on call and a hot appendix was waiting for him in the OR. Levine had done the workup, then called him. The symptoms and the CAT scan findings were typical. The case probably could have waited until the morning but all the OR's were full and he would have had to bump an elective case. Better to get it done.

He sighed…a surgeon's life.

He was almost out of the lot when he heard it, a faint shuffle of feet. He stopped. The sound didn't. Three of them, he thought, two ahead, one behind. After the events of the past couple of years, Kurtz had seriously thought about applying for a carry permit. So far, he had resisted the idea. That might have been a mistake.

He briefly considered wedging himself between two cars, where they would be forced to come at him one at a time, but no, that would deprive himself of the main advantage of his training and skill, which was mobility. Also, if they had guns, he would be a sitting duck.

Regardless, he thought, if they had guns, he wouldn't have much chance.

The footsteps grew louder. Kurtz sighed and moved into an open area between two rows. He pulled out his cell phone and glanced at it but didn't have much hope. The parking lot was five stories high, built of concrete and steel. Cell phones had never worked inside the lot. Sure enough, he had no connection.

They rounded a corner, two big, white guys, dressed in jeans and leather jackets. One was blond, the other black haired. They stopped, smiled and kept on coming. Kurtz glanced behind him. The third guy was standing on the ramp leading up to the second floor. He was smaller than the others, also white and he was carrying something in his hands that Kurtz couldn't make out.

The two in front didn't say anything. They spread out a bit as they approached.

"Can I help you?" Kurtz asked. Might as well ask.

One of them smiled. The other frowned. Neither said a word. At least they didn't have guns. Their hands were empty, no holsters under their arms or at their waists.

He had about two seconds left to size up the situation. On the off chance that this was an innocent encounter, he stepped to the side, but nope, they turned and kept on walking slowly toward him.

Kurtz sighed. "Just to be certain we're on the same page, here, I'm going to give you boys a chance to back off. You have until I count to three to turn around and walk away."

They looked at each other, smiled and stopped. The blond one said, "I figured you'd be smaller." He chuckled softly. "It won't do you any good." The other one shook his head. They looked at each other, then looked at Kurtz and took one more step.

No time like the present.

Kurtz spun, hit the blond one in the abdomen with a roundhouse kick, completed the motion, dropped and went for the dark haired guys' legs. The blond staggered and almost fell. The other one seemed to have had some training. He jumped over Kurtz' kick and executed one of his own, a side kick that would have taken his head off if it had landed but Kurtz was able to move just enough for the guy's foot to miss by an inch.

The blond guy staggered to his feet, made a sound midway between a roar and a groan and charged in, his arms spread wide. Kurtz turned, grabbed one outstretched arm, dropped and launched the stupid shit over his head. He went flying, landed hard and rolled, groaning and out of commission for at least a few moments.

By now, the other guy was almost on top of him. Desperately, Kurtz wrenched his body to the side and flipped back to his feet. The two circled. The dark haired guy came in with a left jab and followed it with a right cross. Kurtz slipped both punches. The guy was pretty good. He actually knew what he was doing.

Just then, two men in white coats turned the corner. They stopped and stared. "Shit," one of them said. He turned to the other and said, "Go get help." The second one didn't wait. He shook his head, turned and ran. The first one took a tentative step forward, then stopped, wide-eyed, obviously re-considering his first impulse. He cleared his throat. "Security will be here in less than a minute," he said.

Kurtz' attackers didn't wait. By now, the blond guy had staggered to his feet. He ran off to the left. The dark haired one also turned and ran. Kurtz glanced behind. The little one on the ramp had vanished.

Kurtz drew a deep breath. "Thanks," he said.

"Don't mention it," the guy said. He drew a deep, relieved breath. "Glad we could help."

Kurtz reluctantly conceded that, considering the circumstances, perhaps he should not be operating on anybody right at the moment. David Chao, grumbling at being awakened on a night he was not on call, wound up doing the appendix and Kurtz went to the police station with Harry Moran, who had arrived twenty minutes after Security. Barent, also grumbling, met them there.

Both Barent and Moran went over the story but in the end, had little to offer besides the obvious.

"One thing I don't understand," Barent said. "The parking lot has surveillance cameras. We've got their faces. That is a really dumb place to attack somebody."

Moran shook his head. "Not so dumb," Moran said. "Look at them."

Kurtz and Barent both stared at the computer screen, where the two attackers' faces were highlighted. "Crap," Barent said.

"What are we looking at?" Kurtz said.

"The shape of the nose," Moran said. He reached out a finger and traced it across the screen. "The cheekbones, the tips of the ears." He shook his head. "Nose putty and derma-wax. They're disguised. Probably wigs and contact lenses.

"Attacking you there, at the hospital, was not an accident," Moran said. "He's sending another little message."

"You can't find me," Kurtz said. "You can't stop me."

"Yeah. Hitting you on the street somewhere could have been random," Barent said. "He doesn't want that. He wants us to know that it's him."

"Except that I was cleaning their clocks," Kurtz said.

Moran looked skeptical. "Were you?" They had already reviewed the films three times over. "You were holding your own, I'll give you that, but neither of them were out for the count and two against one is still long odds. Not to mention the third guy."

The third guy had stood back and watched. The third guy wore a hat and dark glasses. "Look at his hands," Barent said.

The hands were in shadow. Exactly what he was holding in them could not be made out, but...Kurtz winced. "Looks like a gun," Kurtz said.

Barent shook his head. "A little bulky to be a pistol. Hard to tell. I think it's a Taser."

Moran nodded. "So, you see, you weren't exactly winning. This guy could have stepped in at any time. He was just waiting to see what the others could do. You were lucky."

Kurtz sighed. Lucky. Did he feel lucky? He was alive and in one piece. All things considered, that was pretty lucky, but most people didn't have random thugs attacking them in parking lots. That wasn't so lucky.

"So," Barent said. "Until we get to the bottom of this, watch yourself."

"Oh, thanks," Kurtz said. "Thanks a lot."

Chapter 18

Bollinger Grande Annee Vielles Vignes Blanc de Noir. The very best. He swirled it around the glass and admired the tiny bubbles rising upward against the light. The bottle had cost him over 500 bucks and he was not, frankly, enjoying it as much as he thought he would because, frankly, he felt like a fool. It was all very well to celebrate a job well done. It was quite another thing to pay idiotic prices for a bottle of fermented grape juice. Oh, it was good champagne. No doubt about that. But was it *that* much better than *Dom Perignon*?

He sighed. Relax, he told himself. Today went well. His little attempts at misdirection had been spectacularly successful and a new day offered new opportunities. He glanced at the clock, finished his champagne and rose to his feet. A criminal genius needed to be fresh and well rested for tomorrow's amusements.

He smiled. Tomorrow…and, of course, the day after and the day after that. He rubbed his hands together, ignoring the faint tremble as he walked in to brush his teeth.

He had a lot of plans.

Over the next few weeks, an assortment of student papers vanished from a professor's office, only to reappear on his desk three days later, torn into shreds.

Some bloody sheets were stolen from the laundry, only to reappear draped over the windows of the medical school cafeteria.

No signs. No clues. Nobody saw anything. Nobody knew anything.

Then, two weeks after Halloween, a nurse, young and female, coming out to the parking lot after the evening shift, was pursued by a howling figure dragging a metal chain and wearing a fright mask. The nurse made it to her car unscathed. She was hesitant to report the incident and did so only at her co-workers' urging. A review of the tapes revealed only that the perpetrator was tall and slim and presumably male.

Ten days later, an anatomically correct doll used to demonstrate fiberoptic bronchoscopy briefly disappeared, to reappear later in a classroom with a very large dildo in its mouth. Big deal. Kurtz, when he heard about it, wondered if this one was really part of the series. It lacked the element of calculated viciousness that the other incidents seemed to have. More likely just a student prank.

After that, there was a gap of another week. This time, a young post-doc employed by the pathology department had been working in her lab, again at night. Her slides, an unusual collection of soft-tissue sarcomas, had been smeared with feces and ruined. An unsigned note had been left, printed in crayon in block letters. It said:

> **I won't quit until justice has been done. You can't find me. You can't stop me.**

A few days after that, a pressure relief valve malfunctioned on one of the ventilators in the ICU. Once placed on the ventilator, an unfortunate patient named Mary Smith began to blow up like a balloon. Fortunately, the respiratory therapist involved was smart enough to disconnect the ventilator before the patient's lungs exploded. The official police take on this one was that the ventilator had most likely been re-assembled incorrectly after routine cleaning, which had taken place only the day before. They might have been right. There was no way to tell.

The newspapers were starting to report things, though none had yet figured out what was really going on. When they did, it wouldn't be pretty.

"We should tell them," Kurtz said. "Keeping this a secret is going to backfire."

The Dean frowned. "You're suggesting that we encourage our patients not to come here."

"No," Kurtz said. "I'm suggesting that the presence of a possibly homicidal maniac is not something that can be kept secret. The cover up is always worse than the crime. Remember?"

"I could say that we're not the ones committing the crimes. While annoying, very few of the incidents so far seem designed to inflict real harm."

"Really?" Kurtz gave him an incredulous look. The Dean, clearly, was in deep denial. "Sandra Jafari could have died. *I* could have died."

The Dean winced. "Sorry. This is true, but harassing letters rarely lead to an attempt at suicide. I suspect that the result in this case was not intended. And as for you, fists and tasers do not indicate an intention to commit homicide."

"No, merely an intention to beat me to a pulp. Hardly worth thinking about."

The Dean reluctantly nodded, and gave a small, sad smile. He sighed. "Of course, you're right. I'll prepare a press release. Just in case."

"Why so pensive?" Lenore said.

Kurtz gave a half-hearted shrug. "When I was a kid, things seemed so solid and stable and secure. You got up in the morning and went to school. You hung out with your friends and came home and ate your dinner and did your homework and went to bed. One day seemed much the same as the next. It seemed like things would never change, but after awhile, as you grow older, you come to realize that little by little, things are different than they used to be, in a lot of ways. Maybe you're no longer friendly with that kid down the street. Maybe you like books or hobbies that didn't used to interest you. Then your grandparents pass away and then one day it occurs to you that your father and your mother don't look as big as they used to, and maybe your dad doesn't have much hair anymore and then you go away to college and when you come home for the holidays, everything looks different."

Lenore paused with a bite of food halfway to her mouth. She gave him a sharp look. "Growing up is like that," she said.

"It's not just growing up. It never ends. Things change." He shook his head. "It's not just you and your life and your own circumstances. What was that quote, 'Most men lead lives of quiet desperation'...?"

"Thoreau."

"Was it?" Kurtz shrugged. "This guy, he must have wanted something. Life, or something, or someone, has disappointed him."

"You sound like you're feeling sorry for him," Lenore said.

Kurtz shrugged again, then he gave a tired grin. "Mostly, I'm feeling sorry for myself. I don't like feeling like an idiot. None of us do."

They were eating at the Spice Market, Jean-Georges Vongerichten's temple to Asian Street food. It was kitschy, with bright lights and bright colors, and loud, but Kurtz loved the place. Tonight, however, he found it difficult to concentrate on the food. He glumly stared down at his bowl of Thai hot and sour soup with shrimp.

Lenore nodded and cut her own appetizer—chicken samosas with cilantro and yogurt—into small pieces. "You've been speaking with Lew and Harry," she said. "You must have theories."

"Of course, but it's pretty much the same theory that we started with. Somebody who has a grudge, possibly against the school and probably against the Department of Ob-Gyn, and certainly against Christina Pirelli in particular. Most of it has been directed against her."

"So, what did Christina ever do to make somebody hate her?"

"Nothing that she can figure out."

"Maybe you're being too logical," Lenore said.

"What do you mean?"

"Academic medicine is not a forgiving game. I've heard you say that. Nobody cares if your mother was dying of cancer or your lab notes burned up in a fire. You either produce or you don't get promoted. Publish or perish. Succeed or die. Isn't that so?"

"Yeah, but most so-called academics don't care that much. In the end, we're all doctors. We take care of patients. That's our primary responsibility and that's what we get paid for."

"It's what you get paid for, but in the end, you're not all doctors. For real academics, if they can't do the research and publish the papers and get the grants, the stakes are a little higher, aren't they?"

Kurtz frowned and stared into space. "I suppose so," he finally said.

"Well, then."

"Somebody has a grudge," Kurtz said. "That's for sure."

"A motive may be insane to everybody but the person who has it. Figure out the motive and maybe you've figured out the crime."

Not exactly a new concept in the annals of police work, but still…Slowly, Kurtz smiled. "Let's order some champagne," he said. "I've got an idea."

"You want to do what?"

"The annual Benefactor's Ball is in three weeks. I suggest that we throw in a commendation to honor Christina Pirelli and the Department of Obstetrics and Gynecology."

The Dean appeared doubtful. "And this is supposed to accomplish what, exactly?"

"It's supposed to get our lunatic angry enough to come out of the woodwork."

"He's done that before. Frequently. We haven't been too fond of the results."

"Before, he was on his own turf. This time, he'll be on ours. I think it's time for us to pick the battleground."

"What do Officers Barent and Moran think?"

"They think it could work," Kurtz was shading the truth, but only a little. Harry Moran had rolled his eyes. Barent had frowned. "Pretty obvious," he said. "The guy would be a fool to take the bait."

"He's nuts," Kurtz had said. "I'm hoping it will drive him off the deep end."

"If you really drive him off the deep end, maybe he'll blow up the administration building." Barent shrugged. "If the Dean wants to do it, we can station some guys in the crowd. Don't get your hopes up."

The Dean looked pensive. "They are starting a new community outreach program, and one of Christina's research associates is doing some really impressive work on the effects of hormonal changes on the genesis of ovarian cancer."

"It's already a benefit. Announce that half of the proceeds will go to a fund a new screening clinic, and maybe a lab."

"Sure," the Dean said. "Why not?"

Chapter 19

The benefit was held each year on the Saturday before Thanksgiving, supposedly to get an early start on the holiday season. Kurtz wore a tuxedo, which he hated, and Lenore wore a dark red gown which perfectly set off her green eyes, blonde hair and lush curves. The Dean gave an impressive speech. Christina glowed. Her research associate, Lydia Cho, seemed dazzled. The food was good, the wine superb. All in all, a perfect evening.

Barent and Moran had promised them some anonymous detectives in plainclothes, but if they were there (Kurtz could only assume that they were there), they knew how to mingle without making themselves conspicuous. The caterer had picked his people for reliability and discretion. Cameras were unobtrusively placed. If anything happened, they would be certain to get it all recorded.

But nothing happened.

The party began to wind down around ten. By midnight, all of the guests had left. Over $250,000 had been pledged.

"We should do this more often," the Dean said.

Kurtz frowned. "Not exactly a victory for the good guys."

"You win a few, you lose a few. Sometimes you get rained out. I'm not sorry that the event remained uneventful."

Kurtz shook his head, "Oh, well," he said.

And that was that. Zilch.

The next day, a note was received in the Dean's office:

> **It was excellent champagne, but I've had better. Obviously, you think that I'm an idiot. You'll regret that. You can't find me. You can't stop me.**

"Well, shit," the Dean said.

Two days later, Kurtz' anesthesiologist called in sick and his first case, a gallbladder, was delayed for over an hour before they could dig up a replacement. You had to roll with the punches in this business, Kurtz knew that. Worse things had happened, but somehow, he was having trouble maintaining his usual cheery outlook. He could feel his hands tremble. There was a twitch at the corner of his eye.

"I'm sorry, Richard," Vinnie Steinberg said. He looked grim. "I'll make a few phone calls. It shouldn't be too long."

"Right," Kurtz said. He decided to take a little walk. He got a cup of coffee and sat outside on a bench in the courtyard, letting the late-November sun shine down on his face while he sipped his coffee. It was cool but still pleasant and a light breeze was blowing. Slowly, he could feel his muscles unwind.

Henry Tolliver wanted the job, Kurtz reflected, but the negotiations were on hold while Staunton sorted out its little troubles. It was common knowledge that Tolliver was also on the short list at Jefferson. In normal times, Staunton and New York could outbid Philadelphia and Jefferson but these were not normal times.

Still, aside from the uproar, no permanent damage had been done…not yet, anyway. Kurtz shook his head. So far, they had been relatively lucky, but it wouldn't last. Kurtz was sure of that. The guy had been doing this for a long time and there was no indication whatsoever that he was ready to stop.

Across the quad, an elderly couple were walking arm in arm. The man wore a rumpled suit and the woman wore a print dress. A small handbag dangled from her free hand. A skinny white kid with dyed green hair and a ring through his nose was intently following them, inching slowly closer. What a jerk…Kurtz rose to his feet and walked up to the kid. "Hey," Kurtz said.

The kid stopped. He looked at Kurtz suspiciously. "What?"

"They're not your grandparents, are they?"

The kid blinked.

Kurtz pondered the situation. The kid was smirking. Kurtz was tempted to wipe the smirk off his face. "They do look like easy marks, don't they?" So did this little idiot, if it came to that. He was about half Kurtz' size. "But that doesn't mean they deserve to get their handbag stolen."

"Huh?" A sneer crossed the kid's face. "Get lost, asshole, or I'll call the police."

Kurtz considered whether or not it was worth it and reluctantly decided that it wasn't. "Kid," he said. "I'll give you one chance. You see, I wasn't born yesterday and I happen to be the police." This was true, though Kurtz was almost embarrassed to say it out loud. Police surgeons did carry the rank of Inspector in the New York City Police Department, though the actual police occasionally resented it and more often considered it a joke. "You've been closing in on the old folks ever since you came in here. Maybe you're innocent. Maybe you're not, but I'll bet anything you like that you have no legitimate business, so take advantage of the fact that I have better things to do and get lost."

The elderly couple had by this time entered the building. The kid glanced at them as they vanished inside and almost audibly sighed. Without a word, he turned and walked away.

Kurtz glanced at his watch. Almost an hour had passed. He was feeling better, he realized. His little encounter with the teenaged jackass had cheered him right up. Maybe by now, his case could get underway. He drew a deep breath of the cool autumn air and went back to the OR.

The new anesthesiologist's name was Jenkins. He was short and middle-aged and obviously pissed off. Kurtz hadn't seen him before but he seemed to know his business. After the patient was asleep, Kurtz said to him, "I guess you had other plans for the day?"

Jenkins shook his head. "I was working on a paper. I was supposed to be non-clinical."

"Sorry to hear it."

Jenkins gave him a sour look over the drapes. "I'm supposed to get a day out of the OR each week. This is the third week in a row that I've lost it."

Kurtz had performed this operation a hundred times before. The camera on the end of the tube displayed the abdominal contents on the overhead screens. Kurtz' fingers moved steadily, and before long, the gallbladder hung by a thread. He slipped a bag under it, put clips on the duct and snipped it. The gallbladder dropped into the bag and he pulled it out through the tiny hole in the abdomen.

"I understand a lot of you are looking for jobs," Kurtz said.

Jenkins gave a weary grin. "We're all looking for jobs."

"Great," Kurtz muttered.

Jenkins shrugged.

Twenty minutes later, the patient was awake and tucked into a corner of the Recovery Room. Kurtz retrieved his white coat from the rack by the door and went out to the elevators. Five minutes later, he was sitting in Bill Werth's office. He felt self-conscious, almost like he was there under false pretenses.

"So." Werth smiled. "What's up?"

Kurtz drew a deep breath. In for a pound… "Have you heard about the threatening letters? The phone calls?"

Werth frowned at him. "Not really. Just rumors. What's going on?"

The Dean had been reluctant to bring anybody else into the inner circle, but Kurtz had insisted on discussing things with a professional.

"I frankly doubt that Dr. Werth will be more helpful than the police," the Dean had said.

"Maybe he will, maybe he won't, but we haven't been doing so well on our own. It can't hurt."

The Dean thought about it for a moment then sighed. "Why not?"

Kurtz leaned forward. "Here's the story…" he said. Werth made a few notes on a yellow pad but listened without speaking. Psychiatrists, Kurtz reflected, get a lot of practice at listening. When he had finished, Werth put down his pen and absently scratched his cheek.

"Psychiatrists are good at coming up with explanations for why people do things," Werth said. "We're not so good at predicting actions before they take place."

"Ah, so you admit that you're all quacks."

Werth frowned, evidently taking the statement more seriously than Kurtz had intended. "I wouldn't say that," Werth said. "The problem is that motives are complicated and an action can arise from many differing motives. Unless you can examine the actual patient, you can only speculate on what might be driving the guy." He shrugged. "Frequently, we're wrong. You want my professional opinion?"

"Yeah," Kurtz said. "Why else would I be here?"

"The guy is not nuts, or at least, he's not exactly nuts."

"Really…"

"He has a reason for doing what he's doing and the reason makes sense to him. It may or may not make sense to anybody else."

Lenore had said much the same thing. "That's it?"

"Some of these guys are motivated by a general sense of injustice. The school represents a corrupt political system, for instance, but that's pretty rare. Usually, it's personal and specific. Something bad has happened to him and somebody other than himself is to blame. Or so he thinks. You and I may regard his actions as disproportionate—therefore, nuts—but I would bet the guy has a reason that makes sense."

"From what Barent and Moran have told me, these guys don't stop. They escalate."

Werth nodded. "The cops never hear about the ones who make a few obscene phone calls and then get bored. Most of this stuff is just stupid kids doing stupid things, but once they reach a tipping point…yeah. This guy has been doing it for at least four months. I think in this case Barent and Moran are right. I don't think this guy is going to stop until he gets what he wants."

"So, what does he want?"

Werth shrugged. "Damned if I know."

"On the TV shows, they know." Kurtz gave a weak grin. "Can't you give me a profile of the guy?"

"What bullshit," Werth said. "Look, you take some would be Hannibal Lecter, a guy who's committed every crime known to mankind and you analyze him, you dissect his thoughts and emotions back to the time his mother deprived him of some ice cream when he was two years old and maybe, *maybe*, you can figure out what drove the guy to do it. Or maybe you can't. Maybe he pulls the wings off flies and tortures little children just because he likes to do it. Sometimes there is no motive, and sometimes the motive, the obvious motive, the motive that he admits to, is just a coincidence. Sometimes he does it just because he feels like doing it. And that's the guy we catch and can talk to and can try to figure out. You want me to tell you what might be driving some unknown lunatic we don't even know? Forget about it. It's just fiction."

"Okay," Kurtz said, "I get it, but now that you've given me the standard disclaimer, why don't you let loose and speculate a little?"

"Sure," Werth said. "Speculate." He let out a heavy sigh. "Why not? Okay, first of all, the guy resents women, he resents academics in general, he resents the medical school and he certainly resents Christina Pirelli. You're right. All of this began once she became Chairman. Did she harm the guy somehow? Not that she knows of, but that doesn't necessarily mean anything. Actions have all sorts of consequences, some of which are unintended. Go back and talk to her. Maybe you'll figure it out."

"That's it?"

"Afraid so."

"I knew all this, already. I was hoping for something new."

"Well, you're not going to get it from me, that's for sure."

"Thanks," Kurtz said. "You're a big help."

"Coffee?" Harry Moran asked.

Lew Barent looked up from his desk. "Sure."

Barent and Moran were old friends and partners. They had shared an office until a few months before, when Moran had been granted a cubicle of his own on the second floor. Moran poured a cup, put in two packets of Splenda and some artificial creamer and placed in on Barent's desk.

"Family okay?" Moran asked.

Barent gave a faint smile. "Since the last time you asked? No change. Grandkid number one is walking. I think he likes me more than my son-in-law, which annoys the little wimp no end."

Moran shrugged.

"What's bothering you?" Barent asked.

"This idiocy at Staunton...I have a bad feeling."

Barent leaned back in his chair and grinned. "Kurtz does have a tendency to jump in with both feet."

"Don't I know it..."

"Sooner or later," Barent mused, "this guy is going to do something drastic."

"Probably. You got any brilliant advice?"

"Not really. Keep doing what we're doing and hope something comes up."

"The essence of police work," Moran said.

"Better to be bored. If it's not boring, we're in trouble."

"Right," Moran said.

"And tomorrow is another day."

"Oh, that's profound."

Barent grinned, glanced at his watch and then rose to his feet. "Yeah, well. Time to go home and practice my clichés."

"Have a good night," Moran said.

Lenore was already waiting by the time he arrived, seated at a little table in a corner. She was dressed in a gray business suit, which did nothing to hide the lush swell of her breasts nor the generous golden hair falling down her shoulders. She was studying the menu, her tongue nibbling at the corner of her lower lip, and Kurtz began to salivate. Lenore hadn't seen him yet, and Kurtz stopped for a moment to silently admire her.

She smiled as he walked up. "I ordered a bottle of wine. Silver Oak cabernet."

"Good," he said, and picked up the menu. The wine arrived. They gave their orders. The waiter smiled, his teeth flashing white, and left them.

"Cheers," Lenore said. "How was the day?"

Kurtz sipped the wine. He had occasionally toyed with the idea of getting into wine in a serious way but in the end, a decent bottle of red tasted like any other bottle of decent red, and the really expensive stuff didn't taste much better. Maybe his palate was simply not capable of telling the difference. "Routine," he said. "Thank God."

On the other side of the restaurant, a short, fat woman in a print dress rose to her feet, clutching her neck. Her face was red, her eyes wide and panicked. She staggered away from her table.

Why can't I have one lousy quiet meal? Kurtz sighed and rose to his feet as well. Absently, he noted that two other men had also risen. All of them were staring at the woman. If they're wheezing, you leave them alone. Any air is better than no air, and if you screwed around, you might make it worse. The woman wasn't wheezing. Whatever glob of food had lodged in her trachea had efficiently and completely blocked it. She staggered toward Kurtz. The restaurant, he dimly noted, had gone silent.

Oh, well, time to do your thing. He picked up a steak knife. The Heimlich didn't always work. He just might have to slit her throat.

Just then, the woman grunted. Her mouth opened. A wet glob of something gross and unidentifiable plopped out onto the floor. She drew a long, deep, shuddering breath and sank down onto a chair. Breathing. She was breathing. Kurtz drew a deep one himself. One of the other men had also picked up a knife, a tall man with black hair, graying at the temples. His eyes met Kurtz'. He grinned. Kurtz grinned back and shrugged. The maitre'd and two waiters were hovering over the woman like frightened birds, no doubt visions of lawsuits dancing through their heads. The woman, however, was crying hysterically, clutching a stout, balding man who patted her on the back. Crying takes a lot of breath. The crisis was over. Kurtz sat back down.

"Oh, brother," he said.

"Would you really have slit her throat?" Lenore said.

"If I had to. The correct term is a cricothyroidotomy."

Lenore put her hand on top of Kurtz'. "My hero," she whispered. "My brave surgeon." Her eyes were shining.

Kurtz grinned. "Suddenly, I'm anxious to get home."

"Not yet," Lenore said. "First, we have to eat. My brave surgeon is going to need his strength."

"More than usual?"

"Maybe. We'll just to have to see about that, now won't we?"

Chapter 20

Central Park had seen its fair share of crime over the years but the place was almost always crowded in the afternoon between Wollman Skating Rink and the Met. Christina Pirelli considered it a safe enough place to get some exercise. Christina was not a fanatic about keeping in shape but she liked to jog in the park.

It was an unusually warm day for early December. The sun was shining. Most of the leaves had fallen from the trees and still lay, dry and yellow, on the grass and the walkways. It had rained yesterday, and the air was still and smelled like decaying vegetation and warm earth. You had to enjoy days like this while they lasted, Christina thought. It was supposed to turn cold tomorrow and this being New York, it just might stay that way until spring.

She had gone a little over a mile, feeling like she could do a couple more, when she first noticed the guy behind her. She didn't think much about him, at first. He was just a guy, but after another half mile, it occurred to her that he was still there, not close, just keeping pace. She frowned. She was tempted to go a little faster but the guy wasn't crowding her and there were plenty of other people on the trail so she resisted the urge. She turned off onto a side path, careful to choose one that had plenty of people on it. The guy turned off with her.

Enough of this. The Fifth Avenue entrance at 59th Street was only a few hundred yards away. Time to go home. The guy apparently didn't follow once she was out of the park. She walked slowly back to her apartment, feeling a little ridiculous. He was just a jogger. The whole incident meant nothing. She glanced at her watch and tried not to think about it. She was supposed to meet John at The Modern in an hour for an early dinner. Her little interaction in the park had gotten her adrenaline flowing, now that she thought about it. She smiled. She hoped that John had a good appetite. Christina had plans for later in the evening. She planned on ordering him around quite a bit.

She was, after all, a chairman, and chairmen have their privileges.

Two days later, her last patient of the afternoon canceled. She went home early, put on her sweats and running shoes and headed out to the Park. The guy didn't show this time and after a mile or so, she forgot about it. The next Saturday, however, after a nice easy mile, there he was. A surge of annoyance flushed through her system. Coincidence? Maybe. Again, he didn't crowd her, just jogged along behind. When she turned off, he turned off, too. When she sped up, he sped up with her. No coincidence, then, but he wasn't threatening her, not overtly, anyway. He was just...there.

She finished her run and exited the park and he turned off, jogging along the path. She stared after him. Tall, lean, brown hair.

Asshole.

Three days later, he was there again, and then again, two days after that. She almost grew used to it, her silent, distant escort. Almost, but not quite.

The next time she jogged, he picked her up at the half mile mark, jogging silently along behind. After another half mile, however, he was inching up. This was a first, and this, she didn't like. She sped up, and he sped up, too.

Suddenly, she was running, but he was running faster than she was and then he was right behind her, right on her heels. She could hear his breathing, easy and regular and she knew that she couldn't get away from him. And then he said, "Soon. It will all be over soon." And he laughed and stopped and she kept running. She ran until she was out of the park, dizzy and light-headed and nauseous, and continued to run until she reached home. She opened the door to the apartment, barely able to hold the keys in her shaking hands, and slammed the door behind her and locked the bolt and slumped to the floor. Then she picked up the phone and called Harry Moran.

Lenore looked exquisite in the dim light, the candles barely flickering. Kurtz tried to ignore the hint of cleavage peeking out of her dark blue dress then decided to stop fighting it. Better to concentrate on the positives, since he was not as happy with the meal as he should have been. They were eating at Buddakan, a palace of fusion *haut cuisine* inside Chelsea Market.

"Basically, this is glorified Chinese," he said.

Lenore nodded. "So? It's really good glorified Chinese."

"We could eat just as well in Chinatown for a third the price."

"Probably not, and this place has a much better wine list."

"Humph." Kurtz moodily stirred his tea smoked sesame beef with his chopsticks. Lenore continued to eat with obvious pleasure, which obscurely annoyed Kurtz.

"Have you ever heard the parable of the Russian farmer?" Kurtz asked.

Lenore paused with a dumpling halfway to her lips. "No," she said.

"We had a resident a few years ago; his name was Ilya Kirilenko. He had emigrated from Russia to Israel and spent about six months in a residency in Israel before coming to the US. He was crazy."

"How so?"

"Let's just say that had an exaggerated opinion of his own judgment and abilities. He not only thought that he knew more than the other residents, he thought he knew more than the attendings. One time, we were doing some sort of minor case and I asked him if he wanted to suture the skin." Kurtz shook his head, still amazed after all these years. "He said, 'I'm not interested in sutures.'

"I said, 'What do you mean, you're not interested in sutures?'

"He said, 'I already know how to suture.'

"So, I said, 'Why don't you show me?' So, he tried and he did a lousy job."

"Suturing is pretty basic, isn't it?"

"Sure, once you know how. This idiot thought that he did, but he didn't. Needless to say, you can't do surgery if you don't know how to suture."

Lenore frowned but didn't stop eating. "Oh, well."

"Yeah. One time, we did a biopsy of a skin lesion on a teenage girl. She had local anesthesia and some minimal sedation. We dropped her off in the back of the Recovery Room and I went to the phone to dictate the case. Suddenly, I hear the girl screaming. I went running back to see what was going on and Ilya was trying to force an oxygen mask on her face and she was yelling, 'Get away from me, you pervert!'

"I said, "What the hell are you doing?

"He said, 'This is hypoxic encephalopathy. She needs oxygen!'"

Lenore looked bewildered. "Did she need oxygen?"

"No. She was wide awake, breathing normally and her oxygen saturation was absolutely normal. He was nuts." Kurtz shook his head. "I apologized to the patient and told him to leave her the hell alone. Jesus."

"So, what does all of this have to do with Russian farmers?"

"Oh. Well, in addition to being insane, Ilya actually had a sense of humor. One time, he told me what he called the parable of the Russian farmer. It seems that there is a very poor farmer. His soil is stony. He can barely plow it. He can't grow enough crops and his family is hungry. One day, God appears to him and tells him that he'll grant the farmer any wish that he wants. The farmer asks for a horse, so he can plow his fields. The next day, a horse appears at the farmer's front door. The farmer plows his fields, his crops grow and his family has enough to eat.

"The farmer has a neighbor, also a Russian farmer. Like the first one, his soil is stony, his crops won't grow and his family is starving. God appears to the neighbor and tells him that he'll grant any wish that he wants. What do you think he wants?"

"I don't know," Lenore said. "A horse of his own?"

"That would make sense, wouldn't it? But nope. The farmer knows exactly what he wants and that's not it. He says to God, 'I want you to kill my neighbor's horse.'"

"Cold," Lenore said.

"This was supposed to illustrate something about human nature in general and the attitude of the Russian people, in particular. After having suffered for seventy years under communism and hundreds of years under the czars, they were simply incapable of conceiving of a better life for themselves; but they still resented anybody who might have more than they did."

"You said he was crazy."

"Nuts," Kurtz said. "Completely nuts."

"But nuts with a sense of humor."

Kurtz nodded. "Yup."

"What happened to him?"

"He finally pissed off too many people. We fired him."

"So much for a sense of humor."

"What else were we supposed to do? He couldn't do the job."

"Nothing," Lenore said. "Nothing at all. If you can't do the job, then you have to go."

"Unfortunately, true," Kurtz said.

"So, what happened to him?"

Kurtz shrugged. "Who knows?"

"And even more to the point, why are you thinking about this?"

"I'm wondering what's driving our current lunatic."

"So how do Russian farmers and dead horses help you?"

"Damned if I know. I'm just thinking."

She gave him a long look then shrugged. "It's good that you're thinking. Keep thinking. Meanwhile, you want dessert?"

"Sure," Kurtz said.

"Good. Me, too."

Ten minutes later, Kurtz paused with a spoonful of almond bread pudding halfway to his lips. A far away look came slowly over his face.

"What?" Lenore asked.

"Hmm?" Kurtz looked at her, looked down at his dessert, carefully placed the spoon down on his plate and sat back in his chair. He let out a breath and slowly smiled. "I've got an idea," he said.

Christina Pirelli stared at the picture on her desk. "I don't know," she finally said. "Maybe."

The picture was that of Roy Cullen, MD, a recently graduated orthopedist who had joined the faculty at Easton approximately six months before Christina Pirelli had arrived at Staunton. Jennie Suarez frowned down at the picture. "I didn't know he was in New York."

"What was it you said about Winston-Salem?" Kurtz said. "Boring? Apparently, you're not the only ones who left Winston-Salem for the big apple."

"What's he like?" O'Brien asked.

Jenny Suarez frowned. "Serious," she said. "Not my type."

"So why did you go out with him?"

"He's got a lot of nice muscles." She grinned. "I liked his looks. It took me only a couple of dates to figure out that he had no sense of humor."

"And how did he take it when you called it off."

"Not well," she shrugged. "What was I supposed to do? It was a mistake."

Kurtz looked at O'Brien, who kept his face impassive, then at Christina Pirelli, who was frowning down at the picture sitting on the desk. "I don't know," she said again. "Why would this guy be stalking me?"

"Because he's a lunatic?" Kurtz said.

"It's a good question, though," O'Brien said. "What did Dr. Pirelli have to do with his breakup, or anything else, for that matter?" He glanced at Christina, who was looking bewildered.

"He does look like the guy who was chasing me," she said doubtfully.

"Call Harry Moran," Kurtz said. "See about some surveillance."

O'Brien looked skeptical but picked up the phone. "Oh, sure," he said. "Let's see about some surveillance."

O'Brien's skepticism proved well founded. Moran heard him out and then said, "So let me get this straight: a girl breaks up with a guy, six months later a campaign of intimidation begins at Staunton and you decide, with no obvious motive and no evidence whatsoever, that this is the guy who's responsible. And you want me to assign a couple of policemen who have actual jobs to follow him around."

"It sounds bad when you put it like that," O'Brien said.

"Right," Moran said. "Call me back when you've got something real." He hung up.

"Well," Kurtz said. "We'll just have to do it ourselves."

Kurtz had read about stakeouts. He knew what to expect and he wasn't looking forward to it. Stakeouts were tedious, frustrating and boring. You sat there with nothing to do except wait. If you were lucky, it wasn't cold, it wasn't raining, and nobody noticed you, but you still had to pay attention. Even if you were sitting in a car parked on the street, your eyes fixed on the guy's apartment, you couldn't do anything else but sit there and watch because the subject might choose that exact moment to walk out his door and vanish.

Luckily (or not, considering the circumstances), Kurtz didn't have to do any surveillance because it turned out that Roy Cullen had left a week before on a two-week vacation to Aruba with his latest girlfriend, a nurse in the Medical Intensive Care Unit. He had been in New York when Christina Pirelli had first been stalked in the park but was safely out of the country during the latest incident.

"Win some. Lose some," Patrick O'Brien said.

"Yeah," Kurtz said. "I know how that works, except that so far, we haven't won any."

Patrick shrugged.

Kurtz grinned at him. "I have another idea."

Patrick sighed. "Of course, you do."

Chapter 21

Color copies of forty-two letters were spread out on the table, loosely arranged by date of receipt. Most of them contained vague threats and promises of formless revenge. All of them except the first two, which were in pencil and as accurate as Christina Pirelli could remember, were written in crayon. Seen like this, all forty-two together, they seemed sinister but vaguely absurd. He had looked at them at least a dozen times.

"What do you think?" Kurtz asked.

Dina Werth was Bill Werth's wife, an Associate Professor of English Literature at City College of New York. She was an attractive, slightly overweight woman, with long brown hair and an olive complexion. She looked up, a frown on her face. "You were right," she said. "This one is from *Medea*."

"Medea..." Kurtz said.

Dina smiled. "*Medea* is a play by Euripides, one of the few ancient Greek plays to survive into modern times. Medea has been betrayed by her husband, Jason. In revenge, she murders their two children and then takes their bodies away to be buried in secret. *It's fate. You're going to die a miserable coward's death, just as you deserve.* That's not an exact quote, of course. It's paraphrased, but then, there are a lot of translations and they all differ slightly." She rose from her seat and went over to a bookcase, hesitated, then grabbed a thick book with a leather cover. She opened it and read:

I take my children's bodies with me that I may bury them in Hera's precinct. And for thee, who didst me all that evil, I prophesy an evil fate. You will die a miserable coward's death as you deserve, struck on your head by a piece of the wreck of the Argo."

"The Argo..."

"The Argo was Jason's ship. You know, Jason and the Argonauts? Jason sailed to Colchis with Hercules and the Argonauts and stole the Golden Fleece."

"There are forty-two letters," Kurtz said. "That seems pretty tenuous."

"It's not the only one. She searched through the pile, held up a note and read: "*Wounds heal slowly, by degrees. I'll be coming for you. Soon.*'" She waved the letter at Kurtz. "This is the first one, correct?"

"So far as she can remember. She didn't start saving them until the third," Kurtz said.

Dina gave a crisp nod, went back to the bookcase, scanned the top shelf and picked out two leather bound volumes. She opened one of them, flipped through, found the page she wanted and held the book out to Kurtz. "Here," she said. "Take a look."

"*How poor are they that have not patience!*" Kurtz quoted. "*What wound did ever heal but by degrees?*" He looked at Dina.

"Othello," she said. "It's not one of Shakespeare's most famous lines, but it's not obscure, either."

Kurtz sat back in his chair. "Any more?"

"Yeah," Dina said. She grimaced and read another of the notes out loud. "*How shall my hatred be shown? Simple. Only your blood will satisfy me.*" She shook her head. "Sort of an asshole, isn't he?"

"Pretty much," Kurtz agreed. "So that's a quote?"

"Yep. This one is a little more obscure." She picked up the second book, opened it and held the page out to Kurtz.

He squinted down at it. "*'But say, Reuenge,—for thou must helpe or none,—Against the rest how shall my hate be showne?*' Kurtz frowned. "I don't even know how to pronounce it."

"It's from *The Spanish Tragedy*, by Thomas Kyd, written around 1585. It was one of the first revenge plays in Elizabethan theater. Supposedly, it was a major influence on *Hamlet*."

"Who would know this, today?"

Dina shrugged. "An English scholar, maybe a theater buff. Nobody else, that's for sure."

"A theater buff," Kurtz said, and he smiled. "After all this time, a real life clue…Thanks," he said.

Elizabeth Reisman, Christina Pirelli's sister, sat stiffly on the couch in her own living room. She was back home in North Carolina but she and Christina both had Skype on their computers. Kurtz and

Lydia Cho sat on a brown, leather couch in Christina's apartment. Christina sat next to them in an easy chair.

"So, let me get this straight," Elizabeth Reisman said. "You think that somebody resents Christina for something having to do with one of us, and that it somehow revolves around the theater." She looked at Lydia Cho and raised an eyebrow. Lydia shrugged.

Elizabeth Reisman looked like Christina, a little younger, a little thinner, but the same dark curls and pale complexion. Christina, sitting in front of her own computer screen and nursing a glass of Chardonnay, looked equally skeptical.

"Yeah," Kurtz said.

"That doesn't seem likely," Elizabeth said.

"It might not have anything to do with the theater, not directly, at least, but both of you, I've been told, like the theater, and this guy, whoever is doing it, obviously knows at least a little about the theater."

"Huh," Elizabeth said.

"Have either of you ever seen *The Spanish Tragedy*, by Thomas Kyd?"

"Never heard of it," Elizabeth said.

"How about *Othello*?"

"Okay. I've heard of *Othello*."

"You've never seen it?" Kurtz said.

"I read it in high school. I've never seen it performed."

"*Medea*, by Euripides?"

Elizabeth shook her head. "Heard of it. Never read it. Never seen it."

Lydia Cho, who had been listening to this interchange with a grim look on her face, leaned back in the couch, took a deep breath and turned to Christina. "You got anything to drink?" she asked.

Christina looked at her. "You mean like alcohol?"

"Oh, yeah," Lydia said. "I mean like alcohol."

Silently, Christina rose to her feet, disappeared into another room and came back with a bottle of Bourbon. She poured a generous helping into a crystal glass, glanced at Lydia's pale face, frowned and added a little more.

"Thanks." Lydia drank half of it in one swallow.

"You've thought of something," Kurtz said.

Lydia sighed, then nodded, her lips set in a tight line. "Yeah," she said. "I've thought of something."

"*Othello*, *The Spanish Tragedy* and *Medea* are all about revenge," Kurtz said. "This is not likely to be a coincidence."

Harry Moran shrugged. Lew Barent sat next to him, eating a burger and quietly listening. Barent had a small smile on his face. Kurtz, who had come to know him well, thought that Barent was enjoying being a spectator on what, to him, was a minor sort of case. "Revenge for what?" Moran said. "If Lydia Cho is correct, the interaction was superficial. They went out on a few dates. They weren't physically involved. They drifted apart. How, exactly, is Christina Pirelli supposed to have harmed the guy?"

"By existing?"

Moran, Barent, Kurtz and Patrick O'Brien were sitting in a booth at the Subway Inn, a homey sort of bar on the Upper East Side. Moran and Barent were officially off duty and they were all sipping beer.

Patrick O'Brien picked a pretzel out of a bowl on the table and chewed on it. "Iago, if I remember correctly, also did not have any obvious motive when he hatched his plot against Othello, his supposed friend and superior officer. Since Iago lacked a definite motive, it's generally assumed that Shakespeare meant Iago to be taken as the personification of pure evil."

Kurtz and Moran stared at him. Barent cocked his head to the side, smiled and poured himself another beer. Patrick O'Brien gave a modest shrug.

"Well," Moran finally said, "most criminals do have a motive, even if it's simple jealousy for somebody who has a better life than they have."

"According to Lydia Cho," Patrick went on, "she went out with this guy a few times while she was in Medical School. He was attentive, too much so, actually. He started to talk about a future on their third date. Around this time, Lydia decided to drop the MD part of her degree and go on with the PhD. She preferred research to taking care of patients. The guy was angry. Apparently, one of his fantasies about the future involved a wife who made a lot of money, so he dumped her. This didn't bother Lydia Cho since she thought he was sort of a jerk, anyway. And that's that."

"So where do Othello and Greek tragedy come in?" Patrick asked.

"Lydia went to a number of plays with him, at least three or four. He expressed enthusiasm for the art form."

"It sounds like he expressed enthusiasm for everything to do with her, before she decided to stop pursuing her MD."

"So why blame Christina?" Moran asked.

"Apparently, according to the guy's fevered brain, Christina is the one who convinced Lydia to give up the idea of becoming a well-paid doctor and go into research, instead. Lydia and Christina both confirm that she was supportive of the decision. She didn't talk her into it, but the guy was convinced that she had."

"Well," Kurtz said, "that is not exactly that." He grinned. "I put a Google search on the guy before coming here." He took a sip of his beer and smacked his lips. "He's dead."

Moran and O'Brien stared at him. Barent shrugged. "About five years after his breakup with Lydia Cho, he drove his car off a bridge in Stockton, Colorado, where he was working as a bus boy in a local restaurant. The autopsy revealed high levels of both alcohol and cocaine in his blood. It might have been an accident but there was speculation as to suicide. Friends and co-workers claim he was depressed."

"Then why are we here?" Moran asked.

Kurtz put his beer down on the table and raised an eyebrow. "He has a brother. The brother works at Staunton."

"Really?"

"His name is James McDonald. He's a pharmacy technician. His work takes him all over the hospital, which is certainly convenient. He also moonlights once a week at Easton."

Moran ate a pretzel and grudgingly nodded. "You have a theory, and it makes a little sense, but it's not evidence." He frowned. "Tell me about the brother. The dead guy."

"Joseph McDonald. He was in a Masters program in Sociology when he met Lydia Cho. Good looking, charming and obsessive. He had a lot of student debts and no job prospects beyond the dim hope of teaching high school, which he did for awhile, until he got fired for having an affair with one of his students. He went on welfare, worked for every left wing cause imaginable and chose Colorado as a place to live because he liked the outdoor lifestyle. He drove a car off a bridge and nobody mourned him, except his little brother, who was apparently the only person alive dumb enough to buy his line of bullshit."

"It's not evidence," Moran said again.

"No, it's not," Kurtz agreed. "Is it enough to put a guy on him, at least for a couple of days?"

Moran sipped his beer, while he considered the question. Finally, he looked over at Barent and nodded his head. "Yeah," he said. "I think we can do that."

Chapter 22

The campaign of intimidation continued. During the next week, three more letters were received by nurses on the OB floor, two harassing phone calls were reported and a package containing a dead sparrow was delivered to Christina Pirelli.

"Low level stuff," Kurtz said.

"I doubt the sparrow would agree," Patrick O'Brien said.

Kurtz shook his head. "Keeping the pressure up."

It was worth a shot but it wasn't worth overtime. A rotating team of NYPD detectives was assigned to put James McDonald under surveillance. It was noted that he left his apartment each morning at approximately 7:30 AM and arrived at work by 8:00. Twice during the week, he went to a local pizzeria during his lunch hour, before returning to the hospital. He got off work at 4:30 PM, took the subway home and, on Monday, Wednesday and Thursday, did not go out again. On Tuesday, he walked to a nearby Barnes and Noble, where he stayed for approximately forty minutes before picking up dinner at a neighborhood Indian place. On Friday, he had dinner with some friends at a local hamburger joint. He arrived home by 10:00 PM and was not seen to exit his building for the rest of the night. On Saturday, he went out shopping, strolled through the Museum of Modern Art and took in a movie by himself. On Sunday, he went running in Central Park. Nothing he did seemed unusual, out of place or suspicious.

Meanwhile, the letters and phone calls continued.

"I don't know," Moran said.

"It could have been set up weeks in advance. We know he's been using intermediaries." Kurtz grimaced. "Whoever he is."

"My point exactly," Moran said.

They continued the surveillance for three more days before Moran called it quits. "Either there's nothing to discover or he's covered his tracks. Either way, this isn't working."

"Right," Kurtz said, and glumly nodded.

"Penny for your thoughts?"

"Huh?" Kurtz looked up at Lenore, then back down to the book lying in his lap. The book had been opened to the same page for nearly twenty minutes. "I'm trying not to take this personally," he said, "but it's not easy. This son of a bitch is calmly going about his business, ruining people's lives, smirking, and playing us for fools."

"You don't know that he's smirking. That's an assumption."

"Hah! I bet you he's smirking right now. He's probably sipping a glass of wine and congratulating himself on being smarter than we are."

Lenore raised an eyebrow, sipped her wine and said, "What are you going to do about it?"

Kurtz drew a slow, deep breath and grimly smiled. "Well, that is the question, now isn't it?" Unfortunately for Kurtz' peace of mind, he had no idea what he was going to do about it. "I'm considering my options," he said.

Chapter 23

"He's twenty-seven years old," Patrick O'Brien said. "He has an above average IQ and he got decent but not spectacular grades. His letters of recommendation were okay but nothing special."

"An underachiever," Kurtz said.

"Apparently."

"How come?"

Patrick shrugged. "Other things on his mind? The letters don't say exactly, but if you read between the lines, he seems to have spent a lot of time by himself. He was into video games, long distance running and wilderness camping. Also, saving the environment."

"Nothing wrong with saving the environment."

Harry Moran made a rude noise. "You ever hear of the Earth Liberation Front?"

"Can't say that I have," Kurtz said.

"How about the Monkey Wrench Gang?"

"Nope."

By this time, Harry Moran had tweaked his sources. "He and his brother were both suspected of being members. They would do things like burn ski resorts in Vail, Colorado and sabotage logging operations, sometimes with dynamite."

Kurtz winced. "I was hoping that he was a more mundane sort of lunatic."

"Apparently not."

"Why didn't all of this come up when he applied for the job?"

"He was arrested only once," Harry said. "He was sixteen at the time, a juvenile, so the records were sealed. After, that, he has no record. He either went straight or he never got caught."

They were sitting in Patrick O'Brien's small office. Moran and Patrick were sipping from cups of the cafeteria coffee. Kurtz, who had just arrived after finishing a case, was wearing a white lab coat over green hospital scrubs.

"Their parents died in a house fire. James was only thirteen at the time. An aunt and uncle took in both brothers until they went away to college. James and Joseph stuck together after that, until Joseph took his header off the bridge."

"Anything suspicious about the fire?" Kurtz asked.

Moran shrugged. "Not that we know of."

"How about the aunt and uncle?" Patrick asked.

"Strongly religious. They belong to a small fundamentalist sect that believes in keeping to themselves and living as simply as possible. No central heating, no modern technology, not even electricity. A lot like the Amish."

"I bet James and Joseph just loved that."

Harry shrugged again. "No idea."

"Any evidence that the kids were abused?"

"None at all."

Patrick frowned down at a file. "His yearly performance appraisals are interesting, more for what they don't say than for what they do. He's competent. He keeps to himself. He doesn't hang around with his co-workers. Basically, they don't seem to like him much but they can't say exactly why."

"How about the paper?" Kurtz asked. "The envelopes, the stamps, the crayon? Any way to identify where he's getting them?"

"Common brands," Moran said. "Available from literally hundreds of outlets. No way to trace them."

"How about if he got them online?"

"Then we could probably trace them, assuming that he used his own name, his own address and a credit card, but only if we had a search warrant. We're not getting a search warrant. Not with what we've got."

"Then we've just got to get more," Kurtz said.

Moran gave him a quick, cynical grin. Kurtz had the uncomfortable feeling that Moran was looking into his soul and laughing.

"Any idea how?" Moran said.

"Not yet," Kurtz said.

Moran shrugged and rose to his feet. "Let me know when you come up with something."

"Right," Kurtz said. "You bet."

He did have one more idea. Not much of an idea, admittedly, but if it worked out, it might help to nail down at least one minor point. Kurtz and Patrick O'Brien were sitting across a table from Lillian Mayberry.

"Recognize anybody?" Patrick asked.

Lillian Mayberry frowned as she looked through the pile of twenty blown up photographs. None of the photos were members of the medical staff of Staunton University Hospital. One of them was the same picture that was on the ID card of James McDonald, pharmacy technician.

"No," she said, after carefully inspecting each picture. "I'm afraid that I don't."

Lillian Mayberry was the supervisor of the Medical Records Unit on the day shift. There were three other clerks on the day shift, two on evenings and one on nights. The day shift clerks had all been shown the pictures and all had failed to recognize any of them except for one clerk, a pretty brunette who frowned down at one picture and said, "Isn't that Justin Bieber?"

"No," Patrick O'Brien said automatically. "It's not." He looked a little closer. "Oh," he said. "Yes, actually I think it is. Well, do you recognize any of the others?"

"No." She shook her head. "Sorry."

Patrick sighed. "That's okay. Thanks."

One of Patrick's men came back for the evening shift, and then another came back for the night shift. None of the clerks recognized any of the men in the photos.

They showed the same pictures to Christina Pirelli. When she came to James McDonald, she frowned and looked at it for a long time. "This looks a lot like the guy who was following me. The hair's a little different. The nose is a little thinner." She hesitated. "If it's him, he's lost weight."

"Could you identify him in court?"

"Not for certain. I wouldn't want to swear to it."

"Oh, well," Kurtz said, the next day. "It was worth a try."

Patrick shrugged. "Now what?"

"I don't know," Kurtz said. "I guess we better think of something else."

Kurtz wasn't expecting much, and he was he was not surprised by the Dean's reaction. The Dean listened to him, nodding, then said, "So you think you know who he is, but you can't prove it."

"Yes."

The Dean frowned. "Our hands are tied, then. You know that."

"I'm informing you of what we've discovered. We've identified a suspect. What you do with that information is entirely up to you."

"Unfortunately," the Dean said, "or maybe not so unfortunately, this medical center is unionized. We can't fire him. We can't retaliate in any way without proof, and even if we could, our goal is to make this campaign of intimidation stop. He can send letters and make phone calls just as easily from outside the institution as inside."

Kurtz shrugged. "Like I said, I'm telling you what we've got."

The Dean looked at him. "Go get more," he said.

Where had Kurtz heard that before? "I intend to."

"Good," the Dean said. Then he gave a lopsided grin. "Good work, anyway."

A large man in a Security uniform stood watch in a corner of the men's locker room. He ignored the assorted hospital workers as they entered the room, grabbed scrubs from the wire shelving, opened their lockers, changed into work attire and exited the locker room. Most of the workers cast speculative looks at the Security officer but nobody felt it advisable to ask him what he was doing there. When James McDonald arrived, the officer gave him a slight smile but said nothing. McDonald opened his locker, changed, closed the locker and exited. The Security officer exited with him. The officer nodded at him, gave a wide grin, and turned away. He walked slowly down the corridor, whistling.

James McDonald frowned.

Two hours later, as McDonald was in the process of stocking the medication dispensary on the 14th Floor, the same Security officer walked down the hallway, smiled at McDonald, and wandered away. McDonald paused. His hands clenched into fists. He drew a deep breath and continued with what he was doing.

Soon after lunch, McDonald exited an elevator, pushing his medication cart in front of him. When he arrived at the nursing station, the same Security officer was waiting. The officer said nothing as McDonald stocked the dispensing machine, then followed him down the hallway toward the elevator. As the elevator arrived and McDonald stepped in, the officer tipped his hat and gave McDonald a small smile.

So it went throughout the day. The same officer would appear at random, gravely watch McDonald at his work, smile and go his way. At the end of the day, McDonald entered the men's locker room and stopped. Taped to his locker was a white envelope. McDonald frowned, reached up, took the envelope and opened it. Written on a white sheet of paper in red crayon, it read:

It's been fun, hasn't it? Enjoy it while it lasts. It won't last long.

McDonald crushed the piece of paper into a crumpled white ball and carefully placed it into the garbage pail in the corner of the room. Then he changed into his street clothes and went home for the night.

"I don't know what you mean," Patrick O'Brien said.

James McDonald put his hands on Patrick's desk and leaned forward. "Your men are following me. I want them to stop it."

Patrick stifled a yawn behind one gigantic palm, cleared his throat and looked James McDonald straight in the eye. "I have no idea what you're talking about," Patrick said.

McDonald drew a deep breath. His lips thinned. He said nothing, turned and walked out of Patrick's office.

Patrick grinned. "Well," he said to the air, "what's the matter with him?"

The Security guard showed up at noon the next day, watching him while McDonald went through the food line at the cafeteria, and then at 2:00 PM while he was working on one of the floors, and again, right before he got off work. Each time, the guard would nod, smile with thinly veiled amusement and watch with seeming interest as James McDonald went about his work. He never said a word.

At 5:00 PM, McDonald arrived home. Picking up the mail from the box in the lobby, he patiently waited for the elevator, then pushed the button for his floor. He took a deep breath. It had been a long day and he was pissed off. Patrick O'Brien, he had to admit, was annoying him. He walked down the floor, opened the door to his apartment, placed the mail on the counter and poured himself a drink. He savored the sharp bite of the alcohol then crunched a bit of ice between his teeth. Idly, he sorted through the mail. One envelope contained no return address. He shrugged and opened it and stared at the letter inside. His hand, he vaguely noticed, was trembling. In blue crayon, the letter said:

> **I'm enjoying this. I hope you are, too. I'll be coming for you soon.**

Chapter 24

"You're looking pleased with yourself," Lenore said.

"Hmm?" Kurtz looked up from the book he was reading.

Lenore pursed her lips and gave him a quizzical look. "I said that you're looking like the cat that swallowed the canary. What's going on?"

Kurtz shrugged. "I could tell you but then I'd have to kill you."

"Oh, really?"

"Yup," Kurtz said.

"Don't press your luck, Bozo."

"Wouldn't dream of it," Kurtz said.

"But seriously," Lenore said.

"Can't talk about it. I really can't."

"Are you kidding?" Lenore said.

"You being a potential witness and all."

"Oh, shit."

"Like I said."

Lenore looked at him, frowned and then shrugged. "Want some more wine?"

"Sure," Kurtz said.

"Let me give you a piece of advice," Lenore said, and poured the wine.

"Yes?"

"Don't get in over your head."

"Wouldn't dream of it," Kurtz said. It was, he reflected, excellent wine.

The next day, Audra Fox, the Assistant Head of Labor Relations, gave Patrick O'Brien a call. "You know a guy named James McDonald, in pharmacy?"

"He was in here yesterday accusing me of having him followed," Patrick said. "Aside from that, I can't say that I do."

"Oh," Audra Fox said, "well, I just got a call from Merryl Packer."

Merryl Packer was a worker in the laundry division of the hospital who just happened to be the President of the Union. She was known to be foul mouthed, ambitious and basically insane, but very far from stupid. "So?" Patrick asked.

"She says that you're harassing this James McDonald. She's filed a grievance." Audra sighed. "She called you 'a fucking pig.'"

"I'm sorry to hear that."

"Yeah, us too." The National Health Care Workers' Union, generally referred to as 1199, from its very first district in New York, was founded in 1932 by a group of pharmacists. It had since spread over the entire United States and was the largest representative of health care workers of all sorts in the country. "Merryl is nuts."

"Nothing I can do about that," Patrick said.

"She's asking that Security cease and desist its campaign of harassment. She's also asking for punitive damages."

Patrick shrugged. "Let me know if I have to testify."

"You bet. So, what's the real story with this James McDonald?"

"We are keeping an eye on him, but nobody's harassing the guy." Patrick paused, thinking uncomfortably that both Kurtz and Moran (or at least, Kurtz) might have their own agenda. "Not that I know of, anyway."

"Why are you doing that?"

"I can't tell you," Patrick said. "I mean it. It's confidential."

"Really…"

"Yup."

Audra Fox sighed. "Well, good luck."

"Yeah. You, too."

James McDonald's nerves were on edge. Today, a different Security guard had shadowed him, a middle-aged, fat white guy instead of a middle-aged, stout black guy, but the cold eyes and the silent smiles were identical. The Security guard had appeared without warning, randomly throughout the day, never speaking, never interfering, coldly watching, then vanishing. Prick.

James McDonald breathed a long, slow sigh of relief, feeling his tight muscles unwind as he turned the key on his apartment door and entered. He wanted, no, he *needed*, a drink, a nice big one.

Something good. Johnny Walker Blue, that would do it, he thought. Settle my nerves. Think about the future. He wasn't going to take this lying down. James McDonald had a history, abilities and resources that Patrick O'Brien knew nothing about. He thought about that, and smiled, as he pondered his next move.

Christmas came and went. Kurtz tried to enjoy the holidays but it was tough. He was on edge, waiting for the next ridiculous atrocity. Lenore set up a small tree in the apartment and they decorated it together. The tree reminded Kurtz of his childhood, when his mother was still alive, before his father became the silent, brooding figure that he remained to this day. Kurtz slowly hung each ornament on the tree, remembering.

He sighed. Lenore, who by now understood his moods, let him be.

On Christmas Eve, they went to a party at Bill and Dina Werth's apartment. A loaded buffet was set up along one wall, a bar along another. People came and went all through the afternoon and early evening.

"Anything new with your stalker?" Bill Werth asked him.

Kurtz glumly shook his head. "Nope."

Werth frowned. "That's unusual. This time of year, you would expect it to get worse. Seeing their victims in a good mood tends to piss these guys off."

Kurtz stared down into his Bloody Mary, finished it and poured himself another. "I don't think he cares what we expect."

Bill Werth shook his head and had nothing more to say.

On Christmas, they met Lenore's parents, plus her Aunt Sylvia and Uncle Milton at a Chinese restaurant on Mott Street.

"When I was a kid," Lenore said, "there was an advertisement. It was in all the subway cars, a little old Chinese man is beaming out at the reader and the text says, 'You don't have to be Chinese to love Levy's Jewish Rye Bread.'"

"Huh?" Kurtz said.

"Unlike our European brethren, the Chinese have never persecuted the Jews, and both cultures encourage education and upward mobility. The Chinese kids and the Jewish kids go to the same schools, they're in the same classes and they join the same clubs. We pretty much grow up, together. There's a real affinity between the two communities, though maybe it's more a New York thing than universal. Also, the Chinese are not Christian, so unlike almost every other store and eating establishment, Chinese restaurants are open on Christmas. I'm not sure when it started, but going out to a Chinese place on Christmas is a very old tradition in the Jewish community. In Brooklyn, there are a bunch of Kosher-Chinese places but we stopped keeping Kosher when I was a little kid, so here we are."

Right. Esther Brinkman was still grumpy over a Reform rabbi instead of an Orthodox one but she didn't keep Kosher. Kurtz stared in bemusement as Lenore's plump Jewish mother deftly used a pair of chopsticks to lift a pork filled dumpling to her lips. The dumpling glistened enticingly with flecks of scallion and chili oil. "Well," he said, "count me in."

A couple of tepid letters arrived during the next week, the usual vague baloney threatening nameless destruction for imaginary sins. James McDonald was ignoring the ever-present security and doing his job. If he was also sending threatening letters and making harassing phone calls, they couldn't prove it. His grievance charge against the hospital was wending its way through official channels.

New Year's Eve came and went. Kurtz and Lenore wandered down to Time's Square but the crowd was insane. They trudged back to the apartment, watched the ball drop on TV and popped the cork on a bottle of Champagne.

Kurtz was a lucky man with a lot to look forward to. He stared at Lenore's serenely smiling face and felt truly grateful.

He wondered what their stalker was doing tonight.

Monday. A new month, a new rotation, a new group of resentful staff members who didn't want to be here, and it was his job to orient them to a new environment, all without wasting time, delaying any cases and especially, all without harming any patients.

"Relax," Mahendra Patel said.

"I can't relax." Jerry Hernandez was in a foul mood. These days, he usually was. Nearly twenty per-cent of the department had already flown the coop. Serkin, blithely convinced that his department was overstaffed, was perfectly satisfied with this situation. Hernandez, responsible for finding actual bodies to provide the anesthesia, at least one for each operating room, all day, every day, was at his wit's end. It had reached the point where making out the next day's schedule took a couple of hours of robbing Peter to pay Paul, and involved an ongoing negotiation with the other Directors at St. Agnes and Easton.

"So called 'academic time,'" Serkin had said, "is a dying vestige of an outmoded practice model. We have an outcomes database that follows nearly two-hundred parameters related to every case that we do, and I'm in the process of hiring research coordinators. If a physician gets an idea for a study, there is no reason why ancillary personnel who are paid far less than that physician cannot carry out the legwork. Meanwhile, the anesthesiologists will be paid to give anesthesia."

Right. Except that if you didn't have academic time then you might as well be in private practice, and the real private practitioners were paid a lot more than the pseudo-academic worker bees that they were all rapidly turning into. If you had to work like you were in private practice, then you might as well get paid like you were in private practice, and obviously (to everyone except Stewart Serkin, anyway), the only way to do that was to blow this shithouse and actually go into private practice. So here they were, with a department vanishing by the week.

Patel smiled. Patel had no worries. All he had to do was go where he was told and do the cases that he was assigned. Since being relieved of his position by Serkin, Patel's life had become a lot simpler, and a lot easier. Patel, Hernandez suspected, was getting considerable enjoyment out of watching the department fall apart.

"Take a deep breath," Patel advised. "If you don't have the bodies, then you don't have the bodies. Nobody is going to blame you."

"Hah! They're all going to blame me."

"Well, maybe." Patel smiled. "I've got a case to start. See you later."

"Uh, Dr. Hernandez?" A tall man with brown hair and a short dark beard, wearing surgical scrubs, a blue surgical cap and a surgical mask hanging from his neck, held out a hand. "I'm Ben Abbott."

"Dr. Abbott." They shook hands. "Welcome aboard."

Abbott gave a tentative smile. He was rotating in from St. Agnes. Today was his first day.

"Have you listened to the online tutorial?" Hernandez asked.

"Of course," Abbott said.

"Good." Hernandez, Vinnie Steinberg and Casey Thompson, the Site Director at St. Agnes had each put twenty-minute podcasts online, which described the physical makeup of their respective OR's and the placement of all the anesthesia equipment. The podcasts had been Steinberg's idea, a very good idea, Hernandez thought. It was Steinberg's misfortune to be working for a guy who was deeply suspicious of all good ideas that he did not think of himself. Steinberg, to Hernandez' certain knowledge, was already thinking of taking his talents and abilities elsewhere. Hernandez would have been thinking the same thing, except that in the past three years, he had taken care of the COO, the Chairman of the Board of Trustees and the Dean's wife. Hernandez was perhaps the only member of the Department of Anesthesiology who was at least relatively immune to their Chairman's insanity.

"Any questions?" Hernandez asked.

"Nope," Abbott said. "I've met my resident. I've put a note in on my first patient. I think I'm ok."

"All right. I'll be here all day. Let me know if there's anything you need."

"Thanks." Dr. Abbott nodded. "Will do."

Hernandez walked off down the hall while Abbott rubbed his hands together and smiled.

This, unfortunately, was a little more serious than casual harassment.

Ordinarily, Lew Barent would have come along but a dead body had been discovered in an apartment in mid-town. It didn't look like murder, more like the unfortunate deceased had suffered a heart attack…except that he had been dead for at least three days before the victim's wife had thought to call it in. Lew had taken Arnie Figueroa, which left a pissed off Harry Moran to deal with Staunton's little problem. "So how much damage did he actually do?"

Moran, Kurtz, Jerry Hernandez and Patrick O'Brien were clustered together in Hernandez' office, which opened onto a hallway off the main operating room suite. "Hard to say," Hernandez said. "We're still sorting it out. The anesthesia work room has been demolished. Three ultrasound machines have been smashed. They cost about 25,000 bucks. Four anesthesia machines have been vandalized. I'm not sure how much actual damage has been done to them yet but if they have to be replaced, they're over 50,000 each." Hernandez hesitated. "We've had to delay all the cases except the ones that were already underway. We're not certain how many OR's he might have gotten into or what he might have done that's not obvious yet. Everything will have to be checked out."

"Any drugs missing?" O'Brien asked.

"Oh, yeah."

Moran gave him a disgusted look. "How did that happen? I thought you were required to keep medications locked up."

"Jesus," Hernandez said, and swiped a hand through his hair. "We keep track of the inventory in the PYXIS machines but a lot of stuff, like the volatile anesthetics, aren't in the machines. They're sitting on shelves in the work rooms. They're not controlled substances. We have to be able to re-fill the vaporizers whenever they get low, which sometimes happens in the middle of a case, so all the carts have a few bottles and there's a cart in every room. Nobody is going to notice if a couple of bottles go missing. As for the narcotics, the residents and nurse anesthetists are required to either lock them up in the lock box in each OR or keep them on their persons at all times. The guy asked his resident for the key. It seems he wanted to show him some new technique and he needed to draw up some meds. The resident gave him the key. Why wouldn't he? The guy was supposed to be his supervising physician."

"All the stuff that the resident signed out this morning is gone."

"What was it?"

Hernandez sighed. "Two thousand micrograms of fentanyl, fifty milligrams of morphine, ten milligrams of midazolam and a thousand milligrams of ketamine."

Moran looked at him and shook his head. "Benjamin Abbott, MD," he said.

"Supposedly."

187

"And where is the real Dr. Benjamin Abbott? I'm assuming that there is a real Dr. Benjamin Abbott?"

"Yeah," Hernandez said. "There is. We don't know. He's divorced. He lives alone. He's not answering his cell phone."

"And nobody here recognized that this guy was a phony because he was rotating in from another hospital and you had never seen him before."

"That's correct."

"But he had a valid looking ID card and he seemed like he knew his way around an OR."

"Yeah," Hernandez said.

"I've sent some uniforms over to his house. They should check in shortly."

"Stick around," Moran told Hernandez. "I may need you to translate."

A minute later, the resident, a bewildered looking kid named Kevin Kucera was sitting across the desk from Moran. Hernandez sat in a chair by Kucera's side. Moran had given Kurtz and Patrick O'Brien sour looks but reluctantly allowed both of them to stay. They were standing against the wall next to the desk.

"What happened?" Moran asked.

Kucera shrugged. "He introduced himself as Dr. Abbott. We discussed the first case. He seemed to know what he was doing."

Moran briefly glanced at Hernandez. "In what way did he seem to know what he was doing?"

"He knew the drugs that we use. He knew the dosages. He asked me if I wanted to intubate with a Mac blade, a Miller blade or a Glidescope."

Moran glanced again at Hernandez. "All reasonable options," Hernandez said.

"He asked you for the key to the narcotics box," Moran said.

"Yeah."

"Why?"

"He said he wanted to show me a ketamine induction. I've never done that."

"It's not the most usual induction but it's not uncommon, either," Hernandez said.

"Why not?" Moran asked.

"Ketamine lasts longer than propofol, the stuff we usually use, and it's psychotropic. It can cause hallucinations."

"Why use it at all, then?"

"It has some advantages. It causes catecholamine release. It supports blood pressure and cardiac output. It has prolonged effects on pain modulation. If you use ketamine as part of the induction, they generally need less pain medication after the case."

Moran frowned. "Is this stuff that a pharmacy technician would be likely to know?"

"Maybe, if he worked in the OR, and if he paid attention."

"So, you gave him the key," Moran said to Kucera.

"Yeah. Why wouldn't I? He was supposed to be my attending."

"And then what?"

"I went to the pre-op area and started the IV line on the patient and then I came back to the OR to see if the nurses were ready for us to bring the patient back."

"Did you notice anything unusual in the OR?"

"Unusual how?"

"Anything broken, misplaced, stolen...?"

Kucera shook his head. "Not that I noticed."

"And where was Dr. Abbott?"

"I don't know. I never saw him again."

Moran frowned at Hernandez, who was sitting with his hands folded, looking morose.

"And when did you notice that the narcotics were missing?"

"People started yelling out in the hallway. Stuff was smashed up. Dr. Hernandez came in a few minutes later with a master key and checked the narc box."

"I checked all the narc boxes in all the OR's," Hernandez said. "This was the only room where anything was missing."

"Take a look at this," Moran said. "Tell me if you recognize this guy." He handed Kucera a copy of the photograph from James McDonald's ID card.

Kucera looked at it closely, frowning. "It could be him. Dr. Abbott had a beard. This guy doesn't."

Hernandez nodded. He had said the same thing when shown the same picture.

Moran looked at Kurtz and Patrick O'Brien. "You guys got anything to add?"

"Nope," Kurtz said. Patrick shook his head.

"Okay," Moran said to Kucera. "Thanks." Kucera rose to his feet and walked out, looking relieved.

Moran's cell phone went off. He glanced at Kurtz and Patrick O'Brien. "Let's hope," he said. He picked up the phone. "Moran," he said. He listened, then nodded. "I understand. Get him to the hospital and get his statement."

Moran sighed, then looked at Hernandez, Patrick and Kurtz. "Dr. Abbott was found, barely conscious, on his living room couch. As he left the house this morning, somebody knocked him over the head, dragged him back inside and tied him up."

"So now what?" Kurtz asked.

Patrick O'Brien had already established that James McDonald had not shown up for work that day. "Now, I think we have enough for a search warrant," Moran said. "Play time's over."

"Amen to that," Kurtz said.

Chapter 25

The victim had indeed died of a heart attack, not unusual in an eighty-year old with a history of coronary artery disease. The victim's wife hadn't called it in because she was suffering from advanced Alzheimer's disease and hadn't realized her husband of fifty-seven years was dead.

Barent took the wife's addled statement, sent the deceased to the morgue and made his way back to the station.

Two hours later, Barent and Harry Moran, armed with a newly issued warrant and accompanied by Kurtz, Patrick O'Brien and three uniformed police officers, knocked on the door of James McDonald's apartment. There was no answer. Moran waited a moment, and then knocked again. Still nothing. He turned to the Superintendent, a small, middle-aged Hispanic man in blue coveralls. "Open it up," he said.

The Superintendent selected a key from a key ring and slid it into the lock. The door silently opened. Barent, Moran and the three officers pulled their guns and entered. Patrick O'Brien and Richard Kurtz waited in the hall outside. Moran had grudgingly allowed them to come along, on condition that they stay out of the way. Both had agreed.

A male figure sat on the couch, only the head visible from behind. Silently, Moran extended his arm. "This is the police," Moran said. "There is a gun pointed at your head. Don't make any sudden moves and put your hands up where we can see them."

The man did not respond. His head remained still. Slowly, carefully, one of the uniforms moved around the couch. A surprised look crossed his face. He grinned. "You might as well put the gun down. This guy isn't dangerous." Moran looked at him, shrugged and holstered his weapon. He moved around the couch. Facing him sat a crudely fashioned scarecrow with a bloody mask covering its face, a knife in its chest and a bottle of Scotch cradled in the crook of its left arm. The scarecrow's extended right hand held a folded piece of paper. Moran reached out, took the paper and unfolded it. In light green crayon, it read:

Wondering what I'll do next? Keep on wondering. You'll never see me coming.

The apartment was bland, Kurtz thought, the furniture functional, modern and a monotone gray. Three bottles of expensive Scotch and two bottles of brandy sat on a sideboard next to a wooden dining room table. There were no pictures on the shelves, no artwork on the walls.

One of the two bedrooms was set up as an office, with a gray filing cabinet and a gray metal desk with a ThinkPad on top of it. "Don't touch anything," Barent said. He and Moran pulled on rubber gloves, then opened drawers. In the first drawer of the desk, Barent found a large box of crayons, most of them barely used, a box of envelopes and a sheaf of blank, white paper, plus two sheets of paper with writing on them. One read:

We reap what we sow. They that sow the wind shall reap the whirlwind

The other said simply:

Soon.

In the second drawer of the filing cabinet, Moran found two University Hospital ID cards, one with the name Richard Lester, MD, the second with the name Benjamin Abbott, MD. Both cards had a picture of James McDonald in the upper left corner. Beneath the cards lay a box of stamps and a photograph of a young man, smiling, with his arm around Lydia Cho, who was looking straight into the camera with a serious expression on her face. The man bore a marked resemblance to James McDonald. Lydia Cho, Kurtz noted, did not look happy.

In addition to the desk and the filing cabinet, a tall, black safe stood in the corner of the room. It had a keypad with a digital lock. Moran, Patrick O'Brien and Kurtz glumly stared at it. No way to figure out the combination. It looked like a gun safe.

"If we open it up and it's empty," Kurtz said, "he may have taken a gun with him, and if it's not empty, he still may have taken a gun with him."

Moran briefly raised his eyes to the heavens and gave an almost inaudible sigh. "This is true," he said.

"Or more than one," Patrick O'Brien said.

"The techs will go through the place and let us know what they've found. Hopefully, they can break the encryption on the computer." Moran cracked a slight smile. "Maybe we'll learn something."

The NYPD's computer tech was a tall, thin guy with sharp gray eyes named Rich Styles. It took him about ten minutes to get into James McDonald's computer. "No encryption at all," Styles said. He sounded offended, as if any self-respecting criminal should have had more security on his computer. "Once I got through the password, it was wide open. Piece of cake." Styles raised his brows, blew a bubble on the wad of gum that he kept in his right cheek, and gestured at the computer. "It's all yours," he said.

In the end, the computer contained a remarkable trove of downloaded pornography, plus various environmental screeds and declarations. Nothing overtly criminal, though, and no hint as to where James McDonald might have gone, where he might be hiding or what he might be planning next.

"Now," Harry Moran said. "We wait."

An all-points bulletin was issued. Word was put out on the street that a small reward for usable information would be forthcoming. A license to possess a handgun had never been issued to James McDonald but a rifle did not require registration. The gun safe proved to be empty, which might mean nothing but at least gave them cause to worry. The suspect was assumed to be armed and dangerous.

Three hours later, a uniform came into Lew Barent's office and said, "Call for you. Line 3."

Barent gave the phone a suspicious look, then picked it up and flicked it to speaker. "Barent," he said.

"Barent? This is Lieutenant Darren Gibson, 24th Precinct. I thought you would like to know that a couple of concerned local citizens have informed us that somebody meeting the description of your suspect has pitched a tent in the vicinity of the Blockhouse."

Barent raised an eyebrow and gave the phone a benign smile. "We in law enforcement always appreciate the concern of local citizens, but aside from a general sense of civic obligation, might anything else have been motivating these concerned citizens?"

"They were reluctant to say. I gather that some members of their organization approached the gentleman in question and were not satisfied with the results of their enquiry."

Barent nodded his head. "Well, we shall definitely look into it. Please give your local citizens our thanks."

Gibson chuckled. "I'll do that."

Barent clicked off the phone, sat back and pondered. The Blockhouse was built as one of a series of fortifications intended to protect New York from the British during the War of 1812. A picturesque but largely abandoned ruin, it sits today in the Northwest corner of Central Park, on a high, rarely traversed wooded ridge. In 1905, a bronze plaque commemorating its history was placed above the door. Within a few years, the plaque vanished, presumably stolen. In 1999, the plaque was replaced and within a few more years, this second plaque, too, went missing. People wandering through the Northwest section of Central Park were advised to travel in groups and never go there at night. It was an excellent hiding place, however, for somebody with outdoor skills who did not wish to be found. Barent thought about this for a moment, then shrugged and picked up the phone to call Harry Moran, Richard Kurtz and Patrick O'Brien.

Chapter 26

The night was clear and cloudless, with no moon. Even though they stood in the middle of perhaps the busiest city on Earth, the Northwest corner of Central Park was still dark. A soft hum of traffic could be heard, which was not a bad thing. Hopefully, it would mask their approach. The tent was pitched against one lichen covered stone wall of the Blockhouse, providing shelter from the wind as well as limiting access to anyone who might choose to sneak up on its occupant. It also, of course, limited McDonald's escape options. He had a small campfire with a grill perched above the flames, on which he was cooking what appeared to be a couple of hotdogs.

Kurtz, Barent, Moran and Patrick O'Brien stood on the top of a small hill and watched through night vision goggles as the SWAT team, clad in black body armor and armed with assault rifles, crept through the woods surrounding a small clearing in front of the building. McDonald wore a parka, boots and dark jeans. He squatted back on his heels, seemingly oblivious to his surroundings, as he cooked his meal.

The team seemed to flit from tree to tree, silently, as they closed in. Kurtz counted eight of them, but he knew that more were spaced strategically around the entire building and even more were stationed further away in case the suspect attempted to run and somehow managed to break through the first line. Barent pursed his lips. Moran silently nodded. He liked the way the team was working. McDonald was surrounded with his back to a wall. He was trapped, though he didn't yet know it.

One of the team members raised his hand. The others halted. Cautiously, silently, the first man inched forward. He seemed to hesitate, gingerly used his toe to push aside a small pile of leaves, which proved to be nothing more than what it appeared. He nodded to the others, all of whom resumed their stealthy slide forward.

An immense clatter of tin cans knocking together came from an oak tree. McDonald raised his head and without hesitation, rolled to the side, came up with a long rifle and began firing.

Policemen do not like to be fired upon. When fired upon, they fire back.

"Christ," Barent muttered. He, Moran, Kurtz and O'Brien calmly stepped behind a series of trees. When bullets fly, they are apt to fly anywhere, and direct sight of the action meant direct flight of a bullet. They waited for perhaps fifteen seconds, until all the bullets had stopped, then they stepped out. James McDonald lay on his back, dead or unconscious. One officer shook his head, frowned and gingerly prodded the body with his toe. Two others stood aside, their weapons held steady. One was speaking on his radio, no doubt calling for an ambulance.

"Tripwires," Moran said. "That was pretty smart, actually." He shook his head and gave a small, tight smile. "But then, firing on the police is pretty stupid." He shrugged and they all walked down the hill.

McDonald had a bullet in his abdomen and two in each leg. Two others had grazed his head. Remarkably, he was alive. He was taken to Bellevue and rushed into surgery.

Kurtz, with nothing else left to do, went home, where Lenore was waiting for him. "Well," he said, "I guess that's that."

Christina Pirelli walked out of the hospital at 4:30 PM after her usual busy day. Christina was feeling pretty good. First Harry Moran and then Richard Kurtz had called to update her on the situation. The schmuck was still unconscious in intensive care but had a good chance of recovering. From a purely humanistic standpoint, that was nice, but on a deeper, more personal level, she couldn't have cared less. Christina Pirelli resented people who sent threatening letters, made nasty phone calls and made actual assaults on people and property. Fuck the son-of-a-bitch. But he would probably recover, so her relief at finally being free from persecution was also free from any residual regret that she might have felt (well, probably wouldn't have felt...) over the poor sad end of poor James McDonald's idiotic criminal career.

The parking garage was five stories high. Since Christina usually arrived before 7:30 AM she rarely had trouble finding a spot on the first floor but today, she had slept in and arrived after eight. She took the elevator to the fourth floor and walked down the aisle toward her almost new Lexus. As usual, the place was pretty much deserted. She barely noticed a man, tall, with brown hair, fumbling at the lock of his car a couple of aisles over. She pulled out her key, pressed the button and heard the lock snick but before she could open the door she realized that the man was standing in front of her. She looked at him and felt the blood drain from her face. "You," she said.

He smiled. "Hi, Chris," he said. His smile grew wider as he raised something that might have been a gun and pointed it at her chest. She barely heard the soft pop that it made as he pulled the trigger. She felt a stinging pain in her chest, felt her legs growing suddenly weak and then everything swirled around her and went black.

"Why?" James McDonald asked. "What did I ever do to you?"

Moran looked at Kurtz and frowned. This was not going as any of them had expected. McDonald's vital signs had stabilized over the night. He was off vasopressors. There seemed no reason not to wake him up and get the breathing tube out, which the ICU staff had done after rounds in the morning. Lew Barent was back at the station house. Moran, Kurtz and Patrick O'Brien had arrived in the ICU for what they all assumed would be a routine interview involving some perfunctory protestations of innocence, followed, once the evidence was laid out, by a grudging confession, followed by fervent protestations of remorse and regret. Moran had read him his rights. McDonald had shrugged and stated that he didn't need a lawyer since he had done nothing wrong.

As the interview went on, Kurtz' worry increased. Seemingly honest bewilderment was not supposed to be a part of the scenario. Of course, maybe the guy was just a good actor. So many sociopaths were, after all, but somehow, Kurtz didn't think so. McDonald wasn't acting calm and contrite. He wasn't pretending that it was all just a sad, silly misunderstanding. No. He was pissed off, and if this was an act, it was not an act likely to endear himself to the forces of justice.

"So, let me get this straight," Moran said. "You've never seen either of these cards before?" He held both ID cards under McDonald's nose, one for Dr. Richard Lester, the other for Dr.

Benjamin Abbott, both displaying James McDonald's smiling face in the upper left corner.

McDonald gave Moran an angry look. "No. Somebody is framing me."

Moran raised a brow at Kurtz and Patrick O'Brien, both of whom gave silent shrugs. "And this?" Moran said. He showed McDonald the paper saying:

> **Wondering what I'll do next? Keep on wondering. You'll never see me coming.**

"Never saw this either?"

"No," McDonald said.

"You didn't show up to work yesterday. Where were you?"

"Hiding out. What did you think I was doing?"

This was not an answer that Moran had expected. He frowned. "And why were you hiding out?"

"Because you assholes are setting me up to take a fall. The letters, the security guy following me around, and then somebody breaks into my apartment. I don't know who and I don't know why, but I recognize a set-up when I see it."

Moran puffed up his cheeks and gave McDonald a moody look. "When did somebody break into your apartment?"

"The other night. He left a note on the kitchen counter. It was just like all the rest, some crap about the past not being forgotten."

"Anything damaged?"

"No." McDonald shook his head. "Just the note."

Moran sighed. He shook his head. He looked honestly regretful. Kurtz suppressed a smile. Moran was good at his job. He knew how to convey a message, which in this case was sad amazement at McDonald's stubborn insistence mixed with an unvoiced contempt at his supposed stupidity in denying the obvious, but all them except maybe McDonald knew that it was just an act. Moran was as bewildered as the rest of them.

"Christina Pirelli has identified you as the man who followed her in the park and attempted to assault her. Drs. Kevin Kucera and Jerry Hernandez have both identified you as the supposed 'anesthesiologist' who vandalized the OR at Staunton yesterday afternoon." Not true, of course. All three physicians had looked at the photo of James McDonald and said it might be the guy. None of them were prepared to make a positive identification.

McDonald's face grew red. He suddenly lunged forward, which didn't get him very far since both wrists were handcuffed to the railings. "You fucking asshole! You won't get away with this!"

"You know, James," Moran said with a sigh. "You're not helping your cause, here. We've got you six ways from Sunday. If you admit it, we can work with you. If you don't, it's gonna be jail time."

McDonald shook his head. "Fuck you," he said. "I've had it. Get me my lawyer and get lost."

Moran shrugged and walked away. Kurtz and Patrick O'Brien followed. Neither said a word until they were seated in Patrick's office. Kurtz poured a cup of coffee, looked at Patrick and Moran. Patrick shook his head. "Not for me, thanks," Moran said. He leaned back in his chair. "Not exactly what I expected."

Kurtz rubbed at his eyes. He could feel a headache coming on. "So, let's assume for just a moment that he's not putting us on. He says he's being framed. He says somebody broke into his apartment and left a note on the counter. Okay, maybe he is being framed. Where does that leave us?"

"Exactly where we were before," Patrick O'Brien said. "Being played for a bunch of fools."

"Oh," Moran snapped his fingers. "Right. I should have remembered that."

"'The past is not forgotten,'" Kurtz said. "'The past is not forgotten. It isn't even past.'"

"Huh?" Moran said.

"What he said, 'The past is not forgotten.' It's a quote from William Faulkner."

Dimly, Kurtz felt an idea trying to percolate through his brain. There was something about this situation that seemed to hover, just out of his reach. He grimaced and rubbed at his temples.

Just then, the phone on Patrick O'Brien's desk rang. He gave it a sour look and picked it up. He listened, said nothing for a long moment, then cleared his throat and said, "Thanks for letting me know." Carefully, he placed the phone back down in its cradle and turned to the other two men. "Christina Pirelli seems to be missing," he said. "She was scheduled to be in surgery this morning and she hasn't shown up. She's not answering her pager and she's not answering her cell phone. She's vanished."

Chapter 27

They found Christina Pirelli's Lexus still sitting in the parking garage, its engine cool. One of the officers who had accompanied Moran, Kurtz and Patrick O'Brien noticed something glittering on the ground. He hesitated, put on rubber gloves and picked it up. He pursed his lips and gave Moran a worried look. "It's a dart," he said, "from a tranquilizer gun."

The parking garage contained surveillance cameras, the lenses of which had been sprayed with black paint. A review of the recorded tape showed all the cameras going dark, one by one, starting at 3:17 PM on the previous day.

John Crane's thinning hair was disheveled, his face grim. He sat at the kitchen table of Christina Pirelli's apartment, along with Barent, Moran, Kurtz and Patrick O'Brien. Christina's apartment was larger than Crane's. Christina had given him a key and they had talked about him moving in but he had not yet done so. Officially, Crane was a suspect, but he had no obvious motive and he had answered all of Barent and Moran's questions without hesitation. He had last seen Christina when she left for work the day before. Neither threatening letters nor any suspicious phone calls had been received in the past few days, and all prior letters had been turned over to the police. Crane had called Christina's daughter to let her know that Christina was missing. She was coming home from college and would arrive by evening.

"This is unbelievable," Crane said.

Moran frowned at him. Moran had been a cop for a long time and he liked to think that he knew what he was doing. He did not enjoy trying and failing to figure out a psychopath. Kurtz sympathized. "You know, we've been thinking of this guy as an idiot," Kurtz said. "Crazy, but basically an idiot."

"That's because he's been doing idiotic things," Barent said.

"But he's not doing them in an idiotic way. He's doing them in a really smart way."

Moran shook his head. Patrick O'Brien grunted.

John Crane winced and hung his head. "This is really unbelievable," he said again.

"And it's obvious, really," Kurtz said. His voice sounded far away. He barely even realized that he had been speaking.

"What?" Moran said. "What's obvious?"

Kurtz shook his head, "Playing us for fools," he whispered. "Of course." He shook his head again and seemed to see them all for the first time. "The past is not forgotten and the guy who's doing this is not an idiot. He's been enjoying this. He's smart. He likes being in charge. He knows his way around a hospital; he knows his way around a medical school, and he knows his way around an OR."

Kurtz grinned. "I have another idea."

"You've had a lot of ideas," Patrick said doubtfully. "So far, they've gotten us nowhere."

Kurtz looked at him and grinned even wider. "Trust me," he said. "What have you got to lose?"

Moran frowned. "God knows, I don't have any ideas." He shrugged. "So, tell us, what's the big idea this time?"

Kurtz said to Crane, "Do you have Elizabeth Reisman's number?"

"Christina's sister? Sure. She has an emergency contact list taped to the refrigerator."

"Could you get it?"

Crane rose to his feet, walked into the kitchen and came back a few seconds later with a sheet of paper, which he handed to Kurtz.

"Excellent," Kurtz said. He opened his cell phone and dialed, listened for a moment and then said, "Elizabeth? Yes, this is Richard Kurtz. Remember me? We met when you were in New York. I have a question for you: what is the name of Christina's ex-husband, the neurosurgeon?"

"You see, Chris, you were supposed to be my wife."

Christina Pirelli did not answer, as her brain was still fogged by the ketamine she had been injected with earlier. He was speaking as much to himself as to his captive, who was tied up in an easy chair, her head lolling backward, staring at the lights flickering across the ceiling in her drug fevered brain.

"A wife is supposed to stand by her man. She's supposed to consider his needs as equal to her own, make a few compromises when it's necessary for the sake of the partnership. Go where he goes, cleave to him and no other. Love, honor and obey."

Christina Pirelli groaned. Her head lolled back and she shuddered as the hallucinations and the words mingled together into an incomprehensible total. He looked at her as his breath came fast and his lips thinned back in a snarl. "God damn it," he said. "I needed you." And he wiped a tear from the corner of his eye with a trembling hand.

His name was Alan Lane, an upper middle-class kid from Scarsdale, New York, who had been the apple of his parents' eye and the pride and joy of Scarsdale High: Captain of the track team, solid A average, President of the debating society, respected member of the film club, the chess club and the woodwind ensemble, followed by four years at Princeton before medical school at Duke and then residency at Chapel Hill, where he met a young OB resident named Christina Pirelli. His parents had initially disapproved of the relationship since Christina was a divorcee, a mother and a Catholic, but Alan Lane had been entranced by Christina's lush figure, ready laugh, no bullshit outlook on life and boundless energy in bed. Besides, she was a doctor. The way he figured it, a neurosurgeon and an obstetrician together should be able to satisfy all of their reasonable, and most of their unreasonable desires.

And what had happened to all that, anyway? After all these years, he still couldn't figure it out. He hadn't kicked her. He hadn't hit her. He hadn't abused her in any way. He was 'too controlling' she had said. He gave her no space. No *space*. What the hell did that even mean, anyway? He asked her what she wanted to do on the rare weekends that they both had off. He asked her what she wanted for dinner. They discussed the apartment they would move into and the furniture they would buy for it and where they would go on vacation. They even discussed how many kids they wanted to have. It was a mystery.

He clenched his hand into a fist, except that the fist didn't work as well as it used to and the hand trembled and that, more than any of the rest of it, had been the last straw. The very last straw.

"Wake up, you bitch," he whispered.

She moaned and she moved her head back and forth and blinked her eyes. He frowned and sat down and picked up a glass of Scotch with trembling hands and sipped it as he prepared to wait.

Three hours later, Christina was dimly aware of her surroundings, though if she let her attention wander, the lights and the sounds that assaulted her brain could easily be overwhelming, but they were not as overwhelming as they had been. Vaguely, through the fog and the confusion, she realized that it would not be a good idea to let Alan Lane know that the effects of the drug were beginning to wear off.

He had gotten up to make a sandwich, which he had eaten at the counter, all the while staring out at a dock and a small boat floating in the water at the end of a sloping, grassy yard. Dimly, through the fog in her brain, she noticed that his hair was just as blond, his eyes just as blue as they had been when she had first met him, all those years ago, the golden boy of the Department of Neurosurgery.

When he was done, he stacked the dishes on the counter, then sank back down on a couch across from the easy chair where Christina lay sprawled. They appeared to be in a den, with large windows facing the back, a large flat screen TV on one wall, a series of book cases on the adjacent wall and two doors into the room, both of which were closed. A cigar smoldered in an ashtray. Sitting next to the ashtray was what appeared to be a large aluminum can.

"Tell me, Chris, have you ever heard of spinocerebellar ataxia, type 3?"

Christina moaned.

"I'll take that as a 'No.'" He sipped his Scotch, then held the glass up to the light and frowned. He had gone through almost the whole bottle during the past few hours and his voice was just slightly slurred.

Surreptitiously, Christina wiggled her toes. She was relieved to find that they responded but not too happy to discover that her legs were tied together. She was leaning backwards in the chair, with her hands in her lap and her feet sitting on the floor.

"It's sometimes known as Machado-Joseph disease. It's the most common type of spinocerebellar ataxia, a defect on chromosome fourteen." He shrugged and took another sip of his Scotch. "It's usually an inherited condition but it must have been a mutation in me because nobody else in my family has it. It was quite a shock, as you can imagine." He grinned at her, though on second thought, maybe he wasn't grinning at all. The room still swirled with intersecting lights, and weird geometric patterns covered the walls and ceiling. "I've become a little clumsy in the past year or so." He held the Scotch up again to the light. The glass shook as his hand trembled. "More than a little, actually. I can't operate anymore. Soon, I won't be able to drive a car and soon after that, I'll be confined to a wheelchair and then…" He shrugged. "That's if I let it get that far." He looked at her and slowly grinned. "Which I have no intention of doing."

Somewhere deep inside, Christina considered whether or not to feel sorry for the sorry son-of-a-bitch, but at the moment, she just didn't have it in her.

"So, I suppose you're wondering why you're here?" He raised an eyebrow in her direction. "Well, you needn't wonder because I'm going to tell you."

He sipped his Scotch and poured the glass full again and shook the empty bottle over the glass. "I always enjoyed the finer things in life, Chris. Most doctors do. We work hard, we've got money and status and respect, and neurosurgeons have more than most. Nothing wrong with that. We deserve it." He gave a rueful smile. "I've got a disability policy but it's not enough to cover my expenses and I don't have a lot of money left.

"I never thought I would see you again, after the divorce, but my career took me to New York, and then, lo and behold, you showed up, too. A chairman. You're a fucking *chairman*. You got a new chairman of neurosurgery, less than a year ago, and you were on the Search Committee. I can't do clinical work anymore but administrative work?" He shrugged. "That I could do, so I applied for the job." He took a long sip of his Scotch, shook his head and grimaced. "Needless to say, I didn't get it. I didn't even get an interview. So, okay, you got a lot of applications, some good people applied. I understand that. It was a long shot. Life isn't fair and nobody promised me a rose garden but I've done some good research and I've got a good CV and you disrespected me, Chris. Again. I'm a little tired of your attitude, Chris. I'm a little tired of you taking things away from me.

"But frankly, I would have done it, anyway, because in the end, having you here, on top of the world, when my world is spiraling down and turning into nothing…well, that's just a little more than I'm willing to put up with. Life's a bitch and then you die, and that might as well apply to you as to me. You know what I'm saying?"

The front door to the room splintered.

Alan Lane grinned and calmly knocked the aluminum can over onto its side. A clear liquid poured out and cascaded, seemingly in slow motion, onto the floor. He picked up the lit cigar and smiled at it. Then he dropped it.

Christina didn't even think. She kicked out at the floor with her bound feet. The chair tipped over backward and she fell behind it.

"Freeze!"

She couldn't see who said it but it didn't matter. Within an instant, there sounded a concussive roar followed by a white blinding light and then the room was engulfed in flames. She coughed and tried to crawl but her hands and feet were still tied so she tried to roll instead and then hands grabbed her and lifted her up and carried her away.

Westchester was out of Barent and Moran's jurisdiction. The show was being run by a Westchester police lieutenant named Steve Girardi. He was thin and stooped, with thick black hair and cold brown eyes. He didn't say much but he didn't have to. His men knew what they were doing. Barent, Moran, Kurtz and Patrick O'Brien stayed out of the way. They had focused a parabolic microphone on Alan Lane's house by the lake and had heard his entire monologue. When they heard enough, they broke in. Nobody had expected the can of ether but Christina Pirelli was alive and except for a few minor burns, unhurt. Alan Lane was dead, the house a total wreck.

"He wasn't really trying to cover his tracks," Moran said.

They were sitting in Christina's apartment, two days later. Christina and John Crane sat close together on a couch. Christina's daughter, a slightly Goth version of her mother, sat on a chair and listened intently. Moran, Kurtz and Patrick O'Brien sat on kitchen chairs that they had moved into the living room. Barent stood by the fire place.

"He left notes on his computer, almost as if he was expecting them to be read." Moran shrugged. "Maybe he was. Well, first of all, he had two kids with the second wife and dumped her after she gained weight. It appears that she no longer 'inspired him.' Alimony and child support took a big chunk out of his income. He did most of his cases at Metropolitan but he was also on staff at Easton. A lot of the Easton physicians also have privileges at Staunton. It was easy enough for him to swipe an ID card and make copies of it. He got himself a brown wig and contact lenses and he wore them whenever he went on one of his escapades.

"The locker numbers and combinations at Easton are listed in a hand-written notebook that's kept by one of the OR nurses. The notebook is in her desk, which isn't locked, in her office, which is only locked at night. One of James McDonald's jobs at Easton is to stock the PYXIS machines in the OR. The pharmacy techs share a locker, so the tech on duty can change into scrubs. Lane got McDonald's locker number, then he got into the locker and made impressions of the keys to McDonald's apartment. He broke into the apartment while McDonald was at work. He did set the poor schmuck up, just like McDonald claimed."

Christina frowned. "How did he know it when you started to focus on McDonald?"

"McDonald didn't keep quiet about what was going on; quite the opposite. He was complaining to everybody he knew. Lane paid attention to McDonald. He knew when we took the bait." Moran glanced at Kurtz, who winced. "He also hired a guy who looked like McDonald to chase you around the park, and of course, with the brown hair, the height and the build, they both looked at least a little bit like him. They were intended to." Moran shrugged again. "A part time waiter and unemployed actor. He seems to think the whole thing was a lark. If you want us to, we'll press charges, but at best, it's petty harassment."

"Forget it," Christina said. "Not worth it."

"The autopsy is interesting. He shot you up with ketamine but he saved the fentanyl and the morphine for himself. He knew how much to take so he'd stay functional but not feel any pain. I don't know if he was expecting us to find him or not, but he was clearly planning on the two of you going up in flames together."

Christina nodded. She drew a long, shaky breath. "I've listened to the recording that you made before you broke into the house. He talks about compromise but he doesn't mention that I was always the one who had to do the compromising. He would ask me where I wanted to eat dinner but only after he had already decided that we were going to go out. Everything we did was like that. He decided that I would work part time after we had our first kid and that I would quit, for a 'few years' at least after the second." She sighed. "He had it all planned.

"And that baloney about him applying to be the Chairman of Neurosurgery? I never knew. He had twenty or so papers, a couple of minor grants and no leadership to speak of. The search firm knocked him out on the first round. We never even saw his application. Jackass." She hung her head. A slow tear dripped down her cheek. John Crane took her hand and gave it a squeeze.

Barent glanced at Kurtz and shrugged.

"We'll be going then," Moran said. "Give us a call if you need anything."

Christina nodded silently. John Crane rose to his feet. "I'll show you to the door."

"You did good," Moran said to Kurtz, once the door had closed behind them in the elevator.

Kurtz shook his head. "We were two steps behind him the whole time. We got lucky."

Moran smiled. "She's alive and he's not. It's over, and that's what counts."

"I suppose so. Anyway, the Dean will be pleased. Things can get back to normal."

"Yup. Have a good night," Moran said, "and cheer up."

"You bet." Kurtz grinned weakly. "Back to work in the morning. A couple of nice routine gallbladders will do me a world of good."

"Nothing like a nice, routine gallbladder," Barent said. He smiled. He had heard Kurtz express this conviction before.

"You said it."

Epilogue

Three months later, Henry Tolliver took over as Chairman of the Department of Cardiac Surgery. He proved to be an able administrator, a good clinician and an excellent steward of the Department's scholarly activities. The Department prospered and the Dean was pleased.

After considerable arm twisting, Peter Reinhardt agreed to stay on as Chairman until Henry Tolliver's arrival, then was granted the sabbatical he had requested and, somewhat to the Dean's surprise, actually wrote his textbook. It was published, received excellent reviews and sold a reasonable number of copies.

A delegation of junior anesthesiologists went to the administration of the Medical School and announced that they would all be leaving unless things swiftly changed in the operating rooms. After considering this announcement, the Dean informed Stewart Serkin that his resignation would be accepted, as of thirty days from that date. Mahendra Patel was appointed Acting Chairman. A Search Committee was formed to find a permanent replacement, on which Henry Tolliver, Christina Pirelli and Richard Kurtz were all asked to serve.

—The End—

Information About the Author

I hope you enjoyed *The Chairmen.*

I graduated from Columbia College with a degree in English before attending Northwestern University Medical School and went on to a career as an academic physician. I was a member of my institution's Appointment, Promotion and Tenure Committee for approximately ten years and I've served on three Search Committees, one for Chief of Surgery, two for Chairman of the Department of Anesthesiology. I began writing many years ago and am now the author of the four books in the Kurtz and Barent mystery series, *Surgical Risk, The Anatomy Lesson, Seizure* and *The Chairmen.* I am also the author of the science fiction novels: *Edward Maret: A Novel of the Future, The Cannibal's Feast* and The Chronicles of the Second Interstellar Empire of Mankind, which to date includes *The Game Players of Meridien, The City of Ashes, The Empire of Dust, The Empire of Ruin* and the soon to be released, *The Well of Time.*

For more information, please visit my website, http://www.robertikatz.com or Facebook page, https://www.facebook.com/Robertikatzofficial/. For continuing updates regarding new releases, author appearances and general information about my books and stories, sign up for my newsletter/email list at http://www.robertikatz.com/join and you will also receive two **free short stories.** The first is a science fiction story, entitled "Adam," about a scientist who uses a tailored retrovirus to implant the Fox P2 gene (sometimes called the language gene) into a cage full of rats and a mouse named Adam, and the unexpected consequences that result. The second is a prequel to the Kurtz and Barent mysteries, entitled "Something in the Blood," featuring Richard Kurtz as a young surgical resident on an elective rotation in the Arkansas mountains, solving a medical mystery that spans two tragic generations.

Preview: Brighton Beach

Chapter 1

During the course of a long and successful career as an undercover cop, Arnaldo Figueroa had developed a talent for passing unnoticed. He was average height, with an average face, thin but not unusually so. He looked nothing like an athlete, though he was, in fact, endowed with superior eye-hand coordination and excellent reflexes and had wrestled in high school and then in college.

He had trailed the three men through the neighborhood at night. The three walked as if they owned the place, looking neither to the left nor the right. Though they were not on their own turf, they seemed afraid of nothing. The three passed four small groups of pedestrians, all of whom stepped to the side and hurried by without looking at their faces.

Wise, Arnaldo Figueroa thought. These were not men whose attention you wanted to attract. Not at all.

The three were big, white and probably Russian. Figueroa regarded the three men as an anomaly. They had no business here…unless, of course, they did have business here, which would be bad news for the denizens of New York City.

Figueroa, whose business it was to keep track of other peoples' business, was curious. He wasn't crazy, though. He followed the three at a discreet distance, flitting from the cover of a tree to a parked van to a screen of bushes, from corner to corner, staying far back. Unnoticed. Hopefully.

The three men stopped in front of a brownstone that was undergoing renovation. Scaffolding covered the sides and a sign reading, "Construction Zone: Keep Out" was displayed in front. The door was boarded up, the building dark and seemingly empty.

One of the three knocked on the door. The door opened. A short, thin man looked at them, puffed up his cheeks and gave an abrupt nod. The three men walked inside. None of them had said a word.

Expected, then. Arnaldo Figueroa shook his head and sighed. This was bad. Nobody scheduled legitimate meetings in an abandoned building.

Turning on his heel, he scurried away. The blare of a car horn a block or so over saved his life. He jerked his head up at the sudden sound and neither heard nor felt the bullet that was intended to scramble his brain.

The car horn was the last thing he would remember for a long, long time.

Richard Kurtz held out his hand. "Sponge," he said.

The nurse handed him a pair of forceps with a folded four-by-four held in the tip. He dabbed at the abdominal wall, decided that the oozing was insufficient to cause any problems, and proceeded to run the bowel. Ten centimeters above the cecum, he found what he was looking for: a hard, solid mass.

Kurtz' fingers moved almost without thinking. He had performed this operation a hundred times before. The mass was isolated and the patient had been adequately prepped, having had an asymptomatic tumor found on routine colonoscopy a couple of weeks prior. The colonoscopist had taken multiple specimens and so far as could be determined by biopsy, the tumor had not spread.

Unfortunately, however, the tumor had spread. Once the abdomen was opened, it could be seen that the liver was infested with multiple, tiny nodules. It was a surprise, since the patient's liver functions were normal and MRI showed nothing suspicious. Kurtz sighed.

The patient was forty-seven years old, young for colon cancer, but it ran in his family, which was why he had elected to have the colonoscopy at such a relatively young age. Not young enough, as it turned out.

"Fuck," Kurtz muttered.

Drew Johnson, the fifth-year assisting on the case, nodded but didn't say a word. There was nothing to say.

Linda Rodriguez, the intern, too inexperienced to know better, said, "How about RFA?"

Drew Johnson rolled his eyes. Radiofrequency ablation was the hot new thing. Like most hot new things, its benefits over the tried and true were hazy and still unproven.

"Too many of them," Kurtz said. "His liver is riddled." He shook his head. "Fuck," he said again.

Might as well do the bowel resection, Kurtz reflected. No reason not to. Chemotherapy, mostly 5-fluorouracil and leucovorin, would probably give him another year or so, and at least he would die without a drainage tube. They took half a dozen punch biopsies of the liver nodules and sent them off to pathology, then Kurtz watched as Johnson clamped the colon above and below the tumor and cut out the offending piece of bowel. Then they waited. Twenty minutes later, pathology called to confirm that the frozen sections of the margins were clear and that the nodules from the liver were indeed the same type of poorly differentiated adenocarcinoma as the mass from the bowel. Once assured that this was the case, Johnson proceeded to stitch the two segments of bowel back together.

Forty minutes later, the patient, awake but sedated, was resting comfortably in the recovery room. Kurtz had already given the family the bad news, a job that he always hated, and was changing in the locker room when the police beeper went off.

He stared at it for a moment, then pushed the small button on the top and scanned the number. It was one that he knew well. He sighed and picked up his phone.

New York City Health and Hospitals/Bellevue, formerly known simply as Bellevue Hospital, was the oldest such public institution in the United States, dating back to 1736. Bellevue had a long and storied history, having been responsible for numerous innovations such as the first city-wide sanitary code in the United States, the first cadaver kidney transplant in the world, the first mitral valve replacement, the first resection of a femoral aneurysm and the establishment of the first nursing school for men. Despite this illustrious history, Bellevue, as a city hospital devoted primarily to the care of those who cannot afford to pay, is today looked down upon by the more elite institutions in the city.

Kurtz, who had unfortunately come to know the place well, did not share this opinion. The care provided by Bellevue, so far as Kurtz' experience went, was generally excellent. Tonight, was no exception.

Lew Barent and Harry Moran met him in the ER. "It's Arnie," Barent said. "Arnie Figueroa."

Kurtz winced. He knew Arnie Figueroa well. "Shit," he said.

"He's been working undercover. We don't know who shot him. It was a residential neighborhood in Williamsburg."

Kurtz by now knew the drill. As a police surgeon with the august rank of "Inspector," his principal job was to oversee the care of injured cops, particularly those injured in the line of duty. In most cases, however, and this case was not an exception, the injured cop was already under the care of perfectly competent physicians who resented having an outsider looking over their shoulder, potentially criticizing the quality of care that they provided and gathering evidence for any professional liability suits that might result from a less than stellar outcome.

Kurtz didn't blame them. His real job, in his own opinion, was to provide a little hand holding, give some reassurance to the other cops and the patient's family that New York City's best was on the case, making certain that everything was being done to the highest standards. Which it was.

As a police surgeon, Kurtz was entitled to come into the OR and observe, which he did as gingerly and unobtrusively as possible. The surgeon, a tall, skinny guy named Allen Wong, didn't even glance at him, his attention focused on the patient's exposed brain. Kurtz couldn't see much of the actual operation, since the surgical field in a neurosurgery case was small and almost entirely obscured by the drapes and the bodies of the surgical team clustered around the field. That was alright. He listened for a half hour or so, gathered enough information to know that the patient was stable and the operation proceeding in as normal a fashion as possible, and made his way back out to the waiting room.

As he entered, the patient's wife, mother-in-law and three kids all looked at him, their eyes filled with desperate hope. They were surrounded by about ten cops, who looked at him with flat, level gazes, clearly expecting the worst.

"It's going well," Kurtz said. "Probably another hour or so until he's out of surgery. He's stable."

Figueroa's wife gave a little sigh and bowed her head over a string of rosary beads. The cops sat back. Kurtz glanced at Barent and Harry Moran, then gave a nod toward the door. The two cops rose to their feet and followed him out.

"No way for me to tell how much of his brain is going to be left after this," Kurtz said. "You know that, right?"

Moran winced. Barent looked away. "Yeah," he said.

"The surgeon is Allen Wong. He's good."

Barent grimaced. "We'll see," he said.

"Yeah," Kurtz said. "We'll see."

Iosif Kozlov was angry. He was angry at the three idiots who had allowed themselves to be tailed to the meeting place of his recently acquired associates. He was angry at the supposedly competent sniper who had shot the undercover cop in the head without, somehow or other, killing him. Not that they had known he was a cop, of course. He had been dressed like a bum, which was what his idiotic henchmen had assumed him to be. It wasn't until the news hit the internet in the morning that any of them had put two and two together and realized that they had shot a cop in the head.

Yes, Iosif Kozlov was angry. In the normal course of things, the still breathing cop would have been swiftly carried away and never seen again, his dead body buried in a landfill or ground down into dogfood. In this case, however, a group of six young men passing by had immediately stumbled upon the bleeding cop and called the police. The Colombians had decided that killing an additional six men, some of whom might have been armed for all any of them knew, just to dispose of some random vagrant, would be an inappropriate escalation. The meeting had been abruptly ended, the building evacuated of both their personnel.

He took a deep breath. Calm, he told himself. His primary enforcer and personal bodyguard, Grigory Mazlov, stood to the side. The three idiots stood in front of his desk, their faces blank.

"Why?" Kozlov asked.

One of the men frowned. The two others remained outwardly impassive. The first man cleared his throat. "We didn't see him."

"Did you see anything? Did you look?"

"We did." The first man gave the two others an uncertain glance. "He was good."

The cop probably had been good, Iosif Kozlov conceded. It didn't matter. He and his men were operating in a foreign country, surrounded by enemies. You stayed alert. You were better than the opposition. You had to be. Or you died.

"Hold up your left hand," Iosif Kozlov said. "All of you."

All of them did so, their faces grim. They were sweating. One of them drew a deep breath.

"It remains to be seen if you can redeem yourselves from this failure," Kozlov said. He opened the middle drawer of his desk and pulled out a bolt cutter. He waved it lazily in front of his face, then put it down on the desk and slid it across. All three men stared at it. "Pick it up," Kozlov said.

Slowly, the first man, the one who had spoken, reached out. He picked up the bolt cutter with his right hand.

"Before we go any further," Kozlov said, "I wish you to understand a few things. First, we must be strong." He stopped, leaned back and stared for a moment into space. "I have reason to know that all of you are strong. Second, we must be brave." He smiled. "And I also know that you are brave, but strength and courage are the most basic, the most common attributes that we must possess. We must also be dedicated, to ourselves and to our cause. We must be obedient to those who have been placed above us and we must be loyal to the organization of which we are privileged to be a part. All of these qualities, you are about to demonstrate. In addition, however, there are other qualities that are not only useful, but vital to the work that we are called upon to do. We must be intelligent. We must understand our environment and our world and the requirements of success, and perhaps most of all, we must know ourselves. We must know of what we are capable and we must know our limitations, as soldiers and as men." Iosif Kozlof's lips quirked upward. "You underestimated the enemy. You are allowed to make such a mistake only once. Do you understand?"

Grigory Mazlov remained impassive, watching all three men with hooded eyes. All three nodded their heads. "This is good," Kozlov said gently. "Now go ahead."

Slowly, the first man put the little finger of his left hand between the jaws of the bolt cutter and squeezed the handle.

Iosif Kozlov smiled.

CPSIA information can be obtained
at www.ICGtesting.com
Printed in the USA
LVHW011343260420
654465LV00003B/592